The Garden of Death

John Paul

First edition, December 2022

ISBN 978-1-5011-7321-9 (paperback)
ISBN 978-1-387-43917-1 (ebook)

This book contains mature content, including graphic sexual situations, brutal violence, sexual violence, drug use, foul language, and gay-themed material.

Lulu Publishing Services – December 2022
www.iamjohnpaul.com

CHAPTER ONE

The evening sky darkened as the sun slowly sank beneath the horizon. Bright orange and red striated the sky and a breeze rolled through the air. A large steel bird flew overhead. The roar of its engines was nothing more than a hum to its elite passengers on their speedy trip from New York, but thunderous to those trapped in the maze of stone below. On the ground the grass was fading from the blaze of the recent summer sun, dry and brittle. A stone wall surrounded this mysterious maze; its craftsmanship was of a generation long dead. More than a century old, this border stood strong at a towering 12 feet tall, forming an intimidating rectangle that engulfed more than 40 acres of decay. On the two shorter ends, the wall was less stone and more black iron. The giant gates were layered in paint, but if you stood for a moment and looked closely, looked beyond all the paint, you could envision them as they stood decades earlier— majestic, masculine, and royal. From outside the garden was a vision of beauty, a remnant of the grandeur of past lives. Inside it was a different sight, a different world completely.

Inside the gates were endless pathways of new tar, black as night and smooth like butter. Flowers bloomed throughout, wild from seeds not planted by man. Their colors were vibrant and alive as they fed off the soil of the dead. More flowers, not rooted in the soil, were scattered about the grounds. They were brown and dry, lifeless as they lay wrapped in plastic or aged paper on top of various graves. Some faded plastic flowers could also be seen near newer tombstones, trying to provide color to a lifeless environment in the approaching autumn months. The grounds were cluttered with trees older than many countries, towering over the headstones. Over 63,525 people lay just below the surface.

The headstones varied in size, shape, and color as well as age and condition. Some stones were so old and worn down by the weather that the carvings were almost unreadable. Some were totally blank. Others tilted to one side or lay on the ground, no longer having the strength to stand. This was a beautiful place, this garden of death, but it was also a scary place. Cemeteries today are much simpler — low, flat, and as exciting as the conversation among the dead. This one, however, had beauty in its history, adventure in its paths, and mystery in its darkness.

* * * * *

Catherine walked through this cemetery almost every day on her way to and from work. She was a simple woman — smart and educated, but free of greed and power. She loved to smell the flowers and read the headstones. Sometimes, when walking through the gardens with her husband, Peter, she would stop and talk to the dead. Not so much to them, directly, but about them, of what she assumed their lives might have been like. They never spoke back, of course, but that did not stop her imagination. She often found life, love, and beauty where most people saw nothing. She saw the good in everyone, and everything. Her husband did not.

It was not just headstones that she would talk with — Catherine would talk to strangers, too. As a nurse, it was in her nature to make small talk with people. She was accustomed to talking with people she knew little about, and unfortunately, she was used to seeing too many of them die. Catherine convinced herself that the real reason she walked through the cemetery so often was to apologize to the dead—for not saving them all. It did not matter that the people in this cemetery had been dead for decades—some even centuries. She found comfort in speaking a few words of cheerfulness to a headstone. It was her own kind of therapy.

On most days Catherine walked straight through the cemetery, sometimes choosing a different path, but always moving without haste. Every now and then she would walk a little slower or sit a little longer to enjoy the peacefulness and serenity of this wonderfully mysterious garden of death. Her son, Nicholas never got to walk with her; however, long after she was dead, he would walk these same paths also pondering and looking for something, or someone.

While sitting on a stone bench, cold to the touch, even with her layers of autumn wear, Catherine watched the birds dance in the sky as the sun set. The colorful harvest backdrop added to the serenity, and mystery of the garden. People passed by, talking to each other and paying little attention to anything or anyone around them. Others walked more slowly, studying the stones and discussing how the deceased might have lived—just as

Catherine had. As the sky grew darker the echo of voices died and soon the only sound was the wind racing through the grass and trees. The breeze felt good, refreshing to Catherine as she sat with the dead.

Realizing that she had lost track of time and assuming that her husband would be worried that she had not come home sooner, Catherine gathered her bag and walked, more quickly than usual, along the dark path toward the west gate. Even at this darkening hour the garden was a palette of beauty and color to her. Once the gate was clearly in her sight, she slowed down to enjoy her final steps through the garden. She knew she should have kept her quick pace, but the plastic flowers were so beautiful and the sight, and words, of the stones were still grabbing the life out of her. Then, suddenly, Catherine was grabbed a bit too abruptly.

Adam jumped out from behind one of the headstones and tackled Catherine. She struggled, dropping her handbag as it spewed its contents all over the ground. Even in her moment of panic she was able to leave breadcrumbs—forever the Girl Scout. Adam picked Catherine up over his shoulder and carried her into the thick brush from which he had just emerged, buried among the headstones, and well out of sight of the path. Catherine tried to scream again and again, but Adam was stronger, and was able to muffle her screams with his large, rough hands. He did not want to raise the dead, let alone alert the living.

It was not difficult for Adam to win the struggle with Catherine, being that she was a small woman. With a thin frame and light to carry, many people would have seen her as an easy target. Her husband Peter always told her that she was too thin. "Not enough meat on her bones," he would say as he put second helpings of dinner on Nicholas's plate. "Not enough meat. You don't want to be like your mother. Eat up son and build those muscles."

Although Catherine struggled, kicking and thrashing as she hung suspended over Adam's shoulder, it did little to stop him. Eventually though, he did stop in a clearing deep in one of the corners of the cemetery. Few people would trek that far from the path, especially at this hour. Nicholas had, many times.

The headstones in this section of the cemetery were mostly blank and falling apart, if not already on the ground in pieces. Some were covered in moss and others were barely legible. It was the oldest part of the cemetery, and no longer visited by any living generation. Nicholas had seen this part many times — even been in this very corner. It scared him, and excited him every time he came here. Especially once he learned that this was where it all happened — where his life began.

A young woman barely out of her teens, nicknamed Hoover, was waiting rather impatiently for Adam to return with Catherine, or anyone. It did not need to be Catherine, but she was hopeful that Adam was not coming back empty handed — anyone would have been fine. Hoover was homeless, a drug addict, and a prostitute. A trifecta of sadness. Through the years she had been beaten and molested, not only by her father when she was a child, but by Adam and many others in her young life. No matter how hard she tried to please the men in her world, they repeatedly told her that she was stupid, and they treated her like she was worthless. Coming out of the womb, Hoover never had a shot at living a good life.

Her real name was Eve, but for as long as she could remember, no one called her by that name. She was forced to blow her father from a very young age and had spent most of her teen years with man in her. Whether she was being beaten, raped, or paid, she was always blowing someone. As a result, it did not take long for a nickname to be given, and to catch on. To her Eve was dead, and only Hoover was allowed to carry on. Some days she would find herself crying, missing Eve.

Hoover was strung out on a cocktail of drugs when she met Catherine. She paced the clearing, scratching her face and body, mumbling to herself, occasionally slapping her face hard, yelling at herself and at nobody—at least no one present, in body. Though she looked disturbed, she was pleased to see Adam and Catherine. Hoover found comfort in Adam, this young man who beat her yet cared for her, even if only for a short time in her life, and in his own way. Adam had few or no feelings for Hoover. She filled a need he had, often. If you could find her friends, as few as she had, they would say that, to Hoover, Adam was the center of the universe, her reason for living. He would certainly be her reason for dying.

Catherine was thrown to the hard, cold ground with a thud unjustified by how little she weighed, that echoed off the headstones. The impact knocked her slightly unconscious, but she remained semi-aware of what was happening. Adam danced around her now dirty body humming nursery rhymes before he jumped on top of Catherine and began licking her face and grabbing her breasts, tearing at her jacket and uniform. Adam was anything but gentle with her as he thrashed and thrusted with great force. He was proving to Catherine, to this young lonely girl and to himself that he was a man, that he had the strength and the power to do what he pleased, when he pleased — a quality that Hoover was accustomed to seeing in her men. For Adam, he needed to feel this power, this rage, to feel good about himself — to feel like a man. Nicholas would one day learn to know that feeling all too well.

Adam's hands were soiled and callused from years of manual labor. They covered Catherine's mouth as he carelessly plowed into her, hard and fast. Harder and faster. As many times as he had done this, his awkwardness always made it look like his first time. His torn jeans barely down to his ankles, while his zipper and belt buckle scraped Catherine's leg, cutting into her thigh with a jagged pain. Her feeble body was unable to handle such ferocity. In and out he went, tearing her skin, her inner walls, with little regard for anything but his temporary satisfaction. He was endowed, and he penetrated Catherine carelessly enough that when the doctors later looked at the torn skin, they thought Catherine had been gang raped.

Weak from being so violently invaded, Catherine lay on the dark dusty soil with her clothes torn open. The white innocence of her nurses' uniform was tattered with dirt and blood. This meant nothing to her two new friends as Hoover followed Adam's direction and went down on Catherine while wearing a large strap-on dildo. Adam fucked Hoover in the ass while she took her turn tearing into Catherine. The three bodies rocking wildly.

Hoover knew that the harder she hurt Catherine the greater the reward she would receive from Adam. She pushed into Catherine with her dirty, cracked, and oversized sized dildo as Adam pushed harder into her. This kind of control over his victims excited Adam. Neither of them worried about protection for Catherine nor for themselves. Hoover was too strung out to fully understand the damage she was doing but knew that more drugs followed her job, one she had performed many times before. Pavlov had long since proved this method successful.

Tears filled Catherine's eyes, and dripped down her face, mixing with the blood and dirt smeared on her from their filthy hands. She tried not to make any noise, although she wanted to scream, not only for help, but also because of the pain. Her head was throbbing, and her groin stung – nothing she had ever felt before.

Time seemed to last forever during this brutal invasion, but in the end, Catherine had been tormented for no more than 30 minutes. Adam and Hoover, who so freely stole life from Catherine, who had no remorse for human life, had finished with her as quickly as they had taken her from the path. Once Adam had sowed his seed, he and Hoover kicked Catherine's frail bloody body around a bit. They both urinated and shat on her, and then left her for dead. Adam got a certain satisfaction, a high from violating her, or anyone. She was going to be another mark tattooed on his wrist.

No sooner had these two haunting creatures of the darkness arrived, were they gone, vanished into the dark world, and out of the maze. Catherine held on to what she believed to be her last breath before she too would join the other bodies beneath her. Fortunately for Catherine, she had a high-pitched voice. With her assailants no longer holding her mouth closed, caking her beautifully shaped pale lips with dirt, her frail, almost mute screams, which were more like baby yelps, were soon heard by Toby, a newly hired security guard roaming the grounds one last time before locking the gates for the night. Had Toby been like any other guard — one who wore headphones, listening to music, and singing loudly out of tune while making his rounds, Catherine would have died — sooner. But Toby was different. He had no Walkman and was singing no song. Instead, he was listening to the sounds of the night, much like Catherine liked to do.

It was the contents of her handbag all over the ground that first caught his attention, and as he bent down to examine the mess, he heard the faint cry for help. It took a few cries before Toby was able to find Catherine hiding in the corner. With her clothes torn open and her body covered with blood and soil, it was hard to determine her condition. If it had not been for her occasional squeals for help, Toby would have easily mistaken Catherine for dead. He was scared. This was not the type of thing he was used to seeing. This was his first week on the job. Cemetery security guard sounded like a much easier, and less stress job than flipping burgers, well until he found Catherine. Suddenly flipping burgers seemed a lot less stressful.

Toby did not try to move Catherine. Instead, he called 9-9-9. He never left her side. Toby gently held Catherine's bruised, frail hand, fearful of hurting her more, but wanting her to feel comfort— to know that she was safe. Toby spoke about the weather; the flowers that grew in his garden, and the garden that surrounded them now. He struggled to maintain his composure as he watched this young woman before him, lying helplessly in torn clothes and fresh blood. Toby removed his security coat and put it over Catherine to keep her warm. As he sat there next to Catherine, Toby was completely clueless to the damage he was doing to the crime scene with his tenderness and kindness. He thought about his mother.

Toby could hear his mother speaking her last few words to her dearest son, a young boy who had grown up making his mother proud. He remembered her voice as he sat on the edge of her hospital bed holding her hand, in much the same way that he now held Catherine's hand. He could hear his mother's frail voice, almost hoarse, yet full of excitement and joy for the son she watched grow up—for the man he had become. His mother had died holding her son's hand. He did not want another woman to die in his hands. He wanted Catherine to speak, to let him know she could hear him. Catherine could only make noises. They were simple noises, grunts or yelps, but it was enough to provide Toby prove that she was still alive as he sat in the dark cemetery waiting for help to arrive.

Within the hour, God's Garden, usually reserved for the dead, was alive with color and commotion. Men in dark polyester uniforms were scattered about, decorating the once dark and lifeless grounds with bright yellow tape. The dark sky, now a mixture of ominous blues and grays, included flashes of reds, yellows, and whites. The echo of voices, muffled by static, bounced off the old stone walls. When the police and emergency teams had arrived, they found Toby, still composed and still holding Catherine's hand, talking softly to her. He concealed his tears from them. They did not need to know about his emotions. The focus was clear—

get this woman to a hospital. He could deal with his own issues later.

Toby was questioned for many hours after Catherine had been rushed off to the hospital, fully cooperating with the investigation. He was concerned, not only for this woman he knew nothing about, but for his job and for others who might wander into the garden, the sacred grounds, only to be violated. Although Toby was new to his job, he was very aware of what went on among the bushes and dark corners of this lovely garden. Prior to him becoming a security guard, he too was a garden crawler. He had committed a great number of sins in this very garden since his days as a teen, and lucky for him, no criminal record reflected any of those sins. His greasy hair and body odor, a combination that would lead any onlooker to believe that he had not showered in days, were worsened with sweaty palms and rattled nerves because of all that had happened on his watch. His overweight body was squeezed into his security uniform, stained with work, food and life. Toby, for all his efforts, looked disheveled and out of place in his uniform.

With the garden lit up and the area taped off, the police began their search of the grounds. They needed clues, some sort of evidence that could explain why a presumedly innocent young woman would be raped and beaten so badly in the garden of God. It made little sense to the average person, but to the investigative team called to the scene soon after the first responders arrived, it meant everything. Catherine was not the first to feel the wrath of Adam – although it would be some time before this team would know him by name. This night Catherine was initiated into a club against her will. The police had been trying to disband the club for too long, but somehow its leader, its God, managed to always stay ahead of the law. The monster.

The police surveyed the grounds very closely. With the cemetery already closed, the opportunity for witnesses was limited, but as with any crime scene, the police knew that somewhere, in the dark shadows lurked onlookers, maybe innocent, maybe not, but they were there, watching, wondering what or who would be discovered. They may not be on the grounds at this moment, but hopefully, if they had been earlier, then soon they would come forth and provide some assistance. The cemetery was a sexual feast for anyone and everyone. Undercover police were making arrests weekly. The labyrinth of tombstones, pathways and hidden trails provided any pervert a buffet of sexual activity.

Soon after the cemetery came alive with police activity on-lookers crowded outside the gates clasping the black iron with both hands, hoping for some news of what was happening within the walls. Many were familiar with the sexual activity that took place within the garden walls every day. Some guilty themselves. They needed to know what was happening in their playground, and that their playground would be open again soon. At this late hour these people should have been home with their families enjoying a peaceful evening in the comfort and safety of their warm homes, not snooping around this cool night for speculations and rumors. The media was also outside the gates, intermixed among the crowd of curious neighbors. Well-dressed reporters with microphones in hand sharing details they'd just acquired with everyone who wanted the skinny on what weeds were growing in the garden, and if any had died.

The ambulance siren echoed through the garden and down the street waking up neighbors as it darted through traffic. Catherine lay on her back, as a cold, hard board held her uncomfortably tight. Tubes were running from her body to machines lining the portable hospital. They flowed both clear and colorful. The rookie paramedic studied Catherine, listening to the beeps and tones of the various machines. He talked softly to her, trying to keep her calm, but it was he who needed a calm voice in his ear. His palms were moist with sweat as he awkwardly continued to tend to her. He was sickened by her sight and by what everyone at the scene was speculating. In the short period of time that he spent in his white uniform tending to the sick and wounded he had not experienced anything so brutal. He wondered why and how he got into this profession. Before he could expand on his thoughts the ambulance had arrived at the hospital. More uniforms, both white and greenish blue, were running around the starched halls looking frazzled, but somehow each remained in control of their movements, their thoughts, and their plans to save Catherine and the others scattered throughout the building.

The back doors of the ambulance flung open. Catherine, still lying on the mobile bed, was pulled out as the stretcher grew legs. She was wheeled through the white hallways, the echo of doctor announcements overhead, and directed into surgery where the doctors spent the next few hours sewing her back together. Catherine wanted to hear her husband's voice, to feel his hands on her face. It was his comfort that she needed most right now. Unfortunately, his hands were comforting someone else's face. It would be hours before the police would find Catherine's husband, Peter. He claimed he was in a work meeting, but the truth was that while his innocent wife was being raped and beaten to death Peter was in a trashy motel outside of town making love to another woman.

CHAPTER TWO

The cemetery remained closed for the next few days while investigators went over the area very carefully. While the focus was on the immediate space where Catherine was found, the police studied every corner of the cemetery in hopes of finding something, anything that might lead them to the monster who left Catherine for dead. A variety of trash and broken sex toys scattered among the tombstones were collected and sent off to the lab in hopes of answers. Without DNA testing, there was no way to determine how long those toys had been lying dead in the cemetery, or if they were even used to violate Catherine. A handful of the officers searching the grounds were regulars to this garden themselves, and not just because of other cases. They visited for pleasure, and therefore knew some of the more secluded areas to search. Though they knew it was long shot, a few were hoping to find someone strung out in a dark corner who might be able to identify Catherine or her assailants.

Unfortunately, the various toys and trash they did collect were found to be fruitless. The best the police came away with was a few hair particles found around the shallow grave where Catherine had been violated, and of course the saliva and semen found on and in Catherine. A few samples were usually all that the police would need to identify these monsters, but with the reputation of the cemetery and the number of people who could have been in the same spot only hours before Catherine and her rapists seemed limitless. Nonetheless, tests resulted in many potential suspects, as usual. The police were determined to close this case as quickly as they could, but month after month they were introduced to more and more cases of dead people in cemeteries, and not the ones already six feet under.

Within a few days Catherine was sitting up in bed, breathing on her own—but waking up in the middle of the night with visions of her monsters— images of Adam and Hoover etched in her mind. Unlike the day of her rape, Catherine now had the comfort of Peter, by her side. Finally, he was fulfilling his duties as a husband. Even with him there, Catherine cried a lot and slept little. A few times she hoped that the police would find Adam and Hoover and punish them in much the same way they punished her — even though she really did not mean it. Given all that she had been through, Catherine remained a kind and gentle person, and wanted nothing more than Adam and Hoover to be brought to justice.

By the time Catherine was released from the hospital the police had her looking at lines of suspects. She was not well enough to trek to the police station, so she was evaluating the creepy line up through a video feed while she safely lay in her own bed, wondering why her husband was, once again, not by her side. He was less and less present in her life at a time when she needed him the most.

Peter and Catherine married young — both in their early 20s. They met at a hospital where they both worked. Peter in the finance office, and Catherine in the ER. Their relationship started out with light flirting as they passed one another in the halls. Eventually Peter got the nerve to ask Catherine out. It was only a few months after their first date when Peter popped the question. Catherine, the youngest of three, and the only girl in the family was over the moon when he did. She fell for Peter hard, almost in love with him by the end of the first date. Peter was kind and gentle with Catherine—a perfect gentleman. He was a kind man, but Catherine made him a better one. He loved how Catherine always saw the good in everything—everyone.

A few months into dating, Peter got a life changing job offer. He feared that he would have to choose between the new job or Catherine. Catherine was excited to hear about Peter's new opportunity, one in a new city far from where they both grew up. Seeing her excitement, Peter got caught up in the moment and proposed. A few weeks later, after getting married in the courthouse, the newlyweds were on a plane bound for London to start a new adventure together.

Once they arrived in London things changed—the honeymoon was over before it even got started. Peter became consumed with his new job and was gone all the time. A stranger in a new city, Catherine had trouble making friends at first, but she eventually got a nursing job at a hospital near the cemetery. Catherine could never confirm that Peter had started cheating on her almost as soon as they touched down at Heathrow Airport, but she had her suspicions. Peter had been to London twice before to interview with his new company. During those visits Peter hooked up with someone different each time — one from a fancy hotel bar, and the other in the same cemetery where Catherine was raped.

Before Peter and Catherine could celebrate their first year in London, Peter and Catherine, newlyweds who should have been so excited to be together in an old city rich with culture and adventure, had stopped having sex — stopped spending any more time with each other than necessary. If their flat had more than one bedroom, they would have been slept in separate beds. Peter spent many nights on the couch — when he was not out all night with some new stranger. Eventually Peter and Catherine moved into a townhouse in Chelsea, and lived in separate rooms, but never divorced. Both were too afraid to be alone. Peter enjoyed his affairs but liked that he had a wife to come home to, even if he paid little attention to her. Being the youngest child, Catherine had never been alone. She went from living with her family to living with Peter, and so she was afraid to leave him, especially in a foreign city. She was too ashamed to call her parents and tell them how her life had fallen apart for fear that they would lecture her on how she moved too quickly — into a marriage and move to a new land that they advised against, repeatedly.

While she had not caught him "in the act," Catherine eventually figured out what was going on with her husband — confirmed what she had suspected for too long. Peter left a woman's business card in one pocket of his pants, and a guy's name and phone number on a napkin in the other. Catherine discovered this evidence when washing clothes one Sunday morning. She was convinced then, when she saw little hearts drawn near both numbers, that Peter was attracted to both men and women — but she did not know how to confront him about it. Catherine had assumed Peter was cheating on her with women but discovering that he cheated with men too was more than she was prepaid to accept. She certainly did not know that he frequented the same garden of death that she walked through so often looking for peace. She certainly did not see Peter lurking in the bushes on more than one occasion as he watched Catherine walking through the cemetery. That was their life. By their second anniversary neither was any closer to changing their new, separate lives together. It took Catherine's near-death experience to change their future together.

Many men were arrested and questioned, and several of them had the unfortunate pleasure of lining up for Catherine as the police worked to help her identify her assailant. Some of the men were familiar with this process, having visited the police station almost as often as they had visited the cemetery. Still, others were shocked and embarrassed. They had committed sexual acts in a holy place, with hopes of never being caught. They prayed that their wives, girlfriends and even boyfriends would never discover their desire to have sex with guys on gravestones — yet now they sat in the police station trying to come up with excuses to explain to their loved ones. The embarrassment of those who were detained, and released, would certainly keep some of them from returning to plant their seed in the garden again any time soon. Some, however, were not deterred, and even stopped by the cemetery on their way home from the police station.

Each of the men was released quickly, but the police were no closer to catching Adam or Hoover, let alone identifying them. Some of the detained men described a woman to the police who would later be found outside of the cemetery walls and tagged as Jane Doe. Hoover would die alone, thanks to a cocktail overdose prescribed by Adam. His DNA was all over, and inside Hoover when she was discovered and yet for all the work the police were doing, Hoover's death was recorded as an overdose of a homeless person and her unborn fetish, and never connected to the wake of death Adam left behind.

As it turned out, the best and only real evidence for catching her rapist was with Catherine the entire time—being kept warm within her. With no luck from the hair samples, the doctors turned to the traces of semen they found in and around Catherine's vagina. The investigating team compared these to the dozens of other samples they had been collecting over the past few months connected to other cemetery cases. As luck would have it, her donor was an avid gardener who enjoyed leaving his seed wherever he attacked, like a dog marking its territory with urine. The only difference between Catherine and the other women and men Adam soiled was that she left the scene alive.

Catherine and Peter read the papers and watched the news enough to know that the city was laced with crime and violence, but like the rest of the city dwellers, they were in the dark about the real dangers of Adam. Everyone was. The killing pattern of Adam had been kept from the media for fear that if it leaked, so to speak, the city would become a garden for even more crazy people to sow their seed. At this point they were no close to determining if the killings were the work of one person, or many. After all the years of spilling his seed and his victim's blood all over the city, it remained a mystery as to how Adam was always able to stay ahead of the police. From what Catherine remembered about Adam, she did not think of him as a particularly smart person. But Adam had proven that he was quite smart, or at least smart enough to keep from being caught, so far.

One month after the horrific scene at the cemetery, Catherine still feared the place. She was so frightened that she only went out in public if she absolutely needed something, and she refused to go out alone. She took time off from work for fear of the outside world. For weeks the media had painted almost every headline and newscast with her deadly

30

adventure, and her lust for survival. Knowing this, she feared her attackers would return to silence her for good. The police, on the other hand were hoping that all the publicity would draw the monster to her again, or at least draw him out. The high level of security Catherine experienced while at the hospital continued at her home. This gave her some comfort, but her fears grew more when she discovered that she had missed her period. She had missed it in the past and would normally not have thought too much about it; however, the doctors' strict orders were to report any discomfort or concerns to him, no matter how mundane they may seem to her. Being a nurse, she fully understood this, and called him.

Catherine was afraid to visit the doctor alone, and unfortunately her husband was, once again, nowhere to be found. His adventures away from home resumed not too long after she returned from the hospital. His excuse was always work. He told her that he could not stay home with her all the time, protecting her. Catherine heard Peter's excuses without really listening. She was used to him not being around and accepted that he no longer cared for her the way he professed in public. Catherine knew that if she was going to get through this ordeal, she was going to have to do it alone. Her parents were too old to fly over to London to assist and her older siblings, both biologists, were out at sea and could not get to her for another couple of months.

Her journey back to the hospital would have been more stressful had the police not been there to escort her. They too had become aware of the amount of time Peter spent away from home during her time of need, but it was not their place to speak up. They were there to offer physical support, not emotional support.

At the hospital Catherine had expected to hear that stress, or maybe even the aftershock of everything that she had been through the prior month was the cause for missing her period. She was prepared for almost any news except for the news that she was pregnant. With her hands covering her pale, lifeless face she wailed loudly, but muffled like when she was trapped in the cemetery. Her tears escaped through her fingers, cascading down her soft small hands. How could this be, she wondered. She and Peter had long since abstained from all sexual activity — well, between the two of them, anyhow. Peter was busy sowing his own seed elsewhere during his wife's time of need. He was good at that. As Catherine explained to the doctor that aside from the violent attack, she had not had sex in quite some time.

This information highlighted what the doctor had feared — that Catherine was pregnant the child of a possible serial killer. He ran some additional tests to determine if he could find a DNA match between the unborn child sleeping within Catherine and the DNA samples the police had collected at the scene, and on Catherine. They found a match. Within the hour the hospital was crawling with men in blue, and still Catherine was unaware of the test results. When she was let in on what everyone else at the hospital now knew for certain Catherine screamed. She thrashed. She hit her belly in frustration and fear before she was restrained and sedated.

"Where is her husband?" the doctor asked the police who escorted Catherine to the hospital.

"We are trying to locate him now, sir," one of the officers responded. "He left their home early this morning and has not contacted her since."

The police had not been tracking Peter. They had been focused on protecting Catherine, hoping that as news about her survival would pull her violator out of the weeds. The police believed that they were getting closer to capturing her gardener. The monster.

While Catherine was being escorted home by two officers, two others who had been stationed outside of her home were now surveying the property to be sure no one was lingering around before she returned. They even did an internal sweep of the house to ensure that no one slipped through a window undetected.

Once back home, Catherine sat alone in the living room, saddened by what was growing inside of her. She sat quietly crying while the police continued to search her home, checking every room, every closet. By this time more officers were stationed outside the front and back of the house, undercover, of course, all there to catch anyone attempting to enter the property and hurt Catherine. They were hopeful that the rapist would have been watching the news, learned that Catherine was alive, and maybe figured out where she lived. After all she had been through, physically and emotionally, the police were now using Catherine as bait with the beefed-up security around her home, and the stories in the news, hoping her rapist would see the news and try to finish what they thought he started when he attacked her.

Catherine felt some comfort in the security of the police outside; just sitting in their cars watching the house, and the people that passed by, chatting about work, their kids, and the weather. But at the same time, she felt trapped, confined like she had been in the cemetery, pinned to the ground, unable to escape. She knew that her every move was being watched by the police and feared that she was also being watched by her rapist. The police finished their search of Catherine's house and then she sat alone trying to figure out how she was going to share this news with her husband, news that would normally be considered wonderful. She kept having flashbacks of that night on the ground. The dark, chilled air and suffocating stench. Feelings of pain and sickness came over her as she once again envisioned and felt the pain of her body being torn open, of being penetrated by such filth. She could taste her own blood as she stood in the clean, bright kitchen. She leaned across the counter crying, waiting for Peter to return. This night, like so many before, and after, he forgot to call. The men in blue changed guard more than once before Peter did make it home.

She dimmed the house lights like so many other nights, checking to see if the police were still watching. They were in their unmarked car across the street. She did not make excuses in her mind about where Peter was tonight. She had given that up long ago. Instead, she now sat in that dimly lit home her husband had worked so hard to provide for her and waited for him. She did not listen to music, nor did she read one of the many books scattered around the house, bookmarks in each. Catherine liked having at least one book in each room that she could pick up and continue reading at any time. She always managed to keep each storyline straight—no matter how much time passed between readings. She sat silently in the living room, letting out the occasional cry, but focused on staying awake to give her husband news that he did not need to hear—not this night.

In the foyer, the old grandfather clock struck midnight, waking Catherine from a nap. She was rubbing her stiff neck from having slept upright when she heard Peter arrive. First, she saw the bright lights then heard the screech of the brakes and then the engine went silent, followed minutes later by the fumbling of keys as he quietly tried to let himself in. She could see the front door from where she sat and watched his silhouette. Once he had the front door securely locked, that final click of the deadbolt, she turned on the living room light. Peter's shoes and tie sailed through the air as he screamed in fright, not expecting his wife to be waiting up for him. Nervous and confused by the news he had already received earlier in the night, and of being caught coming in so late without warning, he went to her, trying so show compassion and concern for her being awake so late, and his coming home at such a late hour. She was not listening. She knew he was with that other woman, or was it a man tonight? She could never keep track of her husband's sexual agenda. He never knew she knew about his fooling around with others, and she wanted to keep it that way—for now.

Tonight, however, she was more concerned with the news she needed to tell him, and fearful of what his response might be. Unsure of how to gracefully share the news, Catherine simply and quickly recited the words of the doctor, announcing to her husband that in eight months they would be parents of the monster's spawn, and no, she was not going to get an abortion.

Of course, this announcement was a shock to Peter, mostly because just hours earlier his lover Jessica shared that she was pregnant, and Peter was the father. Jessica's husband, James, knew nothing of her affair with Peter, and he would spend the rest of his life thinking that he was the biological father. This meant that Jessica, as much as she detested the idea, had to have sex with her husband so he would never question whether he was the father or not. Jessica's husband would never know about Peter.

It was ironic that the very night Nicholas was conceived on the cold hard ground, forced into existence by a serial killer raping his mother, Oliver, was conceived on a large comfortable and warm bed draped in flannel, given life by a father violating his oath of marriage. Still feeling the anxiety and stress of hearing about his own baby tonight, learning that Catherine was also pregnant was too much for Peter to digest, especially at that late hour. Earlier in the night he spent hours trying to convince Jessica to abort. Even though she realized that she would have to lie to her husband for the rest of his life, she still thought that was a better option than killing a bastard child. The irony and the sadness about the entire ordeal were like something out of the movies—right out of the Lifetime studios. But regardless of how nutty it all seemed—how bizarre, and coincidental it all was, Peter had to figure out how he was going to manage two babies from two different mothers and keep it all a secret.

Eight months later two young women lay in two different beds, in the same hospital, unaware of the other. Both were hurting; crying out in pain—and not just because they were about to give birth. For a change, they each had their husbands beside them. One pretended to care and was fearful of what would come out of the womb. The other was clueless and thrilled at the notion of being a new dad. As the mothers-to-be focused on their breathing techniques and occasional pushing, just rooms away from each other, their husbands paced the same hall waiting, wondering what their new future had in store for them as dads. Peter knew, as he stood there with Jessica's husband, whose name she never shared with him, that he needed to be there for Jessica as much as he was for Catherine. Peter was confident that he would never get to see his own child if he didn't introduce himself to

Jessica's husband. With sweaty palms Peter met James, and they shared a moment of joy that they were both about to become fathers for the first time. And when the halls filled with the sound of crying babies both men knew the time had come.

James invited Peter in to meet his wife and new son, Oliver. Jessica was not pleased to see Peter, more so because she was not presentable. Peter took one look at the baby and shed a tear as he congratulated them both. Then, hanging his head low, Peter went to see Catherine—to meet the spawn, Nicholas.

CHAPTER THREE

Though it took longer than the police had hoped, the man responsible for Nicholas's conception — someone who had spent his whole life eluding the police, raping and killing without a care in the world, was finally caught. Although it would be months before anyone fully understood the scope of his rage and destruction, the public would come to learn that Adam had killed more than 150 people spanning a decade. He would be forever remembered as one of the most prolific serial killers in the United Kingdom. Some of his victims were men, others woman, and some even young children. While his murders made the news sporadically throughout the decade, his identity remained a mystery to the police for years. Though the scenery was consistent, the method of killing was not, making it hard for the police to conclude or even suspect that all the killings were connected. The only connection between each killing was that each crime, each invasion of privacy — each victim of the great gardener of death was found in a cemetery, but not the same cemetery. If it were not for the fact that Catherine had survived, Adam would still be sinning; still sowing his seed in some garden of death. Instead, he now rests in a garden himself, well beneath the cold hard soil.

In the final weeks of his life, Adam had become desperate for money, more so than usual, and had visited a sperm bank—something he did often—just before planting his seed in Catherine. Between the sperm banks and the cemeteries, Adam had been leaving deposits all over town—all over the region, but no connection had been made between he and the killings because there were never any witnesses—just a lot of sperm. Because the murders appeared somewhat random, and not all of them involved intercourse, the police had few leads and did not necessarily think to connect the dots of the older murders because of the donation Adam left behind with each victim. That changed with Catherine—the lone survivor of Adam's rampage through life. The police compared the sperm samples from previous cemetery crime scenes to those left with Catherine to narrow down the search for the monster. It was a long shot that turned out to be the total money shot.

Once the police made a match between the sperm found in Catherine with deposits at several of the older crime scenes, they expanded their search for matches at a couple of sperm banks. Eventually they were monitoring all the local sperm banks and hospitals in hopes of unveiling the mystery gardener. It would take many weeks, but thanks to Adam's need for cash and drugs he was making deposits more regularly. Ironically, it was not in a sperm bank or hospital where the monster was caged. He was arrested in the very same cemetery where he violated Catherine, only this time he was trying to sell ecstasy to a couple of undercover cops pretending to be male hustlers. Had it been one cop Adam could have gotten away, but since this was an organized operation trying to shut down the sex and drug exchanges going on in the cemetery, he never had a chance. He was surrounded by men in blue within seconds of pulling the baggy filled with little white pills out of the pocket of his tattered jeans.

* * * * *

The product of an alcoholic mother and nonexistent father, Adam became a ward of the state at a young age. By the time he was six years old his father had been killed in a hunting accident—not that he was hunting, but rather, he had the misfortune to be hiding from the police in the north Vermont woods during hunting season. He was mistaken for a deer and gunned down by an out-of-town hunter trying to enjoy the start of his retirement. As for Adam's mother, she was not very present in his life—always drunk or high on meth. Life in the remote trailer park he called home was not an exciting place for a toddler. When Adam turned seven years old his mother was sent to prison for drugs and prostitution leaving no place for Adam to go other than a state-run orphanage—a place he called home until he turned 18. He did get to live with several foster families, but for a variety of reasons, he always ended up back at the orphanage. He was too broken for anyone to permanently welcome him into their family.

On his 18th birthday, unlike most of his past birthdays, Adam received a gift—the gift of freedom. He was released from the state—free to live a life without oversight. He felt more alone than ever before but began his journey, one that would take him to Boston in hopes of a new life—a new beginning. Adam had never been outside of Vermont before turning 18 and had a lengthy petty crime record as a teenager—typical vandalism and harassment crimes—which never helped his case in finding a foster family. His crimes turned more violent and hateful once he left Vermont. He was finally able to give into a dark side that had been growing within him for most of his youth. Just because he had not been out of Vermont, and just because he was trapped in an orphanage did not mean that he was not in touch with the outside world. He did attend a public school, he had odd jobs once he turned 13, and he spent more than his share of time on the internet—not just looking at porn.

Scientists and historians alike would eventually spend many hours studying Adam's life trying to understand how he turned out as bad as he did. Even today millions of kids are born into poverty each year. Some have both parents, some have one. Many end up with none and are part of the system if a relative is not willing to step up. These unfortunate children grow up without much of anything, some without any love, and many of them grow up to become low-level criminals. Most get stuck in a life of poverty then perpetuate it by marrying young and bringing too many more children into the poor lifestyle. Others get out— some, not a lot—and are able to make a better life for themselves. Usually, a teacher or an adult sees a spark in the young child's eye and helps them achieve something great—something better. But, as tough as it is for so many millions, so few were as broken as Adam. Somehow, he was more broken than any other, and carried the weight of a life unloved on his shoulders.

By the time Adam reached Boston he was quite familiar with how to manipulate his prey. From the young age of 16 he was selling his body for money—he knew how to get what he wanted and to give you what you think you wanted. While the nuns at the orphanage believed Adam had been working an after-school job between school and returning home each evening, he was really in the woods getting blow jobs from anyone willing to pay for the treat, or jerking off for them—either way, doing work that gave him the money he knew he would need once he was a free man. Adam was well endowed. Add his large penis to his tall, toned teen body, handsome baby face, and his confident, carefree attitude, and Adam was a pervert's dream.

He was smart enough not to have intercourse with anyone while underage, and he rarely ever wanted to get that intimate with anyone, even for money—although that changed once he was of legal age. In Boston he became a regular male escort to some wealthy patrons—both men and women. With his newfound steady income and no sense of responsibility in a new big city, Adam was easy prey for the dark underworld of sex, drugs and violence. Although he felt right at home on the dark side of the street, he was smart enough to keep the drugs and violence away from the escorting, unless a customer was into the dark side too. Thanks to his good looks, or maybe it was the size of his penis— Adam was given the opportunity to join one of his more regular, more wealthy Johns on a business trip to London. Within a year Adam had gone from never leaving Vermont to crossing the pond to a bigger, older, darker world. The business trip included first-class tickets, a first-class experience, and ended with a first-class murder.

* * * * *

After everything Adam had been through and all that he managed to get away with, he had finally been captured. The media had been following what would become his story since long before Catherine was found in the cemetery, but it was after he was captured that the public became fascinated with Adam's story. Every news outlet was looking for an angle — something to give them the ratings they needed and the audience they craved to stay relevant.

Adam was the main headline in all the newspapers, local and national, making front page news for many weeks. He was talked about on every news and talk show across every television channel. He had become a celebrity. The security at the police station had increased, and they were on high alert for anyone trying to get in and jeopardize the case. For as many fans as Adam had over his celebrity status, there were just as many people who wanted to hurt him — wanted him to pay for what he had done.

The police spent many days questioning Adam about Catherine and about his history of crime. He denied everything, at first. Eventually he gave to the police interrogations and admitted that he and Hoover had hurt Catherine. When he saw how well the media took his confession Adam began to start talking about all his crimes as if he were readying his CV to the police. With every revelation the police found that they were connecting more and more unsolved murders and the media gave Adam the stage he never wanted. His name became a household name. Adam admitted to making dozens of deposits at several sperm banks around the city. He could not name them but admitted that he visited many in the 10 years he spent living on the streets of London. The police were able to charge Adam for many cemetery murders, and the raping of Catherine. In fact, long after Adam was dead, the police continued to uncover facts and clues that pointed many unsolved murders back to Adam.

With Adam's confession Catherine's husband, the police, and her doctors all wanted Catherine to have an abortion. They all wanted to kill her unborn child, to end a life once they confirmed that Adam was the father. They were no better than Adam. Catherine refused any such idea. She would not go against her morals to satisfy anyone, even if it meant bringing a new monster to life.

Once charged of his crimes, the police were hopeful that Adam's case would move through the court system rapidly. No one wanted this case to linger any longer than it had, and certainly no one wanted the continued media hype that had been generated. To some, Adam was a hero—a master of murder. To others he was nothing more than a sick, demented soul who needed to burn in Hell. Unfortunately for all the haters, the criminal justice system was mismanaged and backlogged which meant that Adam would spend more time in jail before he would have the chance to meet any judge. Once it was decided that Adam would have to spend many months in jail before he could make his defense, the police decided to transfer Adam to a more secure prison, but Adam never made it to the new prison.

A young, rookie officer was fascinated with Adam's story—Not in a "I want to be like you" way, but more of a "How did you do it?" kind of way. The officer and his girlfriend talked about Adam all the time, and when the officer learned that he would be the one to escort Adam to the van on transport day he was so excited. He even sent a text to his girlfriend to let her know. Hearing this news, she texted back a bunch of questions she wanted him to ask Adam. Overly excited as if he were meeting his favorite celebrity, the officer fumbled with cuffing Adam, too star-struck to see clearly, giving Adam the upper hand for a moment. Before the officer could ask his first question, he was painting the floor red with his own blood. He lay there breathing heavily, trying to comprehend what had happened, how Adam had overtaken him so quickly, so easily. He thought about his girlfriend. He thought about his mother, and in his final breath he thought about his mistake as his eyes watched Adam move down the hall away from him, carrying the gun that just put a bullet in his neck. That one shoot echoed through the police station, and all the officers knew it was Adam. Without hesitation the dispatcher called for all units to return to base as everyone was trying to find safety. Adam, on the other hand, was trying to get out quickly. He filled the station with the beautiful sound of gunfire followed by screams and loud thuds, leaving a wake of death on the cold floor behind him as he ran towards freedom. Adam had only one goal, and he was not going to be captured again—not alive.

Adam managed to keep the police station captive for a few hours, long enough for the media to smell the gun smoke and come running with cameras rolling. Their celebrity was helping boost ratings for them again, but Adam struggling to find an exit—struggling to give the media any cliffhanger or closure. Alone, frightened and tired, tears escaped from Adam's eyes. He yelled to his mother, his father and to people only familiar to him. He could have ended it all quickly by taking his own life, but instead he chose to live, to prove, if only to himself, that he was strong, determined, and capable of taking on the entire police force. Outside, the station was surrounded by a blue wave, bright camera lights and hundreds of concerned faces— onlookers amazed by all the activity of this once quiet part of the city. Gunshots were periodically heard inside followed by more screams, but not from Adam. He was not looking for hostages, but instead was focused on killing anyone who stood between him and freedom, regardless of how innocent or involved they were in his web of chaos. His only thought was of the front door to the police station. He needed to get away.

By the time he had finished, Adam had killed eight officers and three civilians. He also managed to wound six other officers. His voice was hoarse from yelling, and his vision blurred by tears. His clothes were wet, soaked with his own sweat and stained with the blood of his victims. He had, without comprehending his own words, confessed to even more cemetery killings, including the location of Hoover, who he had already confessed to killing in a drug induced rage just a few days before he was caught. In his final moments Adam was confessing to so much more violence than the police knew anything about.

After his unplanned confession, Adam, with a gun in each hand, taken from officers he killed, shot randomly as he ran through the station toward what he thought was freedom. More police had entered the building by this time and were focused on pushing Adam into a corner — a corridor with no way out. He was monitored through closed circuit TV as police continued to pressure him to surrender, slowly forcing him in the direction that they wanted him to go. Blood and tears swirled new colors on his face. The stench of urine wrapped his leg as it flowed down his smooth, hairless body and onto the floor around his foot. It was then that he knew he had lost this battle. He could see the blue uniforms, some smeared with partners' blood, others covered in armor, but all moving closer, all stronger than Adam. He knew that this was the end, the freedom he sought outside the walls would not come with a heartbeat. With one last shot Adam's body collapsed to the floor and the pool of yellow mixed with his own dark red blood. He never got the chance to meet his son, Nicholas.

CHAPTER FOUR

The monotone voice echoed through the starched white hall almost void of life. Peter stood motionless, staring at the operating room doors. His long auburn hair was tangled, and his clothes were well worn. It was evident that he had not thought about his appearance that evening. He stood silently, almost deaf to the passing doctors and the echoing voices, just staring at the doors with eyes squinted and a face expressing his tiredness, confusion, and pain.

Bodies wrapped in pale blue suits or white jackets rushed around him, all of them mumbling medical lingo. They were speaking another language—one that his wife could understand. He knew, however, that it had something do with what was happening on the other side of those doors—something to do with his unborn bastard. Every time the doors opened, he tried to steal a view, jerking his body this way and that looking for any indication of life.

Peter thought about Jessica, just down the hall holding his biological son. Tears rolled down his face splashing in a puddle on the sterile tile beneath him and the joys he had shared with his Catherine, as few as there were, sped through his mind. He was unable to capture a single moment and hold on to it to help him through his pain. Eventually his body went numb, and he had to sit down. With his hands over his eyes and elbows resting on his knees he sat, crying more heavily now as if he knew what was truly happening on the other side of the doors—visions of the cemetery and Adam filling his head. His sniffling and groans of sadness joined the monotone voices and together these sent him into a blissful, yet very uncomfortable sleep in the chair. Many hours had passed before a nurse woke Peter. He was startled at first, but when he heard the monotone echoing, he remembered where he was and panicked.

"Excuse me sir, but I must ask that you follow me. The doctor would like to see you." Silence.

"Please, sir ... you really must come with me now."

Peter looked at the woman and then at the doors. He could see only darkness through the tiny windows and jumped up at the nurse. Startled, she leapt back and scolded him as if he were a child in school, pointing her finger at him and ordering him to follow her. Dazed and confused, Peter reluctantly gave in, dropped his head, almost in shame, and proceeded through the now empty halls, almost dragging his feet like a little boy. His head was filled with horrific thoughts of blank tombstones.

"Where are we going? Where is my wife? I demand that you bring me to my wife." He was trying to sound commanding, but the nurse could hear the shudder in his voice, the crackle that let her know this man was not strong, not now, and probably never was.

"Oh my god ... the child, where is the child?" His tone grew more tense and his voice got louder as the two walked through the halls. He was still trying to fully wake up and was becoming very irate with the nurse. She continued her pace, quietly leading Peter to the doctor.

Finally reaching their destination, the nurse opened a door and signaled Peter to enter. Once inside she closed the door swiftly, yet quietly, leaving Peter and returning to her other duties. Like his mistress, this nurse provided no comfort in

Peter's time of need and left him alone as soon as she possibly could. In the short walk from OR to the doctor, this nurse felt sympathy for Catherine, not because of the outcome so much, but more so for her having to have lived with such a miserable man. Peter continued to yell to the nurse through the door, crying at the same time. He did not know if he was crying tears of fear or anger, but it felt the right thing to do at the time, and he could not have been more right.

"Please sit down, sir."

Peter jumped at the sound of the deep, strong voice. He thought he had been left alone. Without any verbal fight, Peter walked across the room and sat across from a large sterile desk. Peter was always too submissive—almost wimpish at times. He tried to act tough, but deep inside his heart and soul he was a little child, afraid of so much, yet eager to touch everything. The two men watched each other for a few minutes in silence, each almost waiting for the other to speak. Peter wanted to yell again but stopped himself. He wanted to know what had happened and where his family was. The doctor sat silently as he collected the words he needed to speak.

"I am afraid that we had some complications, Mr. Lawson," the doctor said in a low voice. "Please stay seated while I explain."

"Your wife, as you were aware, was not in the best of health. It was, in fact, a risk for her to try to have this child, and I must regrettably tell you that your wife did not survive the surgery."

Peter sat motionless with tears rolling down his quivering face. He did not know whether to yell or hit something or someone. Every time he opened his mouth only spits of mumbled words escaped.

"What about the …"

"I am pleased to say, however, that your son was born in good health. His weight and heartbeat are excellent, and he has been moved to our maternity ward. I know that this must be very difficult for you, but when you are ready, I will take you to see your son." After a few minutes of silence, the two men headed toward the maternity ward.

* * * * *

Months after Adam took his last breath Nicholas took his first. Father and son would never get the chance to meet in person. Anyone who knew the true origin of Nicholas—knew the wrath of Adam—would say that Nicholas was his father reborn. Peter knew that Nicholas was not his biological son, and he knew that across town his true biological son was going to grow up never knowing him. Soon after his last motel sex-a-thon with Jessica she ended their affair. The media attention that Peter and Catherine received thanks to Adam was much more than anything Jessica wanted to get involved with, especially if she was going to convince her husband that Oliver was his own child.

Peter did the best he could at raising Nicholas, whom he named after Catherine's late father. He felt it fitting to do so. However, where Catherine's father was a decorated war hero and a gentleman of an era long past, her son would grow up to be the tyrant she never expected but should have known given that he had a good bit of Adam's DNA. Soon after Nicholas was born Peter moved back to the States to get out from under the dark cloud of London.

Shortly before Peter and Nicholas returned to the States, Jessica, James, and Oliver had relocated back to Greenwich. Peter remembered that Jessica had a home in Connecticut and knew that she and her husband were only in London for a short period of time. Peter was hopeful that one day he would get to meet his son, so he chose to move to Connecticut as well.

Oliver and Nicholas grew up in the same town but went to different schools. Oliver was enrolled in the local private prep school where he received a top dollar education and was taught the skills necessary to be a refined gentleman while Nicholas was left to fend for himself in the local public school system. Looking back, their paths crossed many times without each other knowing the twisted connection they shared.

CHAPTER FIVE

Twenty-Two years later.

Outside, the sky flashed brightly, almost immediately followed by the roar of thunder. Inside, the room was dark, except for the glowing red numbers on the clock—two dots flashing, temporarily getting lost in the darkness. Heavy curtains covered the floor-to-ceiling windows, allowing an occasional yellow flash into the room— they were not the best blackout curtains. Oliver was sleeping, but not soundly. With each roar of thunder his body twitched as he struggled to free himself from yet another nightmare—the same nightmare he has almost every night. As the storm grew more intense outside the wind rattled the one partially opened window, ruffling the curtains. Thunder roared again. While quite loud for the rest of the occupants, Oliver was in a deep sleep, trapped by his nightmare, not able to hear anything in the outside world.

In those moments when the real world and the dreamworld collide, a thunderous clap both outside the window and inside his dream startled Oliver. He sat up suddenly, releasing himself from his prison of the night. His chiseled naked body was dripping in sweat and entangled in the sheets—he was still trapped. When the random flash from the lightening filled the room, Oliver could see the wetness covering his body. Propping himself against the headboard, he cried quietly listening to the storm, surveying his room whenever the lightening provided a glimmer of brightness in his otherwise dark space. It was at these moments that he could see the mess throughout his bedroom. Anyone who did not know Oliver would think that the storm had ravaged his room, wildly throwing things without care. Books were scattered, mixed with clothes, both clean and dirty. But this is how he lived—organized chaos.

As he sat in bed Oliver thought about his father, and about Elizabeth—the two people he loved very dearly who had recently left him, left this world. He was crying for the joys he wished for in his dreams, and the happiness he was certain once existed in his life. He cried for the pain and suffering, and unanswered questions of his nightmares. His sweaty body coated in goose bumps shivered as he cried more, now with only dry tears.

* * * * *

Elizabeth would have been one year older than Oliver, if she were alive to celebrate life. The only child of Oliver's aunt — his mother's only sister, Elizabeth was like a sister to Oliver. Growing up in the same town they had the joy of spending a lot of time together. They went to the same schools and shared many of the same friends. They were each other's best friend and shared all their secrets — well, almost all of them. All through high school the two spent a lot of time together. So, it was crushing to Oliver to learn that Elizabeth was going to college in another state — not the same college Oliver was planning to attend. Sure, it was inevitable that they would grow up and lead separate lives, but that did not stop Oliver from feeling betrayed, somehow.

While Elizabeth and Oliver had spent a lot of their teen years together, they did have different lives. Elizabeth was raised by a single mother — her father was killed when Elizabeth was still a baby.

Her dad had run to the market to get more diapers when a car full of drunk teenagers ran a red light, smashing into the side of his car. The force from the SUV hitting the sedan sent his car rolling over five times before stopping upside down. Her father was dead before the car stopped flipping. The driver of the SUV, the star quarterback, was not wearing a seatbelt, so he went through the window with such speed that his skull was crushed by the force. He was dead before he hit the ground. The head cheerleader, class president and daughter of the principal were three others in the SUV. None of them made it to graduation that year. There was an abundance of alcohol in their blood, and empty beer bottles and cans in the SUV along with a receipt from a local liquor store on the edge of town that often sold to minors. The owner of that liquor store was arrested, tried, and convicted of murder on all five accounts. He spent a year in jail before hanging himself in his cell.

Elizabeth was too young to remember any of this, but read about it when she was older, and had heard different versions of the story, more than once. As a result of the actions of people she never knew, Elizabeth was not allowed to get her driver's license, nor was she allowed to have alcohol. The first restriction she could live with, but the latter soothed her throat more often than her mother would ever know.

Elizabeth's dad did leave a life insurance policy behind for she and her mom. That combined with the small settlement Elizabeth's mom received from suing the liquor store owner before he killed himself, provided them enough to live—modestly. This was in great contrast to how Oliver lived. His mother married a wealthy hedge fund manager. They lived an extremely lavish lifestyle—one that embarrassed Oliver most of the time, especially when he was around Elizabeth and their friends.

Elizabeth was very smart, which scored here a full scholarship to Emory University where she would study molecular biology. Although far from Oliver at that point in her life, they stayed in contact and got together every time she returned home, which was almost never. By her senior year they saw each other once or twice a year and talked once a month. School and life got in the way of them both keeping the connection alive. Just weeks before graduation she was gone. Well, her body was not, but her smile, her wit, her laugh—they were all gone, for good. And, while it had been almost a year, as the anniversary of her death approached the police were no closer to catching the killer. The life Oliver and Elizabeth let grow apart that was hanging heavy on Oliver now as he grieved the loss of his father. He had been sick for some time, and it was clear that any time with him should be considered the last time. While that script played out longer than the doctors predicted, it was still a shock when Oliver got the call from his mother. His father went peacefully in his sleep not long after Oliver graduated from college.

* * * * *

Although the storm continued for many hours, Oliver did eventually fall back to sleep. He struggled to stay awake, afraid of returning to his nightmare; however, the weight of stress and of life sat upon his eyelids, forcing his tired body back to sleep. Fortunately for Oliver, this time his sleep was sounder, and the storm had finally calmed. Outside, the sky continued to cry, almost as if for Oliver's suffering, with a steady downpour of acid tears.

Hours later a colony of birds chirped a symphony in the tree by the open window as the gray sky opened to the rising sun. Beams of light, bright and golden, found their way around the curtains to partially fill Oliver's room—so much for being blackout curtains. One beam of light stretched across Oliver's face, warming his cheeks and drying any remaining tears. Eventually he sat up, acknowledging that once again Mother Nature was waking him. She kept him from feeling his entire nightmare the night before and was now struggling to keep him from sleeping all day.

Aside from the few beams of sunlight, his room remained dark. Without turning on any light, Oliver untangled his clammy, naked body from his blankets and began an adventure across the chilled room toward the bathroom. His body was a gorgeous sight. As he moved across the room different beams of light revealed his toned features—a living statue of David—a body that most would kill for. In fact, one did.

His floor was a jungle of books, papers, and clothing, among other things, but he was familiar enough with his own jungle to know the path between his bed and the bathroom. His foot, still enjoying the peacefulness of sleep, was weak as it touched the cold hardwood floor. A tingling sensation ran up his leg, and he almost fell to the floor. Grabbing the bed post, Oliver stood tapping his foot on the cold wood, trying to end the sensation, and put life back into his large, tanned foot. He bent over and rubbed the long thin toes, each very cold to the touch, but smooth with just a tussle of hair on their knuckles. He felt the icy cold metal around one toe which triggered a thought about Sebastian, and he smiled. Once he was certain his foot was alert, ready for the stride to the bathroom, Oliver continued his journey.

* * * * *

Sebastian was the first guy Oliver kissed. He was a senior year in high school and was doing a semester abroad as part of a student exchange program. As part of the program Oliver lived with Sebastian, his younger sister, and their parents in Notting Hill in western London. Sebastian's mother worked in the UK office of the same firm Oliver's dad worked for in New York, so his parents did not have to worry about Oliver living with complete strangers. Oliver had been questioning his sexuality for a few years trying figure out who he was, and what he wanted. Sebastian had already come to terms with his bisexuality by then.

Oliver's semester in London provided an more hands-on education than he expected. From the first day Oliver and Sebastian were inseparable, and almost immediately they were in love, or at least what teenagers considered love. Oliver experienced the emotion and passion that comes with kissing a boy for the first time. While the two did not have intercourse, they did explore each other's bodies in ways that Oliver had never experienced with a boy or girl before. At their young age they were certain that their love was real, was everlasting. Sebastian gave Oliver a ring, a beautiful sterling silver ring that hugged Oliver's right index toe to this day — a reminder of what love was or could have been. Sebastian wore a similar ring, each inscribed with their joint initials commemorating their bond, Oliver's first love.

Oliver won the battle across his room without any bumps and scraps, and once in the bathroom, standing in total darkness on cold tiles, grabbed himself, aimed and fired into the dark still air. Seconds later he realized that he was, once again, watering the bathtub. He finished and flushed his bright yellow deposit with hot water. Then he managed to find the sink to splash cold water on his face before returning to the warmth of his blankets. At the sink, Oliver stood, embracing the cold white porcelain, staring at the dark blurry vision before him. His reflection was lit only by a faint nightlight hanging from the wall next to the vanity. Its bulb was near the end of its life and provided very little clarity to the dark room. His hair was tangled and blonde — bright as the sun. His face was clear of any blemishes. His hazel eyes stunning. The kind of eyes you cannot stop staring at because of their vibrance and beauty. He was the mirror image of a father he never met, but with highlights of his mother. Oliver was born a very handsome boy, and he knew it. He was not egotistical about it but accepted this gift and used it to his advantage, only too often, as he grew up.

As he stood staring into the mirror, struggling to make out the dark image reflecting at him, he thought about the past, and the scars on his wrists — the only flaws on his well-maintained body. He had no other imperfections, and he continued to sculpt his body every day as he maintained less than 3% body fat. He thought about the day he painted the bathroom red, sprays of it everywhere, dark and thick, and how it swam across his tanned body. Why had he done it? What could make a teenager who had it all—all but answers—do such a thing? He wondered then, and still wondered now. It was not planned—the attempt to take his own life. Well, not then, and not that way. Oliver struggled, like so many teens, to find his place in life. But unlike many, his mind was often in a dark space filled with dark thoughts, or at least what he thought or perceived to be dark thoughts. There were many occasions when he would find himself thinking about guys ... naked. But his friends didn't know. Elizabeth didn't even know. He was the only child, raised in a rigid home with strict values—values that did not include boys liking boys. Ironically, cheating on your spouse was a value overlooked by his mother, and he suspected by his father too. But homosexuality was a sin—there was no way around it, no other way to say it.

Oliver's uncle was gay—his paternal father's only brother, Samuel, who came out when he was a teenager. Sure, times were different that far back, but it did not stop Uncle Samuel from coming out as gay during his junior year in high school. He was the quarterback, the star basketball player, and fastest runner on the track team. He was even class president one year. All of that mattered to his parents, but when Uncle Samuel came out to Oliver's grandparents, none of that mattered. They stopped talking to him completely. They sent him away, almost immediately to a conversion compound in another state. Oliver heard this story from his father only once and never from any other family member. No one talked about or to Uncle Samuel from that day forward. This frightened Oliver, and as a result, he spent a lot of time in his teenage years fighting urges and feelings for fear of joining Uncle Samuel far away. Oliver often wondered what became of his uncle but was always too afraid to ask.

The thought of that moment when his own life was so close to death filled his head with lonely thoughts. His own reflection sickened him now, and so he returned to the warmth of his blankets. The hatred drilled into him by his parents and grandparents occasionally found its way out of Oliver, and when it did, he would get drunk and wake up with self-inflicted bruises. Fortunately for him none left any scars aside from the ones on his wrists.

Once back in bed Oliver pulled the blankets up to his waist and sat in the cold dark silence. He ran his hands over his sculpted abs and thought about Sebastian again. It got him a little hard. He quickly changed thoughts and was trying to make sense of his nightmare—the nightmare that haunts him many nights a week. The nightmare is not about one event—they never are. Instead, it was a collage of visions and memories that frightened him. At 22, Oliver had lived through so many horrific events in his life. He often wondered how he survived. Why did his parents come home early from the opera that night so many years ago? Had they not, would he have died—drowned in a pool of his own blood? Why did his parents hate one another? And since they hated each other so much, why did they stay together until his father's death?

It was not long after his paternal father had died that his mother came clean about her affair. She felt it was important that Oliver know the truth—or maybe she thought it would help wash away some of her guilt. All these images and their stories created Oliver's' dark sleepless nights. His days were spent trying to figure out how to combat the dark clouds of his nightmares and find the rainbow of his dreams.

CHAPTER SIX

Nicholas was 15 years old when he saw Elizabeth for the first time—it was at the local independent coffee house, 'Cup of Joe.' She was the most beautiful girl he had ever seen, and he had already seen his share of porn. Nicholas went by the coffee house every day afterward in hopes of seeing Elizabeth. She was not always there, but when she was, he would watch from across the street, and sometimes he would go in for a coffee to get a closer look at her—to smell her and hear her voice. To Nicholas, she was a goddess—and angel. He would find himself thinking about her when he touched himself in the shower. Those visions could make him explode in ways that his magazine centerfolds never could. He would come to discover that only his thoughts of Oliver made him explode more.

Although Nicholas found Elizabeth attractive, he did not approach her. He assumed she was out of his league, and while he did not give a crap what people thought, he believed that she would reject him immediately. And he knew what happened when people rejected him ... they got hurt—badly. Many died. So instead, Nicholas watched Elizabeth from afar. He would learn her schedule, and her routine so he could have more opportunities to see her. It would be a long time before he even learned her name.

One day as Nicholas was running past the 'Cup of Joe,' he saw Elizabeth and Oliver sitting inside by the window, laughing ferociously. Elizabeth and Oliver were sharing stories from summer camp, and the hilarious pranks Elizabeth's cabin mates had pulled on their bunk leader, but Nicholas did not know what they were talking about, nor did he care. He was instantly jealous of Oliver, although he had no idea who Oliver was then. He wanted to be the guy sitting across from Elizabeth laughing, but he knew that would never happen. At the same time, he was also jealous of Elizabeth because Nicholas had never seen a more handsome boy as Oliver. Nicholas would have enjoyed sitting across from Oliver laughing about something stupid and being close enough to Oliver to have their hands brush across one another, or their knees touch under the table as their bodies jerked in laughter. This was not the first time that

Nicholas found a guy attractive. He had seen his share of porn, after all. Nicholas struggled with who he thought about more after seeing Oliver for the first time. He did not know anything about either of them—not factual anyway—only what he made up in his head. It would be some time before Nicholas would learn that Elizabeth was older, and Oliver was her cousin. It would be even longer before he would learn that the boy that he was falling in love with could be his brother.

Nicholas would eventually grow into the handsome, muscled god that he is today, but back in high school he was a tall, quiet, almost scary teen boy who had few friends. When Nicholas was not stalking Elizabeth or Oliver, he was busy with typical awkward teen issues like being bullied by the athletes, yelled at by the cheerleaders if they thought he looked at them too long, and of course conceiving ways to kill them all.

Elizabeth graduated a year before Oliver and Nicholas and went to off to college at Emory University. Her first year was tough, as it can be for some freshmen moving so far away from home and being all alone. But she settled in faster than she thought and found herself quite happy living in the

South. She returned north for her first Christmas in college, but that was it. The rest of her time off was spent exploring who she was, what she wanted. Oliver visited her a couple of times and fell in love with Atlanta. He especially loved hanging out shirtless in Piedmont Park. He and Elizabeth would argue over who was getting more attention when they would spend hours enjoying the weather, and sights of the park.

Nicholas also made a few trips to Atlanta to see what Elizabeth was doing and keep tabs on her, but by now it was so he could see more of Oliver. One summer day in Piedmont Park, Oliver and Elizabeth, and a few of Elizabeth's college friends were enjoying a picnic when Oliver noticed Nicholas. He could not see him very clearly, but could see his toned body, and was aroused. Nicholas was shirtless and walking a dog he borrowed from the dog park on the other side of the park. Then later he was wearing a shirt, and without the dog. Then even later he was shirtless again, and with a different dog. That is when Oliver began to think that Nicholas was watching them. He liked being watched, a little, and wondered if he would have noticed Nicholas at all if Nicholas had not been shirtless. Oliver asked Elizabeth if she knew the shirtless man with the various dogs, but she did not. Nor did she even recognize him, even though he had been watching her for many years. Nicholas caught on that he was being watched while watching Oliver and Elizabeth, and left the park, but did not stop watching them from a greater distance. Oliver thought about Nicholas a lot after seeing him in the park, and even went back to the park a few times without Elizabeth in hopes of running into him, but never got lucky. What Oliver did not know was that Nicholas was there, in the park watching Oliver, still. Oliver left Atlanta without ever seeing teenage Nicholas or his cousin again.

A month later as the fall semester was beginning, Elizabeth stopped going to her classes, stopped answering her phone, and her email. It was not like Elizabeth to ignore her cousin. After feeling ghosted for 24 hours Oliver reached out to Elizabeth's mom to see if she knew anything. She did not, and of course, she panicked at the thought of her only child missing. She called the school, and she called the house where Elizabeth lived hoping that one of her roommates would know something. They did not. Then she called the Atlanta police.

Within two days the police were interviewing everyone and anyone who might have known or seen Elizabeth. Nicholas saw all this excitement coming to life outside Elizabeth's house and kept his distance. He wanted to be nothing more than an onlooker, not someone the police decided they wanted to question too. This was not his first rodeo.

Days turned into a week, and still no one had seen or heard from Elizabeth. Campus security video did not provide any clues of where Elizabeth might have gone, but some footage did give police a good idea of the people Elizabeth interacted with on the last day she was seen thanks to all the security cameras around campus. Aside from being harassed by a few frat boys, she was seen talking with some girls, and then one person, in a hoodie, wearing an unbranded backpack, never showing their face to any of the campus cameras. The campus police found it impressive and concerning that someone was able to evade every single campus camera. There were hundreds of cameras around the campus. It is almost impossible to go unnoticed, and yet there it was — in grainy black and white — a great deal of footage of a mystery person.

The police were able to find everyone from the video recordings who interacted with Elizabeth on the last day she was seen—everyone except the person in the hoodie. And the more interesting part of their investigation revealed that no one the police spoke with could identify the person in the hoodie. Hundreds of students wore hoodies. It was as if he were an illusion. It had taken Nicholas many visits to Atlanta to understand where all the cameras were, and how to stand in just the right place for each one.

The police had given up on the idea of any ransom note days after Elizabeth went missing. They had not ruled out death just yet. Two weeks after Elizabeth disappeared, a note was found. It had not been delivered to Elizabeth's mother, or the police. Instead, the letter was found buried in a stack of old mail in the hall of her rental house. No one thought to look there because it was buried on a table with other junk mail that looked like it had been there for months. An odd place to leave a ransom note, unless of course you really did not care about the ransom, the police thought.

The letter was written poorly, a combination of crayon and random letters cut out from magazines and pasted together. The note made little sense to anyone and asked for nothing. It made no mention of Elizabeth's condition, reason for disappearance, or whether she would ever be returned. Instead, the note mentioned how much the author loved Elizabeth, but in the end loved someone else more and needed Elizabeth out of the picture. It made very little sense to the police, or Elizabeth's mom. The police were unable to find any fingerprints on the note. A handwriting analysis comparing the crayon lettering to everyone they thought could be involved, including Oliver, turned up nothing. The police later discovered that the note was computer generated.

The random note file had been saved on a flash drive that was left in the computer lab on campus, which was used by many students. Narrowing the search for a suspect would have been impossible for the police had it not been for the additional files also on the disk. With this new evidence, the police were on their way to solving this crime, or so they thought.

The police were interested in one of the frat boys already interviewed now that the disk had surfaced. The other files on the disk were a few

English paper assignments—essays and poems, a resume, and a love letter. While the ransom letter was directed at Elizabeth, the love letter, and some of the poems were meant for someone else—a frat brother. The person who the police believed to be the owner of the disk claimed ignorance about it all—saying it was all fake, and that he was being framed. He was very nervous about all the attention since he was still in denial about his sexuality and his love for one of his frat brothers.

Elizabeth's body was finally found almost three weeks after she had gone missing. In the fraternity house where the boys on the video recording lived, some of the brothers smelled something rotting in the basement and when they could not see anything after a quick look, one of them called the campus police. The one to call was a criminal justice student, a studious, nontypical fraternity boy who knew very well what a dead rotting body smelled like—a combination of rotting meat and fruit. The police could smell the corpse, but like the fraternity brothers, could not see any body. It was not until they tore into a part of the basement wall that they found Elizabeth's body, tangled and squeezed in between the joints, just thrown into the wall and boarded up. Elizabeth's body had been severely beaten. Many of her bones had been broken, and her breasts had been severed, in addition to multiple stab wounds and other bodily marks. Her blood had been mostly drained out.

The police apprehended her suspected murderer quite easily because of a wallet found in the wall with Elizabeth's body. The wallet and disk with the note found earlier belonged to the same person. And while the student had been questioned already and proclaimed his innocence, the evidence was stacking up against him. It was not long before the boy and two of his friends were arrested and put on trial. They continued to claim their innocence through the entire trial. They did admit to having sex with Elizabeth but professed that it was totally consensual even though they all had sex with her at the same time—on occasion. This trial brought more confessions by more boys about their relationship with Elizabeth—at least their sexual relationship. She had slept around, through most of her college years and even prostituted herself at times for quick cash to feed a small drug habit she acquired in junior high. No one knew—not even Oliver—about this darker side of Elizabeth. Nicholas knew since he was always watching her.

The boys were eventually found not guilty. The wallet had been reported missing before Elizabeth was reported missing. None of the credit cards had been used in some time, and the only bank receipt in the wallet was five weeks old. As for the flash drive, it turned out that the other files on the drive were all forged as well. They did in fact belong to the frat boy, but they were files from over a year ago found on a disk formatted only a month ago. Logs pulled from the computer lab showed that the boy never logged into the campus computers, and his fingerprints were not found on the flash drive.

The night of their acquittal, while the three slept—the whole house sat dark, and warm with a slight stench of alcohol, and cleaning agents still flushing out the old smell of death in the basement. Quite suddenly the house caught fire and was engulfed in flames—no one woke again. This tragedy lit the campus ablaze. Arson could not be proven, nor ruled out, even though the authorities blamed a leaky gas line. And again, no activity out of the ordinary was found on any camera footage. From Elizabeth's disappearance to her death and then the death of the fraternity boys, the police were left with no evidence or a single clue about who was responsible for any of the carnage.

Nicholas watched the entire Elizabeth drama unfold from the shadows. This was one of his more elaborate kills—one that required months of prep. He was certain that he would be caught if he did not take the extra precautions. Getting into the fraternity house proved to be the more challenging part of the entire farce. Fortunately, he was able to attend several parties, and private events, in the house to scope out the layout, and to cause enough chaos in the basement to have a wall knocked out by two guys fighting over what they would have trouble remembering later. But their roughhousing put a big enough hole in one of the walls to require a repair man. And thankfully the boys were drunk most of the time that they never noticed Nicholas in a fake beard and wig pretending to be the carpenter hired to repair the wall.

The burning of the frat house was not part of Nicholas' original plan but given the amount of time he had to spend in their getting every part of his plan to work correctly, a few weeks into the performance he knew that these were lose ends that had to be severed and coordinating the kills of each of them would take too long—so burning down the house made the most sense. It also eliminated any trace of Nicholas even being in the house.

The coroner would conclude that Elizabeth had not been raped, and in fact had not had sex for some time leading up to her time of death. She had no drugs in her system, and only some semen on her clothes, which could have been placed there by Nicholas. So, did she know her killer? Everyone who knew Elizabeth had been questioned endlessly. Everyone, that is, except the person in the dark hoodie. That one player remained a mystery to the police, and it did not make sense to them how that was possible.

By the time the flames of the frat house had been extinguished Nicholas was gone, too. He had completed what he set out to do on campus, and more. He had an agenda, and with Elizabeth crossed off the list, he was on to the next victim. That meant heading to London. He had some unfinished business to complete before he would eventually get to Oliver.

While Nicholas was flying halfway around the world a package was being delivered to the prosecutor's office. The box was delivered by a courier service and was immediately handed over to the police since the courier was unable to say where the package originated, or who sent it. The police opened the box to find a dark hoodie and a note. Much like the ransom note, this note was computer generated. It was a cursive font with the words "Better luck next time, gents."

The hoodie, the box, the note — everything was sent to forensics immediately. The courier was forced to strip down to his underpants and hand over all his clothes in the off chance that he did encounter the killer. The police felt so close to solving the case that they did not want to overlook even the smallest detail. Yet much like every other clue Nicholas had left for previous police and prosecutor teams, the police found no evidence of Nicholas on anything. They were no closer to finding Elizabeth's killer.

CHAPTER SEVEN

Oliver's thoughts were interrupted by a thunderous knock on his bedroom door, which was repeated several times before he finally acknowledged it.

"Yes," Oliver responded in a scratchy, tired voice.

"Are you awake Oliver?"

"Does it matter?"

The door crept open slowly, and a figure appeared from behind it, continuing to whisper.

"Good morning."

"Is it?" Oliver asked.

With the door completely open, a silhouette of Oliver's roommate, Howard, stood in the door frame and while Oliver could not see his face, he could see his beautiful figure.

"Do you want to join us for breakfast?"

"No thanks, I can't eat right now."

"Did you have trouble sleeping through that storm? I'll tell you what—Reed gets even more horny and excited during thunderstorms. I am surprised we did not wake the neighborhood."

Again, Oliver turned this head toward the door trying to see Howard's facial expression, but he still could not. He knew that Howard was wearing a smile, a huge smile—he always did after sex. Sometimes Oliver wondered if Howard thought of anything other than sex.

Oliver and Howard were roommates, first in the dorms and later in this house. They met as freshmen and had been best friends since. Oliver was more of a wild child than Howard, but then his upbringing reflected that. It was Howard who remained the calm one, in most cases, and was always trying to keep Oliver from making stupid mistakes. Of course, Howard too had a wild side— sometimes too wild. Through their early college years many people, including some close friends, thought that the two of them were dating. Howard was openly gay and had been since his very unpleasant outing in high school.

* * * * *

Howard's basketball team had finished practice, and all the boys were all in the locker room. After practice, the showers were packed with naked teen boys talking about an upcoming game, girls, and sex. But this day Howard's body decided to change—he was finally going through puberty. Soap in hand, and dripping wet like his teammates, Howard was busy washing away the teen boy odor. As he did, he was thinking of Edward, the most handsome boy Howard had ever seen.

Edward was a year older, and had already gone through puberty, putting on muscle in all the right places, and not an ounce of fat on him. Edward had a clean blonde bush growing around his big penis, and Howard just loved to look at it in the showers. Howard took his time under the water, secretly watching Edward. Before he knew it, Howard was hard—for the first time and was pointing right at Edward standing under the shower head next to Howard.

Aside from the gushing of water, the room was silent for a moment before laughter filled the room. All the boys were pointing at Howard's crotch, then at Edward, and laughing. Luckily for Howard no one had their phone handy because it happened in the showers. Embarrassed, Howard ran to his locker, put clothes on over his wet body, and sprinted all the way home. It was the worst Friday of his life but ended up triggering the best weekend of his life. He spent that weekend thinking about what had happened in the showers, and why. He knew — had known for some time but had been afraid to admit it.

The following Monday Howard walked into school with the confidence of a victorious warrior. The first boy to try and tease him about the shower incident was shot down as Howard confronted him point blank. Boys get boners. It is part of life. This one happened to have happened at the worst possible time, in the worst possible place, but it helped Howard proclaim who he was, what he was, to the entire school. He embraced his homosexuality and never looked back. Edward never showered near him again.

* * * * *

Howard had his share of lovers, and one-night stands all through college, and he was attracted to Oliver — everyone was. It was not uncommon for one of them to return to the dorm room any night to find the other swimming in the sweat of two overly active bodies under the sheets. The guests seemed to care more about it than Howard or Oliver ever did. While Howard did not particularly enjoy seeing the sweaty, naked flesh of a woman, he tolerated it (a lot like Oliver did), mostly because Oliver pretended not to mind seeing sweaty, naked men with Howard. Oliver continuously emphasized his love for the female body to Howard, but Howard believed that Oliver was hiding some deep thoughts and desires. One drunken night Howard decided to try to bring those desires to the surface.

The two were staying in one Saturday night and were living in their rental house by that time. They had recently moved in and did not have any other roommates yet. Oliver had to finish a term paper and Howard, well, he had more personal plans for the evening. Howard ordered Indian takeout, which he knew Oliver liked very much, and convinced Oliver to take a break from his studies for a relaxing dinner. Oliver agreed, but never expected what he got, although in his thoughts—his dreams, it was something he had hoped for—even longed for since the first time he saw Howard freshmen year. Howard served dinner wearing only boxers. The two ate on Oliver's bed because Howard brought everything into the room before Oliver could stop working and join Howard in the kitchen.

The next several hours that evening were spent sitting on Oliver's bed eating great Indian food, drinking pinot noir, and engaging in deep conversation. None of this was particularly unusual in their friendship. The two often roamed the house almost naked, and though Oliver never admitted it, seeing Howard's sculptured and smooth Asian body in boxers did excite him. To pry as best he could, Howard took their conversation down a very personal path. He suggested that they share "first time" stories. Howard started the conversation not only to set the tone, but because he loved sex and any topic relating to sex.

Oliver found many men and women attractive for a variety of reasons but remained amazed to learn of some of the people Howard and his other friends considered handsome. Oliver's taste in men was specific and limiting. Howard had seen Oliver looking at good looking guys now and again when they were out together at a bar or club, and he had a feeling that Oliver was holding back from telling him, but Howard would never push Oliver to talk — well, almost never. Howard planned to see that evening through, and to get closer to Oliver than he had ever before. After many hours of talking, and many bottles of wine, the two had become quite drunk, which was Howard's plan all along.

Oliver himself was not wearing much clothing that evening. He had showered long before dinner and convinced himself that he was going to be in front of his computer all night and saw no real reason to dress beyond boxers. This excited Howard.

Without any real warning, in the middle of their "first time" stories, Howard found what he thought to be the right moment, and he leaned into Oliver, grabbing his neck and kissing him on the lips. Oliver, drunk and confused, went along with what the two were sharing for almost 30 minutes, but when Howard moved his hand down and grabbed Oliver's crotch, Oliver pushed Howard back.

"Howard, what the hell are you doing?"

"Come on, Oliver. You were enjoying it as much as I was. Admit it."

Oliver, partially erect, got up and walked out of the room and Howard watched as the slightly erect plaid boxers stomped past him. He grinned.

"I am sorry, Oliver," Howard yelled.

"Oliver?"

The house sat silent.

"I do not want to talk about it, Howard," Oliver yelled, now standing at the entrance to his room, his boxers once again limp, and his mind suddenly sober.

"I understand, but—"

"I said drop it! I have a lot of work to do. Thanks for dinner, but I would appreciate it if you would leave me alone now."

"Okay, okay, but I want you to know that I wouldn't force you to do anything you felt uncomfortable doing. I just thought that you were cool with it, that's all."

The next morning the two hardly spoke about what had happened. Howard never tried anything like that again. He realized that Oliver was not ready and might never be.

Within a few days the two were back to old buddies, but they had grown up. They had discovered something new. For Howard it was the realization, or at least assumption, that Oliver was straight or at least bisexual. For Oliver it was the emotion and feeling of being touched by a guy other than Sebastian. Neither knew how to share their discoveries with each other so they ignored them for the moment. While they might not have been able to put into words how they each perceived or received the experience, it was clear that it brought them closer together. Their friendship, their bond had grown stronger, even if neither knew it at the time.

What Oliver never admitted to Howard that night or any night after was that he had enjoyed what they shared and would have loved to see where that kiss would have taken them, but he was more afraid of others and his family at that time to even try. Although Oliver was not one to have regrets that one evening and what might have been would haunt his dreams for many years.

Soon they added more roommates to the house, which certainly removed all hope of ever repeating that night with each other, so they both assumed. It would be much later when they would share another moment together — one that would not only truly test their friendship, but their deeper love for one another.

Oliver could hear Howard in the kitchen making breakfast. Then he heard Reed shuffle down the hall and past Oliver's room. Reed stopped only long enough to say good morning to Oliver as he continued toward the kitchen. Reed was the newest member of the house and was quickly welcomed as part of the gang.

"Are you okay, Oliver?" Reed asked.

Oliver shrugged even though Reed could not see him.

"I'm fine. I'm a fighter —"

"Yeah, but not a lover. I've heard it all before. Yadda, yadda, yadda, blah, blah, blah. You are a strange one, Oliver McPherson, but I think that's why I like you."

After no response from Oliver, Reed left Oliver to ponder his thoughts while he went in search of his boyfriend in the kitchen. Reed knew that Howard and Oliver had a very special friendship, which, while he did not always understand it, he respected it. He also knew that Oliver was very accepting of Howard and Reed living together, which added to Reed's openness around him. Oliver liked Reed for the most part, but at times he tolerated him for the sake of Howard. Reed was attractive, strong and very masculine looking, but was much too feminine acting for Oliver's liking. Oliver had no problem with guys liking guys, but he could never quite understand why a guy would want to act like a girl. This confused him even more as he sought after his own sexual identity.

Reed knew nothing of the past between Howard and Oliver, and never would — at least not from Oliver. Oliver enjoyed spending time with Howard and Reed because it allowed him to see for himself that what they did, and who they were, was okay. That being gay was okay.

Still not ready to get out of bed, Oliver wondered who else was home. As he sat wondering, his thinking was interrupted by a new sound — a voice that he did not recognize. This new voice stopped only long enough to say hello and ask for directions to the kitchen.

"The kitchen?" Oliver asked. "Follow the fucking smell of dead pig. You can't miss it."

"Oliver!" Camilla yelled as the strange man acknowledged Oliver's unique answer and continued in the same direction as the two men before him. This one wore confusion on his face unlike the smiles before him. "Oliver Jackson McPherson, why must you always be such an asshole?" Camilla continued. Her voice got louder as she got closer to Oliver's room.

"Good morning, Camilla, and how are we this lovely morning?" Oliver asked sarcastically through a big grin. "Who is our new friend?"

"Why must you always be so rude?" she yelled in a loud whisper.

"It's in my nature," he laughed. "So what's his name?"

"It is not your nature. Sometimes I—"

"Stop avoiding the question," Oliver interrupted. "Who is he?"

"His name is Miles, and he is not so new, but you are never home so you would not know that, would you?"

Oliver smiled and got out of bed again. He headed for the door to give Camilla a hug.

"Will you put some clothes on, you pervert," Camilla squealed as she gazed at the naked, sculptured flesh reaching out for her.

"You're no fun. It is as if you have never seen one of these before," Oliver said, grabbing himself with one hand as he snatched a pair of plaid boxers and a T-shirt from a stack of clothes near the door and put them on. They headed toward the kitchen hugging one another.

"It is dead pig, you know. I wasn't being rude," Oliver laughed.

"Yeah, but did you have to say fucking?"

"Oh please, as if you two weren't fucking like wild pigs yourselves last night. I'm sure that your latest boy toy can handle a little rough language now and again."

"Sometimes I hate your bluntness, but I suppose you're right."

"Even about fucking like wild pigs?"

"You are so disgusting."

"That might be true, but I'd bet I'm also right." The two laughed as they entered the kitchen.

"You two spend so much time giggling like little schoolgirls. What could always be so funny?" asked Reed.

"Don't bother asking," Howard said. "I have been trying to figure out those two for years. It is best to let them laugh. I don't think we'll ever be able to know or understand them completely."

"It's Miles, isn't it?" Howard asked, waving an egg in Miles' direction. Miles smiled and shrugged in acknowledgment.

"Well, how would you like your eggs?"

"Whatever is best for you. I'm easy."

Howard, his back now turned to everyone, grinned excitedly as he cracked the egg.

"I know you have a shit-eating grin right now Howard," Camilla whispered as she stopped right behind him on her journey to the refrigerator. "Don't even think about it." She slapped his ass and laughed.

Miles was the latest on a long list of boys in Camilla's life. She was a very attractive woman, but being an only child, she grew up spoiled and very picky. All through college she found, time and time again, that every man had a flaw, and she would only accept the perfect man to spend eternity together. Unfortunately for her, she believed Oliver was that man.

* * * * *

Camilla and Oliver met at their college freshman orientation. Camilla was a sophomore and filling in for a friend at the college newspaper orientation booth the day they met. Oliver at the time was a young, eager freshman entering a whole new world. Having been involved in some activities during high school, such as the yearbook and newspaper, Oliver thought it a good idea to get involved with similar activities in college. That is when he saw Camilla. Her smile was visible from across the room—big, bright, and sparkling white. Nervous and somewhat intimidated by such beauty, and not having Elizabeth by his side anymore, Oliver walked around orientation, stopping to check out other booths, but not really paying much attention to them. He kept glancing back toward the beauty standing around stacks of newsprint. Eventually there were no other booths to visit. So, he ventured over to Camilla.

They talked for hours that day about childhood, world peace and the media over beers at a local bar. Camilla was not attracted to Oliver from the start. It was a feeling that grew quickly as the two spent more and more time together in their college activities. For Oliver the friendship was his only interest, although he found her very attractive too. He was enamored with her beauty but was discovering that boys were what he was mostly attracted to once he was in college.

The two traveled together, studied together, and on occasion even slept together. Well, they shared a bed. They never engaged in any sexual activity. Their sleeping together was usually the result of an all-night bender resulting in both unable to drive anywhere and literally staggering into bed, sometimes still dressed where they would find themselves sweaty, sore, and hungover the next morning. A kiss would pass their lips on occasion, but nothing more. The stronger their relationship, their friendship, became, they grew to be like siblings, not lovers. For Oliver, Camilla had become a replacement for Elizabeth. This relationship provoked lots of jealousy from both as they dated other people and did separate things through college. This was a time for them to experiment, to find themselves and the person right for them, but nonetheless, jealously surrounded and haunted them both.

Their friendship was strong and withstood any obstacle they encountered. As the years passed and they became better friends, the two shared stories about past relationships, sexual interests and experiences. Oliver never confided in Camilla about his real desires—not then. He needed time. Their friendship continued to grow and though to the rest of the world it seemed obvious that Camilla and Oliver should have dated in college, with every passing day it became clearer to the two of them that they had something better than dating. They had something that would last longer, that would remain stronger—a bond with a person who would still love you for all your faults. The two felt like soulmates.

Even soulmates can be separated. They both knew the day would come when college would no longer be the bind that ties, and their lives would have to move to a new level. This frightened them both. They still had so many topics to discuss, so many things to say to one another, intimate things. After graduation Camilla traveled Europe searching for herself, and Mr. Right. She returned with a deeper understand of herself, but without Mr. Right. Oliver had graduated shortly before she returned.

Unsure of what to do for work or where to live — the world being her palette, Camilla found Oliver where she left him, and moved in with he and Howard.

CHAPTER EIGHT

The large, virgin snowflakes were falling lightly but steadily from the dark starless sky. Christmas was over, yet many decorations and lights still lit up the buildings around town. A new year was only hours away. Radio stations played holiday music and all the television stations were reporting live at various points throughout the city waiting for the big moment. People were pondering resolutions as they gathered at parties and restaurants to ring in the new year.

Nicholas sat in his rented flat wearing an old pair of jeans and drinking a beer. He did not have on any socks or shoes. Wet and stained, these sat on the floor by the furnace, drying. His shirt, torn and stained, was also on the floor. He sat in his recliner by the window watching the television but listening to the radio. He too was pondering a resolution. He had spent the last three months watching, listening and following his next victim. Back in the States the police were no closer to catching who murdered Elizabeth. They still had no leads or suspects.

Another one of Nicholas' murders going unsolved. The list was growing.

Only the television and the streetlights outside the living room window lit his first-floor flat. The bright yellow streetlight shown through the window and reflected off Nicholas's hairless, muscled chest and washboard abs. A passing car would add light to his flat as it came over the hill. The lights reflecting in his beautifully bright green eyes. He wore a smile on his slightly stubbled face as he guzzled another beer.

* * * * *

He was riding the adrenaline of his most recent kill. The smell of death and the fresh blood still soaked his jeans. He knew this euphoric feeling well and thought of the first time he felt it—that first time he played with himself, not really knowing what he was doing. He had just gotten out of the shower and was naked in his room, sitting at his desk trying to catch up on schoolwork. What started out as a scratch turned into a rub and eventually into something so orgasmic that he let out a scream as the white cloudy, sticky mess shot into the air. Unlike other teens boys, Nicholas did not have "the talk" with his father about sex and his body. Peter, as the two grew older, focused less on Nicholas and more on himself, often forgetting that Nicholas was even around. Much like his real dad, Nicholas was being abandoned by his paternal parent, too. As Nicholas remembered that first orgasm, he also remembered the more euphoric feeling he got from his first kill — a jock named Troy who threatened to beat him up one day in high school.

* * * * *

Troy was walking alone down the street. Nicholas could see him from his bedroom window. It stuck Nicholas as odd that Troy, handsome in his own right, was not with his jock buddies that day. Nicholas could not recall then if he had ever seen Troy walking alone. The sun struck Troy in such a way that Nicholas saw, for a moment, just how handsome, and alone … and sad Troy looked as he walked.

Without thinking, Nicholas decided to follow Troy. Nicholas had just finished cleaning up the newly experienced explosion, so he got dressed and raced out the door. It took Nicholas a few blocks to catch up to Troy, and then stayed many steps behind him. The two walked for almost 20 minutes. After many turns, almost as if Troy knew he was being followed and was trying to lose Nicholas, the two finally ended up deep in forest of the local park, alone together. Troy stopped suddenly, but Nicholas had not, and was caught by surprise when Troy called him out for following him. Troy was aware of his tail for many blocks and was luring Nicholas into the dark woods purposely.

The two boys were close enough for Nicholas to smell Troy's cheap cologne. That was the first time Nicholas took a good look at Troy and all his facial details. He noticed the scar on his chin, small, but a marking that was unmistakable — a skateboarding accident from years earlier. He noticed the sadness in Troy's sky-blue eyes — eyes that should have been striking — seducing even, but instead they were almost defeated. Nicholas was able to see that Troy was not handsome, but not ugly either — quite plain, but in a jock sort of way.

Troy, while cursing Nicholas for following him, took a swing. Before that day Nicholas would have accepted, quite reluctantly, the punch, but as he saw Troy's right arm come swinging out toward him, almost in slow motion, Nicholas pulled his body back, and as Troy's arm sailed passed Nicholas, he took his own right fist and jammed it into Troy's right rib cage, knocking Troy to the ground. While Troy was hunched over on the ground Nicholas looked down at him, and for the first time felt a rush almost as powerful and orgasmic as that first cloudy explosion in his room. He wanted more of that feeling.

Seeing the baseball bat sticking out of Troy's gym bag, Nicholas grabbed it and swung up from the ground, striking Troy in the face, sending his body flipping backward, leaving Troy lying on the cold dirt trail. Nicholas could see that the impact of the bat hitting Troy in the face had broken his nose. Blood was pouring out and over Tory's face like a tub overflowing with water. Troy was much heavier than Nicholas and had broken his nose more than once before. Troy got up, and even with blood pouring from his nose, was prepared to fight Nicholas—mostly because Troy saw Nicholas as some younger punk who was no match for the star baseball pitcher.

Troy was just being the teen jock with a brain still not fully grown or mature enough to understand the lifelong destruction his words and actions could cause. These were not the first time he was destructive verbally to Nicholas, or anyone else. Unfortunately for Troy, he was no match for the rage, the emotion, the desire to kill that lived within Nicholas. With Troy's metal bat Nicholas beat Troy to the point of him being almost unrecognizable. The nose was just the start. Troy lunged toward Nicholas many times, Nicholas swung the bat to the right leg, then the left, sending Troy back to the ground, on his knees before Nicholas. Anyone looking from the wrong angle might have seen Troy kneeling before Nicholas and thought he was about to give Nicholas a blow job, but it was Nicholas who gave the blow to Troy's head as he swung again and again striking Troy with such speed and strength that with just a few swings, some of Troy's teeth shot out of his mouth.

When it was all done Troy's body lay misshapen on the ground. Both of his knees were shattered. Both of his legs were broken. All the bones in both hands were crushed. His head had been hit so many times that it had huge indents from the bat, and his neck was snapped. Troy lay on the ground, feeding it with his own blood, and all Nicholas could think of was how aroused it made him feel. In the excitement of the moment, Nicholas felt a second wet explosion in his pants, erupting without touching himself.

When Troy took his last breath Nicholas just walked away, taking the bat with him. When he was on the other side of the park Nicholas threw the bat into the lake and returned home as if nothing happened. Troy was discovered before Nicholas sat down for dinner. A recently divorced young mom was jogging through the park when she found the mangled, bloody body. She screamed loud enough to draw attention to herself, and Troy. Within hours the park was alive, much like the cemetery had been all those years earlier when Adam attacked Catherine.

* * * * *

The sound of sirens filled the chilled air outside, squealing loudly as if celebrating the new year early. Nicholas could see the blue lights, he could feel the blue lights, reflecting off the walls in his flat as police cars sped past leaving black trails on the smooth, white ground. Nicholas smiled. He finished his beer, crushed the large can with his left hand and dropped it beside the chair. The noise of the aluminum hitting wood echoed throughout the sparsely furnished room.

He was thinking about Elizabeth, and how her gravestone might be covered in snow by now. He thought about Oliver and wondered how he was spending the first holiday season without his dear cousin. The beautiful image of both filled Nicholas's thoughts as he stretched out in the recliner working towards another eruption. More sirens passed, and again the room filled with beautiful reds, whites, and blues. The radio was playing the latest dance hit. Time ticked on toward the burial of another year. Still thinking about Oliver and Elizabeth, Nicholas grabbed his shirt off the floor, wiped his chest clean and headed through the flat to take a shower, dropping the shirt back to the floor. The television program was interrupted by a special news bulletin — one that caught his attention — about two men murdered in Greene Park just down the street from Nicholas' flat.

The television volume was low, but Nicholas could see the picture clearly, and hear most of the report being repeated as he got out of the shower. He stood naked in the hall between the bathroom and bedroom watching the screen. He ran his hands over his face and pushed his wet black hair back over his head, revealing a devilish but sincere smile at the television. He moved into the bedroom, leaving clearly defined footprints of water on the hardwood floor behind him. He knew the water would stain the floor, but he did not care. No footprint can identify a killer.

In the bedroom, with windows open and blinds up, and only a small lamp lighting the room, Nicholas stood in front of his bedroom wardrobe door looking at the full-length mirror, admiring the sculpted body before him. His reflection revealed a scar on his right hip. He ran his left hand over his chest, down over his scar and rubbed his groin for only a moment. Feeling the scar sent horrific memories swimming through his mind, and a single tear escaped, gliding down his cheek. A pair of pigeons sitting on his windowsill were watching him. Seeing their reflections next to his he quietly picked up a towel from the floor, turned around and whipped it at the birds as they fluttered to escape.

Once groomed, Nicholas put on a tuxedo, and as he walked out of the bedroom, he picked up an invitation that lay on the corner of the desk. He grabbed his keys and the remote off the coffee table, turned off the television, threw the remote onto the recliner, and walked out the door, locking it behind him. He left the radio on, quietly singing dance tunes. Nicholas lived in an old warehouse that had been converted into lofts on the north border of Greene Park. He was subletting from a young doctor on assignment in Asia. No one was in the hall or the elevator, an exposed ironclad and wood elevator that sat in the center of the building. It was nearly eleven, and everyone was either asleep or out, more than likely, at a party. Nicholas wondered what adventure would ring in his new year, and whether he would run onto Sebastian tonight. After all, Sebastian was the reason Nicholas was in London.

As he opened the main door to his building, Nicholas felt the chill of the air, and large white flakes as they bit his warm skin. His eyes watered. He buttoned his overcoat and tightened the scarf around his neck. Nicholas stood on the stairs looking across the street toward the park as another police car sped by. He descended the stairs, leaving only his boot prints in the smooth untouched snow. He turned and walked in the same direction as the police car. He continued to be attacked by weak, innocent white flakes.

Within a few blocks Nicholas returned to the scene of the crime. It was hard to miss with all the flashing lights and people gathered around. Jokingly, Nicholas asked an onlooker if this was a good place to see the fireworks display ringing in the new year. The woman looked at him oddly and explained, in more detail than he wanted, directions to Trafalgar Square. Of course, Nicholas never actually asked for directions to the square. The woman then proceeded to spell out her version of what had happened in the park without Nicholas asking. His smile had been reduced to a smirk, but only momentarily, as he was scolded by his storyteller for smiling at such a gruesome event. Nicholas left the woman, who continued to babble, not realizing that, like her husband, Nicholas had left her alone in the cold world.

Nicholas tried to get closer to the scene but was stopped by yellow tape strung between the trees to keep spectators away from the scene. The police ran around frantically, trying to keep people back behind the tape, and photographers from taking pictures. Although the moon was bright, helping officers see, floodlights were brought onto the scene. Forensics and other departments too were spread among the brush looking for clues, for any evidence that would help solve this mystery. Police scanners spat codes and phrases familiar to only those clad in blue, and as more police arrived on the scene, more footprints danced on the new snow, covering older layers of evidence. While pessimistic about finding anything in the snow, the police remained positive that the bodies would reveal something, anything that would lead them to the monster who took their lives. Some wondered if these deaths were linked to the recent random acts of human slaughter that had haunted the city. London had more than its share of murder each year. No one person, or group, had been as prolific as Adam had been 22 years earlier, but copycats popped up every few years, usually getting caught quite quickly. In recent months there had been another spike in cemetery murders and the police were having a harder time solving those.

One officer was silently standing guard. Nicholas approached him with curiosity but was unable to get the officer to say much. Nicholas asked lots of questions, looking for specific answers. These were questions that the average onlooker might not necessarily think to ask, especially since they were not at the scene when the murders took place. If this officer had not been a rookie, he would have realized that Nicholas knew more about the scene than anyone dressed in blue polyester.

Nicholas was looking for answers to questions that this officer had not even heard among his own peers yet. Still, he remained militant in his duty to stand guard and keep unauthorized people from crossing the yellow tape. Nicholas ended his little mind game with the officer after only a few minutes. He was already late for a party and did not want to bring in the new year without Sebastian. Before leaving Nicholas did manage, however, to get the officer to admit that there were only two people, just as the news report stated. He felt comfort in getting the officer to say something about the case. Nicholas thanked the officer, patting him on his snow-covered back as he walked away, leaving his handprint, blue in a sea of white.

Nicholas arrived at the address on the invitation moments before midnight. He stood at the base of the steps and looked at the building, lit with happiness and drunkenness. Silhouettes dancing in the windows reflected on the ground outside. Nicholas slicked his hair back, smiled and headed up the stairs. As he walked through the front door, he was met by a beautiful young couple who handed him a glass of Champagne. The chanting of numbers echoed through the large loft. As the countdown descended, getting louder and louder with each number, the couple who offered the drink to Nicholas, stood closer to him as people converged in the living room preparing to sing in the new year. At the stroke of midnight, the couple kissed Nicholas. The women, drunk and staggering, landed her wet gift left of his mouth, leaving an impression of her lips in deep red on his cheek. The man, also drunk, but a perfect marksman, kissed Nicholas on the lips forcefully, slipping his tongue into Nicholas's mouth. Nicholas responded by grabbing the man's head and pulling him close, returning the gift with equal passion. As they released one another, the man, somewhat more sober from the incident, looked at Nicholas, who only smiled and responded with greetings of a "Happy New Year" before he continued through the crowd leaving the man to ponder the excitement of what just happened.

Nicholas mingled with the crowd of strangers, saying very little. He was more interested in hearing what the party people had to say about the murders. He knew only the hosts, Claire, a waitress at a neighborhood coffeehouse and her boyfriend Chris, a rising artist. Colors of his imagination covered canvases throughout the loft. Some bright, vivid and alive while others were dark, almost void of color and life. It was these painful expressions of chemicals and color that most intrigued Nicholas. It was his first time to the loft. He had only met Claire a month ago when he started stopping at her coffee shop each day for a hot tea and scone. Claire struck up and maintained the conversations between them both each day before getting Nicholas to commit to come to her party. She did not want an ex-patriot to celebrate the new year alone.

The guests, all artists, musicians or students, sang together throwing colored flakes and streamers into the air inside while white flakes continued to fall outside. The conversations Nicholas overheard of the murders in Greene Park became more violent, and less factual, as the crowd became more drunk. Nicholas added his thoughts and comments too, looking for reactions. He got thrills by pushing the envelope on the murders he committed. By 2:00 a.m., people slowly began leaving and Nicholas caught a glimpse of the couple he first met when he arrived. He had watched them throughout the night but never talked to them. He watched them leave, then he too began his slightly slurred good-bye speech to his hosts.

As Nicholas left the building, buttoning his coat to keep out the sharp chilled air, he once again captured the couple, imprisoning them in his glazed eyes. He stayed behind them some distance as the two staggered through the park. Nicholas was intoxicated, but not drunk. He knew what he was doing. He watched the couple as they disappeared into the park, not far from where the police had assembled earlier—old snow still dyed red. The moon was bright and almost full, lighting the sky — a hazed orange backdrop to the falling white flakes. Nicholas followed the footsteps impressed into the freshly fallen snow, losing sight of the couple for only a short time. When he found them again, they had stopped in a small clearing to rest. The three startled each other as Nicholas emerged from behind some dead branches hanging low over the path.

"Bloody hell! Just scare the fucking shit out of us, why don't you?" spat the women in a drunken slur. Her East End accent was very strong.

"I am terribly sorry," Nicholas said. His breath warmed the underside of his nose and palms as he blew into the cupped hands covering his face. Starring at the couple, he stood eyes slightly closed, looking cold and alone, determining whether they remembered him. They had.

"I say my good man," sang the young man. "You're the one from the party, aren't you? We never did formally meet back there," he continued in a less drunken stupor. "I'm Sebastian and this lovely lady is Judy. What's your name?"

Sebastian was tired, worn out from the drinking and the long walk through the park. His face was flushed from the cold air. His exhaustion vanished with the sight of Nicholas, and suddenly Sebastian had a second wind, a new spirit about him. He was excited—shaky, but excited. He was about to get the opportunity he never got back at the party.

"Eric," Nicholas stuttered as he stood tall, yet cold, thinking quickly and smiling.

"Well, it is a pleasure to make your acquaintance, Eric. You are American, aren't you? I don't know many Americans. Do you live here or are you just visiting?" asked Sebastian exchanging handshakes through his thick mittens handmade by his mother. They were a gift the Christmas before. Thick and snug, the dark colored wool kept his fingers warm from the frosty bite of the air.

"We live just on the other side of the park. We moved in together a few months ago but, we aren't married. We are not ready for marriage. Hell, who is?" He smiled and shrugged. His accent melodically filled Nicholas's icy ears, rambling on about everything and anything. Sebastian winked at Nicholas, acknowledging that he was rambling and lightly slugged Nicholas on the shoulder. "So, what is your story?"

"I am visiting relatives in Oxford," Nicholas lied after a slight pause, realizing that Sebastian was more nervous now than drunk. "I decided to come into the city or a few days of fun to celebrate the new year."

"Have you got a place to stay tonight?" Sebastian asked eagerly. "You should not be out this late alone in the city, especially in this park. Have you heard about the murders? What am I asking — of course you have. Everyone has... haven't they? Sebastian continued his diarrhea from the mouth, unable to stop talking. He was nervous.

"We do not generally invite strangers to spend the night with us, but since you are a friend of Claire's, I do not see why not. You are a friend of Claire's, right? Of course, you are. Why else would you be at her party? "

Nicholas accepted the offer and the three continued through Greene Park. He helped Sebastian carry Judy, who was too drunk to hold a conversation, at least one comprehensible, or walk by herself. As they approached the south entrance of the park they were stopped by a homeless man, cold and with little clothing to keep him warm. The man was barefoot. His feet were kept warm with layers of filth and dirt. He was asking for change. His hands, also worn, with fingers extending through torn gloves much too small for the hands they tried to keep warm, already extended. This man continued to babble, pleading for help — the stench of alcohol mixing with his dirty body odor and the cold air, as the three passed him silently, trying to ignore him. Sebastian was horrified at the man's condition. They stumbled up the stairs of the first building they came upon. Nicholas supported Judy as Sebastian fumbled through his pockets for his keys. After much searching, he found them and the three walked up two flights of stairs to the flat. Sebastian and Nicholas carried Judy into the bedroom and left her on the bed, removing only her shoes and coat. She mumbled words of love to Sebastian and pecked his cheek with her now chapped lips. She was not totally aware of Nicholas's presence. The two men then moved into the living room, closing the bedroom door behind them.

"Would you like some coffee, Eric?" Sebastian asked.

Nicholas declined but followed Sebastian to the kitchen. Sebastian and Nicholas talked about sports, the weather and about Judy, filling the air with meaningless noise. Nicholas did not care for the chatter. He had other, more bloody plans.

Nicholas had been watching Sebastian for a couple of weeks by the time they finally met. It took more work than expected for Nicholas to hunt Sebastian down. He had moved since he was last in contact with Oliver.

Sebastian was thinking about the kiss that he and Nicholas shared earlier. Nicholas stood, leaning on the counter opposite Sebastian, smiling to Sebastian's back as if he knew what Sebastian was thinking. Nicholas thought about that earlier kiss too. He was thinking about the passion that was in the kiss, not necessarily for him, but passion within Sebastian, and he wondered if Sebastian and Oliver had shared that level of passion so many years earlier. Nicholas could see that Sebastian loved Judy but was not committed to her, and he wondered how long it would be before Sebastian would be cheating on Judy, if he was not already. The smile Sebastian saw on Nicholas's face when he turned toward him was heart melting, and at that moment Sebastian wanted to kiss Nicholas again. He had no idea that Nicholas was deep in thought.

"Are you okay, my friend?" Sebastian asked, watching Nicholas's body quivering.

Leaning against the counter, Nicholas focused on Sebastian and remembered where he was. Running his hands through his hair, rubbing his face along the way, he recomposed himself.

"Sorry," Nicholas said in a low voice. "I am fine now, thanks. I think I will take that coffee after all." He looked at Sebastian, who fully realized the beauty of the fiery green eyes that stared back at him.

"One extra strong coffee coming right up."

While Sebastian continued to prepare the coffee, Nicholas approached him from behind and put his arms on Sebastian's waist. Sebastian dropped the bag of coffee beans on the counter and stood motionless. The sound of little brown beans bouncing across the counter, and to the floor, echoed through the kitchen. He felt Nicholas's hands, strong and warm now, rub his crotch through his trousers. Nicholas's eyes had an evil green glare as he smiled at the back of Sebastian's neck, wanting to taste this young boy's blood.

"So, did you like the kiss at the party?" Nicholas whispered, slowly kissing the back of Sebastian's neck.

"Yes. Yes, I did, Eric," Sebastian stuttered. Judy keeps telling me to experiment more ... even with men. She says that it would add more excitement to our sex life. We are both bisexual, but she is more experienced, and has had many more partners, both men and women. I am hesitant, not because of the diseases, hell you can get those from anyone now. It is just that, well ... I don't know. I mean, I've wanted to for some time, but you know, I just ..."

"Shut up, you're babbling. If you want an experience that you will never forget, then forget about the coffee." Nicholas grabbed Sebastian's crotch and squeezed. They both smiled, Sebastian of joy and Nicholas of power.

Sebastian turned around to face Nicholas and the two looked at each other silently for a moment. Sebastian nervously made the next move with a small kiss on Nicholas's lips. Nicholas responded almost hurting Sebastian as he forced his mouth around Sebastian's, pushing his tongue through Sebastian's tightly puckered pink lips. In his innocent excitement, Sebastian frantically began taking off his clothes in the kitchen. Within a few minutes Sebastian stood in his underwear nervously kissing Nicholas. His trousers were tangled around his ankles, unable to get past his shoes. A gold chain necklace hung around his neck holding a cross that rested peacefully on his chest, just above his pecs.

Sebastian had a beautifully athletic build for a 22-year-old who did not visit the gym often. He was slightly shorter than Nicholas and stood on his toes to fully enjoy Nicholas's face and lips. He met Judy two years ago at university; his first time away from home without his parents, not including his trips to visit Oliver. Sebastian had been a quiet and respectful child — a mother's dream. He had experimented with sex and drugs in his teens, everyone did, but it was not until his university years, and his meeting Judy that he became a bit of a wild child. His parents, even now, saw only the innocent child, and had always been blinded to Sebastian's non-Christian ways.

Nicholas stood shirtless now — his rented tux jacket and shirt on the floor. Running his hands up and down Nicholas's bare, sculptured chest with the excitement of a child playing with a new toy, Sebastian had the same feeling he felt with Oliver the first time they touched each other. Nicholas wore a devilish grin; the same one he wore when he watched the news report on television earlier that night—the one he wore whenever he killed. He knew what he was doing and was in full control—as he liked it. This man before him would die tonight. Sebastian slowly got down on his knees and cautiously unzipped Nicholas's pants, exposing Nicholas to the slight chill of the kitchen air, keeping him warm with his hands. Nicholas wore no underwear and was partially erect—moist. Sebastian looked up at Nicholas as he played with his new toy. Nicholas winked at Sebastian, who then took Nicholas into his mouth. Nicholas smiled, thinking of his painful past. A single tear rolled down his face as he moaned to orgasm—almost gagging Sebastian.

Nicholas then pulled Sebastian up at the waist, placing him on the counter. Sebastian, wiping his face clean, licking his lips like a kitten licks its paws, felt weak and excited by Nicholas's strength. Without taking his eyes off Sebastian, Nicholas grabbed a knife from the cutting block on the counter and slowly moved it toward Sebastian's crotch, dragging the blade along the countertop. The metal screeching on the tile echoed through Sebastian's ears. He could see a darkness in

Nicholas's eyes. The tip of the knife was cold to his inner thigh as it touched Sebastian. He shivered. Nicholas slowly ran the knife under the elastic band of Sebastian's-stained white briefs. Holding them with his other hand he pulled then away from his skin with great force and sliced the briefs open, fully exposing Sebastian's erect youth. Sebastian sighed with relief, and excitement, as Nicholas held Sebastian down with force. Sebastian, leaning back on the counter, his elbows supporting his body, closed his eyes and moaned in ecstasy. Nicholas jerked Sebastian with one hand, still holding the knife in the other. Sebastian, leaning back with his eyes closed, moaned with joy.

"That feels so good, Eric. Don't stop. "Oh, yeah, that is so bloody good."

Nicholas said nothing, but continued, faster, harder. He was releasing his anger through this sexual encounter. He was expressing hate, not love, or even lust, for Sebastian right now. Sebastian continued to moan has he felt shivers running through his body filling him with a feeling he never felt so intensely before. He never felt this good when he and Judy had sex. As Sebastian climaxed, he screamed with excitement, joy, and pain. At that same moment Nicholas had jammed the large knife into Sebastian's throat, slicing his Adam's apple and coming out through the backside of his neck. Sebastian silently screamed, his mouth open but no sound escaping, as he spewed, red and white, all over the kitchen ... all over Nicholas.

After slowly pulling the knife out of Sebastian's neck, Nicholas proceeded to stab Sebastian in the stomach, in the groin, and in the chest repeatedly. As Nicholas stood back, showering in the blood, he was crying. He was crying for his mother and for Elizabeth. He was crying mostly for Oliver. Standing in the center of the kitchen, now away from Sebastian, Nicholas's face was bloody, his hair was matted red, and his eyes were dark. The walls, floor and ceiling were all sprayed red. The coffee beans, some still bouncing around the floor, now swam in a dark red pool. Nicholas smiled. He stood, leaning forward, with his mouth open and tongue stretched out trying to taste the spewing blood, then slowly slid down to the floor, sitting in the thick red pool, crying. He wanted to yell, but silently he whispered his love for Oliver. He cursed his father for the man he had become, and scolded Sebastian for being so handsome, and in love.

Sebastian lay on the counter, his now limp body stuck to it with his own blood, lifeless.

After a few minutes, Nicholas remembered that Judy was still sleeping in the other room. He stood up, grabbed the knife, and went to her. Passing through the living room Nicholas left his red shoe prints on the white carpet. He noticed a supply of drugs on the center table, something he had missed when he first arrived. Seeing some cocaine, ecstasy, and other narcotics, Nicholas grabbed a needle prepped for injection, not knowing exactly what was in the needle. In the bedroom he stood over Judy for only a moment dripping her lover's juice on her, thinking again of Oliver. Then he put his bloody hand over her mouth and nose, holding her down with all his strength to stop her from breathing before stabbing her in the neck with the needle. Her eyes opened wide as she gasped for air. Within minutes she was foaming at the mouth—all into Nicholas's hand. He let go and watched her body spasm a few times before going limp.

Still dripping with blood, Nicholas stabbed the limp body a dozen times to be sure that she was dead. He stripped off the rest of his tux and put it in the rubbish bin next to the bed. He stood over Judy's dead body for a moment, naked, crying, yet somehow still smiling. Then he went into the bathroom and took a shower to wash away his sins. He dried himself without rushing and put on some of Sebastian's clothes, which were a little tight. Grabbing a box of matches from the bedside table, Nicholas dropped a lit match into the rubbish bin. He found a can of hair spray and sprayed some into the bin. A flame rose into the air, lighting up the room and, for a moment, Nicholas admired his latest bloody creation on the bed. As he left, he kicked the bin, still lit with flames, across the room. It made a thunderous noise at it hit the wall, spilling its contents on the rug, igniting a larger fire.

He smiled as he walked out of the flat, quietly through the building and toward the same park the three had emerged from earlier. Behind him he could hear the crackling of the flames getting louder, larger, engulfing the flat. Had the building been older, Nicholas's goal of burning his art would have been successful. However, this was a newer structure, a building fitted with an advanced sprinkler system. Before the flames could destroy the whole building, Judy and Sebastian were showered with an intense spray of icy water, extinguishing the flames, mixing their blood with the charcoal remains of their flat, and washing away any evidence that Nicholas had ever visited. By the time fire fighters arrived Nicholas was in the warmth of his own flat, uneasily resting in another nightmare.

Nicholas was very careful not to be seen by anyone in the building, but only a few steps into the park he was met by the same homeless man they met earlier that morning. Nicholas, full of adrenaline from his recent kills, offered the man a meal on the other side of the park. The man eagerly accepted, not realizing he was walking toward death. Once the two were near the center of the park, away from any people, Nicholas, standing behind the old man, grabbed him by the neck with both hands, damp and cold. With all his strength, Nicholas made a quick twist. A snap echoed through the early morning, empty park. The man fell to the ground, silently landing on a soft bed of snow. He looked content, sleeping peacefully, yet lifeless. With no remorse, Nicholas continued his journey home.

Nicholas stayed holed up in the rented flat for the next few months. He wanted to lie low and let the city digest the five new deaths. He realized that it was becoming harder and harder not to kill. But at the same time, it was becoming less exciting. When he first started killing, each kill meant something. They were personal. They still were, but he was growing impatient on his journey to get to Oliver.

Nicholas watched the news for any information on the murders. The two from New Year's Eve got the most coverage, and the homeless man's death got almost no mention. Judy and Sebastian's deaths were buried under the story of a building fire. Nicholas was both frustrated and excited. He liked to hear about his kills in the news. It was the affirmation he needed to see and hear — the fuel for his life. When his kills were downplayed, or worse, nothing more than a sound bite, he got angry. For a man who struggled not to get caught, he spent a lot of time obsessing over not being in the news.

CHAPTER NINE

The stones, in all sizes and shapes, stood drunkenly, all around Oliver. Some were small, almost impossible to see in the thick grass. Some stood tall, but feeble. Others rested to one side or the other, fighting gravity. Each, while existing for the same reason, stood as an individual, unaware of the others. Some had carvings, others had only the remains of words no longer readable. Some wore sheets of green, almost moldy, while others were covered with droppings of birds long since dead. The surroundings were eerie, but at the same time, a feeling of comfort and intrigue filled Oliver's mind. He found peace walking these paths especially after a long flight.

He walked along the winding labyrinth, losing himself in thought, getting to know every soul he passed. Some stones were so old all he saw was a blank palette. Oliver sat and studied those palettes, each offering a thought of color or imagination, each clearly a mirror as Oliver continued to discover himself. Who would have thought such a place of mourning would offer such a peaceful setting? Catherine did a couple of decades ago. Oliver felt as though he finally found a haven of rest, a place he could come and be free—free to think about his life without the restraints and restrictions of the outside world.

Oliver had passed the iron and brick wall surrounding the garden on many occasions when he visited Sebastian, and again when he lived in the city for a semester during college. He would stop sometimes to investigate this new world, his face peering through the black iron rods, feeling the chill of the dead reaching out—trying to draw him into their home. When Oliver did venture through the gates he discovered an underworld of sex, and of voyeurism.

As he rounded one corner Oliver saw two men sitting in front of each other, surrounded by tall blades of grass. They would not have been noticed had they not moved as Oliver passed. One of the men stretched back, the weight of a sculptured body wrapped in wool resting on his palms, spread on the moist, cold soil. The other leaned forward drinking the juice of the first. Oliver watched as one showered the other and the ground—a geyser of the first, while the second drank joyously. Oliver was aroused, and as tired as he was from his flight, he felt the need to quench his own thirst.

Oliver continued to move through the garden so the two men would not see him. He remained amazed at how unashamed men were in public, in this sacred garden. As he turned another corner, he noticed two more men standing at a short distance from one another. Oliver watched as the two men looked at each other, then looked away, and then back at each other. Occasionally they both looked at Oliver, which scared the shit out of him. He was trying to not be seen, and yet two men who were cruising each other were suddenly cruising him. Oliver watched as the two moved toward a dark phallic monument almost totally shielded by tree limbs, limp and sad. Curious to see what these two would do, Oliver moved closer, and thought he had found a better spot to stay hidden—he wanted to be the voyeur, not a participant.

These two boys sat next to one another on a stone bench at the base of a larger-than-life tombstone, their bodies almost touching, side by side. They looked at each other occasionally, never speaking. Even if they had, Oliver was not close enough to hear what they might say. Oliver watched as one slid his hand down the sweatpants of the other. Rhythmically, the young man thrashed around in his neighbor's sweats. Oliver watched the face of the man being so beautifully beaten. He was beaming eyes closed, mouth open, but smiling. Silently, the boy expressed his euphoria. After a few moments, the first boy pulled his hand out of the second boy's sweats, bringing with him a big new friend. He swung his ball cap around and lowered his head to his neighbor and drank the juice offered in this sacrifice. The victim sat in complete relaxation wearing a smile of satisfaction before quickly pulling his sweats up. The first boy swung his ball cap back around and wiped his mouth with the back of his hand as he sat back against the black cold monument. His green eyes glowed beautifully under the bill of the Atlanta Braves baseball cap. Nicholas was excited that Oliver was watching and wondered if he recognized him. He did not.

Oliver sat in amazement that the two boys performed such a ritual, knowing they were being watched. Fearful of moving and rustling the grass, Oliver sat motionless, afraid to blink. Almost as quickly as they came, the two adjusted themselves and left in opposite directions, another sacrifice to the gods. For a moment after they had gone, Oliver thought about the bright green eyes. He was so fixated on the eyes that he paid little attention to the rest of Nicholas's face.

Oliver sat, starring in the direction of the monument in wonder and amazement. He wanted what these two boys just had, but not here — not like that. He wondered how people could submit to such a dirty act in a cemetery without guilt.

Convinced that he had seen enough sinning for one day Oliver went in search of the exit from this sexual playground. The images he witnessed flashed through his mind over and over as he found himself getting more lost in this vast jungle of stone. He ran without knowing where to run. He had been here a dozen times before, but now he was lost. Soon each stone, while individual before, looked like the next and Oliver stopped. He felt a panic attack coming on. Looking in front of him, Oliver noticed the black phallic monument again. He had been moving in circles. There was no longer any sign of the earlier entertainment. Out of breath, confused and upset, he sat to rest.

With his face in his hands hovering over his lap, Oliver sat silently, trying to clear his mind. Soon he felt a presence over him. He looked up to find a young man sitting quietly on the other corner of the monument. The man smiled at Oliver and moved toward him, finally sitting next to Oliver. Suddenly Oliver feared that he was about to be the next sacrifice to the gods. He wanted to cry but, his tears were pushed back by the beauty, and youthfulness, of the creature beside him. Thoughts of lust and sin ran through Oliver's mind. He could not understand why he did not get up and run away. He tried, he thought. He sat there, motionless, as the young man slowly unzipped Oliver's pants. Even in the cool air sweat glistened on Oliver's forehead, and that excited his new friend as he gently thrashed inside. He could see the innocence in Oliver's eyes. He did not want to hurt Oliver.

Oliver suddenly became aware of all that was around him. He felt like all the dead were watching, cursing him for such a disgusting sin. Yet he sat there with his eyes closed, letting this man violate him. Oliver moaned as if he were dying. It felt so good. When he finally opened his eyes, he noticed a body lying in the grass behind some stones a short distance in front of him. He wondered how he had not seen that before. He could just make out the face as he filled his new friend's hand with his warm self. Oliver was confident that the man lying on the ground was the man he saw earlier — the one without the ball cap. Oliver noticed blood running down the face of this man. Oliver jumped up and screamed. His violator freaked, wiped his hand on Oliver's pants and ran. Oliver zipped his pants and ran, too.

Oliver finally found his way out of the cemetery and ran all the way back to his hotel. He never stopped or looked back. The sinister acts of the cemetery suddenly got very real, and he did not like that one bit. He called the police when he reached the hotel but gave them very little information. Oliver did not want to get involved in anything. He was not aware of the growing number of dead bodies the city was dealing with — bodies that left no clue as to what happened, or why. He did not want to get involved in solving any murders. At least that is what he kept telling himself. He did not want to talk with the police and explain how he found the dead body. The police did not need to know that Oliver was busy trying to tame his own monsters, and he certainly did not need to help them find theirs either.

After calling the police and taking a shower — he felt violated and disgusted — Oliver sat quietly in his hotel room pondering why he went to the cemetery in the first place. He and Sebastian had walked through it a few times together — cruising guys — but never participated or saw the sort of activity he saw today. When he had finally relaxed and enjoyed some food delivered to his room, Oliver realized that he should help the police — or at least see what they discovered — from a distance.

He returned to the cemetery and was surprised to see it sealed off and alive with police activity. Oliver was most intrigued by the two guys he watched that afternoon in the cemetery. Did one kill the other? Should he at least tell the police about the other guy? Could he remember what the other guy looked like? Sure, he could — well at least he could remember those eyes, but not much else. Could that guy really have killed the other one? Was it planned or a spur of the moment killing? Did he need to be worried that he could be next? Oliver had so many questions. After all, he did get court side seats to the sexual activity, so he could identify the guys, sort of.

He knew the green-eyed guy was watching him as he jerked his sacrifice that afternoon, and that was beginning to scare Oliver. Those green eyes. Maybe he did need to tell the police more, but how could he do that now? After calling the police from the hotel, but not offering his name, he couldn't just walk up to them now and say something, could he? Sure, he could. He could say that he was walking through the cemetery, cutting through really, to get to Chelsea. He was saving time when he saw something, someone. He did not have to say he was the one who called the police. Oliver was having trouble getting the image of the bloody face out of his mind. As he contemplated what he should do more police arrived, and the crowd around him, outside the gates grew. Oliver summoned the confidence to tell a story, so he walked in the direction of one of the officers who was walking toward the gate. Oliver looked up and saw the green eyes again.

Oliver stopped and starred. A policeman? The guy breaking the law earlier was a policeman. How was that possible? As Oliver approached him, they locked eyes briefly, but Oliver quickly looked away and kept walking. His heart started racing, and the hairs on his skin stood up. Suddenly Oliver felt that he was in trouble—over his head once again. He picked up his pace, looking behind him to be sure the officer was not following him—he wasn't. When he was certain he was a safe distance and was not being followed he ran even faster all the way back to the hotel. A few days later Oliver was on a plane heading back to the States.

His visit to the cemetery, not that cemetery, and his visit to London was for Sebastian. Oliver learned about Sebastian's death months after Sebastian was embalmed and silently resting well beneath the soil of a less creepy cemetery—one outside of the city and rarely frequented for sex. Once he did get the news, he was one the next available flight to pay his respects to his first love— his first kiss.

Over the next week the police continued their investigation. Some detectives were convinced that as random as this recent murder appeared, it was somehow connected to others in and around the cemetery. They just could not figure out how or why. Some of the older police officers remembered the days of Adam, and feared a copycat was at large. So many deaths and yet so few clues.

CHAPTER TEN

A few months after Nicholas saw Oliver in London—after they almost, finally met, Nicholas returned to the States. It had been almost a year since Nicholas had spoken with his father only a handful of times. As the plane touched down Nicholas noticed a missed call, and voicemail once he turned his mobile phone back on. The voicemail was from his father, Peter, asking him to lunch. It was not often that the two got together anymore. Once Nicholas graduated college, the two grew more distant. Though Peter remained a widower for most of Nicholas's childhood, he did remarry when Nicholas was a junior in high school, to a woman who was only ten years older than Nicholas. They did not get along, Nicholas and his stepmother Melissa—mostly because he did not respect her.

Melissa was young and dumb, and Nicholas was convinced that she only married Peter for his money. She did not finish college. She was a "bleach blonde, big breasted, thin waisted barbie doll," as Nicholas referred to her when anyone asked.

Nicholas was convinced that Peter thought he was marrying up, in the looks department anyway. Everywhere the family went, guys gave Peter the manly nod as if to say, "Look at you, man—you scored big." It infuriated Nicholas to see how much Peter had changed once he married Melissa. Nicholas was surprised at how superficial and shallow Peter had become as he aged. The stories Peter told Nicholas about his youth, and the photos Peter shared with Nicholas—those of he and Catherine when they were young painted a milder, more liberal picture of the younger Peter. Even what little dating Peter did during Nicholas's childhood was tame compared to the man he had become once he reached his late 40s.

Nicholas called Peter back while waiting for his luggage and agreed to meet Peter at his office the next day for lunch. Punctual as always, Nicholas arrived at Peter's office just minutes before he was expected. And, of course, Peter was not ready. He was in a meeting that should have ended more than thirty minutes earlier. When Nicholas arrived, he could see Peter in the conference room with a few others. One was drawing on the white board, and another was yelling into the phone speaker. It was muffled, so Nicholas had no idea what they were discussing. As he walked around the conference room, he caught Peter's eye, and Peter held up both hands flashing "ten more minutes" with his fingers. Nicholas nodded and headed toward Peter's office. As he sat in Peter's office Hunter walked by. He popped his head in to tell Nicholas that Peter was going to be another ten minutes—not knowing that Peter had already told Nicholas. Nicholas accepted the information as if he were hearing it for the first time and exchanged small talk with Hunter.

"You never called," Hunter said.

"Never called who?" Nicholas responded, confused by the statement but thrilled to be having a conversation with Hunter.

"Me, of course."

Nicholas had completely forgotten that Hunter had written his number of a piece of paper last summer when Nicholas visited the club where Hunter moonlights as a cashier on the weekends. The paper had gotten buried in the bottom of Nicholas' jeans pocket—the jeans that he later burned because they had blood on them.

"Sorry man," Nicholas responded, pretending that he remembered getting Hunter's number. "I washed the jeans without emptying the pockets — ended up with a lot of bills and worn-out paper in the drier. I am not very good with laundering money," he continued with a smirk and a laugh as he explained that he had also been out of the country for a couple of seasons.

The two continued to share small talk, and after a while Hunter, being the younger of the two, took a chance and asked Nicholas out to dinner. Nicholas agreed. He had been hoping to get to know Hunter more last summer, but his priorities about Oliver got in the way.

"Give me your phone," Hunter said. Nicholas pulled out an old flip phone from his pocket — his latest burner phone — and handed it to Hunter, who proceeded to enter his contact information.

"You have no contacts in here," Hunter remarked.

"It's a new phone."

"I am honored to be the first one then," Hunter responded with a smile as he handed the phone back to Nicholas. Then he grabbed his own phone to accept the text he just sent to himself.

"I will text you tomorrow."

By the time the two had finished talking Peter had joined them in his office, and in true Peter form, he did not apologize for making Nicholas wait for more than twenty minutes. Nicholas and Hunter shared some additional glances before Hunter left. Peter shuffled papers around his desk, looking important — or distracted — Nicholas could not figure out which. Then he checked his email before he and Nicholas headed out for some lunch.

"There are some documents I need you to sign, son," Peter said matter-of-factly as they headed to the elevator. "Trust and Will stuff — nothing to worry about. I thought they were on my desk and ready, but that is not the case. I will bring them home tonight. Are you still joining Melissa and me for dinner? We want to hear all about London."

The last thing Nicholas wanted to do was dine with Melissa. Her nasally voice and big boobs were an embarrassment, and he was convinced she got dumber as she got older. "Yes, I'll be there, but I don't want to argue with her again. She needs to remember that she's not my mother."

The restaurant was around the corner from the office, so it was not long before the two were sitting, facing each other without the distractions of work, or Barbie, for a change. Peter asked Nicholas to lunch because he wanted to talk about money. When Catherine died, she left quite a bit of money to Peter. He knew her father had some money set aside for each of his children but did not know then that her parents had set up a trust for her that had grown over the years. Peter took that trust and invested it further, turning a six-figure trust into an eight-figure one over the last 22 years. Nicholas never knew about the money. He knew they never wanted for anything but growing up he and Peter lived a simple life—nothing extravagant except for the occasional fun vacation.

Peter was telling Nicholas about the money because Peter was dying. For a young man approaching 50 married to a woman in her mid 30s Peter thought he had a long life ahead of him that included retirement at 60, then cashing out to live a livelier life. But karma caught up to him after all this time. He abandoned Catherine all those years ago when she needed him most, so it was time he too suffered. A week earlier Peter's doctor gave him the news—he had stage 4 colon cancer. The doctor said the outlook was not good, and that he might have a year to live, at best.

Peter sat silently for a moment reliving the time when he got the news — stunned that he had no idea — no pain or discomfort and could not figure out why he was being punished — why he had to die so soon.

"I did not want to discuss this with you at dinner," Peter said. "Melissa does not know yet. I wanted you and I to talk about it all first — to tell you the news first. I am retiring in two weeks and will live out my last days trying to enjoy what life I have left in me.

"The new documents for you to sign basically give Melissa a small sum of money — enough for her to live modestly after I die. Those funds combined with a small insurance policy I set up when we got married will take care of her. It is your trust that I am modifying — transferring over the money that your mother left when you were born. It has me as the trustee, and I am going to hand it all over to you."

Nicholas wore an expression of confusion, disbelief, sadness, and anger on his face. A flood of emotions all swirling together. A trust? For him? He wondered how much money his father was talking about but knew that answer would come soon. He was angry that Peter did not tell him sooner about the cancer. He should have known the day Peter learned, but he was out of the country, and this was not news Peter wanted to share over the phone. Nicholas wanted to yell at Peter for being selfish with the news, but also wanted to hug him. While they did not have the best relationship over the years, Peter did raise Nicholas, and for that Nicholas felt some compassion and love for the man.

"There is a $1M trust set up for Melissa, and I have a $2M insurance policy for her. That should be plenty for her to live a good life," Peter continued. "I wanted to make sure she had something because I do not believe you would help her out. You two have never been close."

Nicholas shook his head in agreement as he digested that large sum of money. Three million dollars is a lot of money, especially for someone like Melissa, who never really had a job in her life. "That is quite generous of you," Nicholas replied to the news.

"Don't worry," Peter said. "The documents are airtight and ensure that is all she gets from me. The rest of the money is tied up in your trust and insurance policy. I have a financial adviser all set up to manage the accounts with you since they are big.

"The insurance policy that goes to you is also $2M, and at last check the trust was valued at $60M. It is all tied up in the market, so it fluctuates," Peter explained as if he were talking to a child. "That is a lot of money for someone in their mid 20s so you will have help managing and accessing it all."

As Nicholas sat, eating his lunch he thought about what that kind of money would do to a person. With that much money how would he stay under the radar of everyone, anyone … the police? Sure, it would help him move around more, but his initial worry was not about how to spend the money, but how to stay in the shadows with that kind of money in his name. With all these thoughts running through his head he looked over at Peter. He looked into his eyes the way he does with his victims as he watches the last breath escape them. As Nicholas sat there staring into Peter's eyes he could see the sadness, the fear of death, and wondered how Peter was going to survive the next year.

Nicholas new that Peter would be in pain for much of his remaining days and wondered if that was the life he deserved. While Nicholas wanted Peter to suffer in some way because of how he treated Catherine so many decades ago, he was not sure that a slow cancer death was what he had in mind. The idea of killing Peter had crossed Nicholas's mind many times over the last decade, and even more so since marrying Melissa—those were thoughts filled with hate. But now, sitting in the restaurant seeing the sadness, and fear deep in Peter's eyes Nicholas felt that a slow, painful death was not something Peter really deserved. His life needed to end quickly, painlessly. Nicholas realized, as he sat there that if he could kill Peter quickly while making Melissa suffer some then maybe that would be the best of both worlds.

Three weeks later, long after the ink had dried ensuring Nicholas would be a very wealthy man, he proceeded to ensure that Melissa would not be as fortunate. He checked in with Peter much more often than before and watched Peter have many more bad days than good ones. Within weeks of his diagnosis Peter's body began to shut down more rapidly than expected. With the news of Peter's illness, and the money she would get, Melissa checked out from her wifely duties—not too dissimilar to what Peter had done back when Catherine needed him most. Melissa was young, and not at all prepared to take care of an ailing man. Nicholas knew that Melissa was now aware of what she would be getting when Peter died, and she seemed, to Nicholas, more focused on how to spend her unearned funds than how to tend to her dying husband.

Melissa started spending more time with her young girlfriends, often dashing off to New York City for a few days to shop. Much like Peter was not around when Catherine needed him most, his new wife was doing the same to him. He girlfriends were more important to her than her own husband, but not his money. When Nicholas learned that Melissa would be out of town the following weekend, he took that as his opportunity to help Peter through his pain and give Melissa some of her own. It was not a lot of planning time, but Nicholas knew he would have to make it work.

When the Friday rolled around the taxi arrived on schedule and was sitting in the driveway idling for longer than the driver wanted. He honked his horn a few too many times, showing his impatience with his fare. Inside, Melissa was making sure that Peter was going to be fine without her, even though he told her repeatedly that between the nurse and Nicholas he would be fine. He was not well enough to walk her to the door, or even watch from the window as the taxi drove off but convinced her that he was well enough for her to go live her life. She didn't really care about leaving Peter but wanted to pretend. Before the taxi could honk again the front door opened and out popped Melissa doing her best Tammy Faye impersonation, stomping out the door with her luggage in tow. She and her friends always put on too much make up thinking that it made them look younger than they really were.

Nicholas watched Melissa get into the taxi and drive off toward the train station. He was in a rented car, parked a few houses down from Peter. He followed the taxi to be sure it was taking her to the train station, and not another man's house — or a hotel. Not that he really cared if she were cheating on Peter. He just needed her far enough way so as not to return home early and unannounced. When Melissa got out of the taxi at the station, and Nicholas saw Melissa and her friends hug and bounce around like sorority girls reuniting for the weekend, he felt confident that this was going to be the weekend that he ended Peter's life. Once the train departed Nicholas knew he would have only a couple of days to execute his plan, which he knew was plenty of time. He had already worked out all the details.

Rather than head straight to his father's house, Nicholas stopped at a coffee shop in the town square. This was the one time when he wanted to be on camera. He wanted to be captured on film far from Peter's at a time that was also close to another date with Hunter. He knew that the day nurse was already gone and would not be returning until 8 a.m. the next morning. He sent a text to Hunter saying that he was doing some work at the coffee shop and would meet him at the restaurant rather than one of them picking up the other.

As the coffee shop filled up with the post-work rush, Nicholas slipped out and took at taxi halfway to Peter's before getting out and walking the rest of the way. Once near the house he slipped in the back entrance, using the key under the doormat. He knew the angle of the security cameras well enough to know how to avoid being seen. He had helped Peter with the security installation, so he knew to adjust the camera angles days before. Once inside Nicholas quietly climbed the stairs to his father's bedroom. As he stood in the doorway looking across the room at the sleeping man Nicholas contemplated what he was doing. Did he really want to kill his own father? He might not have been his biological father, but he had played the role of 'dad' a lot over the past 22 years.

Peter stirred a bit in his bed. The pain made it uncomfortable for him to sleep for long periods of time. He mostly catnapped these days. He opened his eyes and saw Nicholas standing in the distance. Peter tried to say something, but the pain medication he had taken an hour earlier made it difficult and exhausting to talk. Nicholas assured him that everything was okay — that he should go back to sleep. Within a few minutes Peter was asleep again. Standing over him now Nicholas could smell him — could smell the decay. With little control of his colon at this point, the once meaty, athletic body turned into a small, frail creature. Nicholas imagined how much Peter must really be suffering and convinced himself that what he was doing was the right thing by killing him. Nicholas told himself this with each kill.

Most of his kills had been about killing for the sake of killing. Over the past few years, though, many of his kills have been to get closer to Oliver— to remove people from Oliver's life—and make room for Nicholas. But with his dad, Nicholas knew that killing him was saving him. Peter had said in so many words weeks earlier, when he told Nicholas that he was dying: "Please promise me that you will not let machines keep me alive. I do not want to suffer, and I do not want to be kept alive beyond my time."

Nicholas knew that he would have very little time to get out of the house, and to the restaurant so every step, every action he took had to be precise. Standing over his father, Nicholas was now in a full body, plastic suit and looked like he was about to administer some toxic chemical to his father. He wanted to be certain that no blood got on any part of him, and he certainly did not want any gun powder residue either. Once he was covered from head to toe, including goggles covering those bright green eyes, Nicholas pulled the small pistol out of this bag and placed it in Peter's hands. Had he been conscious, and unmedicated the cold metal would have startled Peter. Instead, he just laid there quietly as Nicholas positioned Peter's hand and arm as if he were a doll. Once everything was in place Nicholas, with his finger holding Peter's pulled the trigger. The bang was louder than Nicholas wanted, and he was hopeful that it did not startle any of the neighbors. He slipped his gloved hand away from Peter's, and slowly stepped back from the bed, trying not to move the limp body.

Once clear of the bed, Nicholas took a moment to look at Peter one last time. His tiny body lay lifeless with a hole in his head, and Nicholas knew he was now at peace. Blood was all over the bed, the sheets, the headboard. Brain parts were dripping from the lampshade on the nightstand. The image was gruesome—a splatter mess. Nicholas was not keen on death by gunshot and almost never killed by this method. It was too loud and too messy for his liking—too impersonal, but he knew this was the only way to ensure a quick death for Peter. Nicholas stepped out of the plastic suit, turning it inside out as he slipped each piece off, in the end creating a small ball of inside out plastic, then put it into his bag. Once Nicholas was certain everything looked legit, he backed out of the room and down the stairs. He looked at his watch—the whole ordeal was done in thirty minutes. He was doing great on time. He slipped out the back door, putting the key back where he found it, and in the dusk, his hooded figure maneuvered through the backyard and out to the park behind the house. Walking through the park at this hour he passed very few people. The ones he did were jogging or walking their dog while talking on their cell phone. No one was paying any attention to the others, and no one was looking at the tall, hooded man briskly walking away from his latest murder. After a quarter-mile Nicholas exited the park, walked a few more blocks, and hailed a taxi back to where his car was parked — not far from the coffee shop. He threw the bag into the trunk of his car and headed to meet Hunter for dinner.

CHAPTER ELEVEN

Hunter lay naked in bed, staring at the ceiling. His sheets covered him up to his waist, as he pondered the past 12 hours. His room was mostly dark. There was a slight odor rising from the pillow and sheets—a mixture of sweat and bodily fluids. He grabbed the pillow and pushed it into his face to get another good whiff. It smelled of Oliver. As he lay in his bed enjoying the scent he wondered if he did the right thing—sleeping with Oliver. Hunter was used to getting looks from guys, and girls. He was good looking. Tall and toned, Hunter was an attractive guy. At 21 and fresh out of college he was eager to take on the world. There was no finding himself now. He did that in college—maybe even before then. He knew from a young age that he liked boys—their smell, their taste—everything about them.

Even though they exchanged glances many times in the club, neither Hunter nor Oliver had approached the other. Hunter because every time he got the nerve to do so Oliver was with his friends.

Oliver because every time he went to the club he was with his friends, and he was not ready for them to see that side of him—he knew it made no sense, and he knew they would love him all the same, but something inside of him kept this one secret from the rest of his life. It was a secret that only he thought was a secret. His friends all knew or assumed—but they patiently waited for Oliver to make the announcement.

Oliver finally went to the club by himself— partially because he wanted time away from his friends and partially because he was hoping that he would see Hunter and make a move to speak with him. Oliver arrived at the club to find Hunter behind the window—his regular spot. They said hello through the chipped glass, as they did each time, they found themselves in this position, and Hunter handed Oliver his change and ticket. The two smiled at each other, and this time as Oliver reached for his ticket Hunter reached out and touched the top of Oliver's hand for the first time. And to his delight, Oliver did not flinch. Instead, Oliver held his hand out a little longer than necessary as if to signal to Hunter that he liked him, too.

An hour later, deep inside the dark club, Hunter found Oliver standing against one of the bars. He was fidgeting with the cap of his water bottle as he slightly moved his body to the deafening sound of the music. His shirt was tied around his belt loop, and his muscles shone in the light thanks to a sheet of sweat coating his skin—he had just come off the dance floor. Hunter saw that Oliver was alone, so he walked up to him and touched his chest, dragging his finger down toward his naval. Oliver was very wet to the touch, but Hunter did not mind. The two tried to have a conversation, but the music was too loud, so Hunter grabbed Oliver by the arm and pulled him away from the bar toward one of the upstairs lounges where he knew it would be a little quieter. Oliver did not resist, and liked that Hunter was taking the initiative.

The two talked for a couple of hours, letting each other into their lives slowly. Neither was necessarily thinking about what would happen next, and though both were hoping the night would end the way that it did, neither had planned it out that way. As Oliver sat listening to Hunter his mind wandered a little thinking about the first time, he found himself attracted to boys. He was looking into

Hunter's eyes, half-listening to him talk. He was lost in the blue sea before him and thought about Howard and Sebastian. He was remembering the good times he had with Sebastian—the intimate moments that he was so unprepared when they happened so many years ago. He thought about the night with Howard—where it could have gone if he had let it. And then he wondered how he ended up here, in a dark club sitting with a handsome boy who was clearly interested in him. As he listened Oliver was mesmerized by the piercing blue eyes, and he remembered another pair of piercing eyes—the green eyes from London. Was it the eyes that attracted him to both men or was it something more, he wondered. Hunter could see that Oliver was deep in thought—somewhere else.

"Are you still with me?" Hunter asked as he waved his hand in front of Oliver's face.

"Sorry. Yes. I am still very present," Oliver spit out trying not to sound like a complete ass. "To be honest with you, Hunter, I am kind of ready to get out of here. Do you want to go grab something to eat?"

"I am not sure we will find any decent food at this hour, but how about coming back to my place? I can whip us up something," Hunter responded, without really thinking about the state of his apartment, or if there was even any food to cook.

Oliver smiled, stood up, and reached for Hunter's hand. "That sounds great. Let's go." As they walked through the club Oliver put his shirt back on, covering up the smooth muscles. Hunter held Oliver's hand hoping that was not going to be the last time he got to see Oliver without a shirt that night as the two headed to Hunter's apartment.

As Hunter lay with his face buried in the pillow taking in Oliver's smell, Oliver was in the bathroom, standing naked, looking into the mirror above the sink wondering if the past few hours were real. He wore a smile bigger than he had ever worn before. He felt exhausted but overjoyed at what he and Hunter had done with, and to each other's bodies, for hours. He could not recall the last time he felt so alive. He finally flushed the toilet, washed his hands and returned to the bedroom where he found Hunter still naked, waiting for him. The two spent the next few hours wrapping their bodies together, soaking the sheets more. Eventually they exchanged numbers, kisses, and a few more gropes, and as much as Hunter wanted Oliver to stay all day — all weekend keeping him warm within his sheets, Oliver needed to go. He enjoyed every minute he spent wrapped in Hunter's arms, and he enjoyed all the conversation between all the kissing, and admiring of nakedness, but that did not change the fact that Oliver wanted something more — someone more. Hunter was a scratch to an itch Oliver had for some time, but Hunter was not the ointment that Oliver sought out. It was not the piercing blue that Oliver secretly hungered for; it was the green.

* * * * *

Nicholas was running late to meet Hunter. He could have sent a text, but he did not want that digital trail out there, even on his burner. Instead, he moved as quickly as he could, and kept Hunter sitting alone at the restaurant bar. Hunter was well into his third martini by the time Nicholas walked through the door. As Nicholas was speaking with the hostess, he scanned the room to see if he could find Hunter on his own. He did find him, but he was not alone. Hunter was talking with Oliver, who was at the restaurant Howard. Howard sat to one side of

172

Oliver and Hunter to the other. Nicholas saw the three men in conversation, but they had not yet seen him. Nicholas needed this date—needed this alibi tonight so he could not turn around and walk out—something he would have done any other night. By the time the hostess hung up the phone to give her attention to Nicholas he had already moved on from her and was heading to the bar.

This was not how Nicholas wanted to meet Oliver, although he already felt he knew him quite well. He wanted their first meeting to mean something—to them both. He wanted the setting to be somewhere special and meaningful. But as he slowly walked toward the bar, he realized that there is no right time, or place for the official introduction. He had been watching Oliver for years. Nicholas thought to himself how funny it was that he had been so focused on how the first meeting with Oliver would go that he forgot to think that Oliver might not have any clue of who Nicholas really was—maybe Oliver did not get a good look at Nicholas in London or did but forgot about those moments since it was months ago. Nicholas decided that he was overthinking the entire situation and just walked toward the bar with an open mind.

Hunter looked up and saw Nicholas heading in their direction. Oliver and Howard had their backs to the front door and therefore did not see Nicholas until they turned around. Hunter's face lit up with excitement, which triggered Oliver and Howard to turn so that the three of them watched Nicholas in his final few steps before joining them. Hunter got out of his chair and walked toward Nicholas to give him a big hug—more so to show Oliver that he had moved on from that one incredible night weeks ago, but also because he always wanted to do that to Nicholas—give him a hug and feel his toned body.

"You made it!" Hunter exclaimed, not yet slurring even though he was well past his typical martini limit. "I was beginning to think I was going to have to replace you with these two fine men tonight."

By this time Oliver and Howard had the chance to get a good look at Nicholas. Howard wiped his lips and let out a quiet meow in Oliver's ear indicating that he very much approved of the fine male specimen joining them now. Oliver just sat there on the barstool staring at Nicholas. A million thoughts were running through his mind. Those green eyes shone bright, and Oliver went a little pale as his pants tightened with his excitement. Was it him? Was it someone else? Certainly, lots of people had piercing green eyes. While these thoughts ran wild in his head, Oliver was certain that to the outside world he was composed and in control of himself. He was wrong.

"Dude, are you okay?" Howard asked when he realized that Oliver was shaking and clearly uncomfortable. "Oliver? Come on, I'm taking you to the bathroom." The two of them fumbled off the stools and headed to the bathroom before Nicholas made it to them. Safe, for now, Nicholas thought.

Nicholas was trying to remain composed and focused given his evening was thrown off track when he saw Oliver. Of all the people he could possibly expect to run into, Oliver was not one of them. He was excited, confused and speechless all at the same time. Hunter, on the other hand, was clueless that Nicholas wanted Oliver more than he wanted him. He was just excited to see that Nicholas showed up—that they were finally having another date, sort of. Meeting Oliver and Howard at the bar was coincidence, and certainly a nice surprise, but for Hunter the night was supposed to be all about

Nicholas—the night when they finally exchanged more than just a few words. It was a time for a full conversation, and maybe more. Hunter had been hoping for this night since the first time he saw Nicholas walk into the club more than a year ago.

"Sorry if I'm late," Nicholas said, trying to calm his voice. He assumed his voice was not calm because in his head it was not. In his head he was thinking fast, talking fast, trying to piece together everything that had happened over the last couple of hours, right up to the point when Oliver turned around. He feared that he was as frazzled on the outside as he was on the inside. Was Oliver his kryptonite?

"It's fine," Hunter said with a little too much excitement in his voice. "I have not been here very long, and I ran into some friends to pass the time." He looked around and, of course, his friends were not there, but Nicholas knew. He watched them bolt to the bathroom as he arrived. He wanted to ask so many questions, but knew that would distract Hunter, and he needed Hunter to focus—he needed the cover, should anyone ask.

The two sat at a table for two, writing off Oliver and Howard—not that they were ever part of the evening plan anyway. Sitting at the small table, a lit candle and rose their only divider — Hunter revealed more of his past than Nicholas had, but that was typical for Nicholas. As the night went on — as Hunter went on, he realized that he was dominating the conversation. Nicholas did not mind. And, after a little while he forgot all about Oliver and Howard and was giving his full attention to Hunter. After all, Hunter was a smart, educated, and very handsome man — just what Nicholas found attractive.

Neither of them noticed when Oliver and Howard finally emerged from the bathroom, and certainly did not see them maneuver around the bar to get out of the restaurant without being seen by Nicholas or Hunter. Oliver lied to Howard about having stomach pains, and he was convincing enough to get Howard to agree that they had to leave immediately. Howard quickly sent a text to Camilla to say that dinner plans had changed, and to meet at home.

A couple of hours had passed as Hunter and Nicholas continued to enjoy each other's company. Nicholas knew he had some cleanup to take care of from earlier in the evening but was having such a good time with Hunter — so much so that he didn't want the night to end anytime soon. When the check finally came, and a few empty wine bottles littered the table both wondered what would happen next. They both wanted the same thing, but neither of them had spoken the words yet. It was unlike Nicholas go be so passive and submissive. As they signed their receipts, another breadcrumb to show where Nicholas was tonight, and stood to leave Nicholas decided he would make the move. He grabbed Hunter's right hand—it was soft and smooth, and a little smaller than Nicholas' hand. He didn't even ask Hunter how he got to the restaurant, he just walked Hunter to his car a block away. By now Hunter knew that he was going home with Nicholas or was hoping that to be true. When they reached Nicholas's car, they were still holding hands. Nicholas turned Hunter around and pushed him against the car, gently. Nicholas leaned in and they kissed, still holding hands. Murder excited Nicholas, and his own kills got him so aroused that he often felt he could kill again in the heat of the moment. Tonight, would not be one of those nights though.

Eventually the two got into Nicholas's car and Hunter directed Nicholas to his apartment.

There was a parking garage across the street, but Nicholas opted to park out front as if to ensure his car was seen—visible to anyone who might want to know his whereabouts. After all, he was trying to lay crumbs—to prove he was anywhere except at his father's house tonight. Once inside Hunter's small but tidy apartment the two began tearing clothes off the other like tigers tearing into their prey. The apartment was no longer tidy, but Hunter did not mind. He was getting closer and closer to seeing Nicholas naked—something he had dreamt of for far too long.

As Hunter lay in his bed naked—his body entangled in silk sheets and the warm, soft strength of Nicholas's arms and legs, he was finally in a calm enough setting to take in the whole night. He wondered how he was lucky enough to be naked in bed with Nicholas—someone he always thought was out of each for him. Hunter was not in love with Nicholas—in fact, he could not recall ever being in love with anyone. But, in this moment, and every moment where he had encountered Nicholas in the past Hunter felt giddy—very excited to be alive. Maybe that was love—maybe just infatuation. Whatever it was, Hunter welcomed the feeling. He had felt this way a few other times in his life — one of them being when he brought Oliver home. Though the feeling was not as intense with Oliver, it was still there. Hunter wanted nothing more than to stay in bed, in the very tangled position he was in at this moment with Nicholas for as long as possible. He lay there in bed listening to the slight hum of Nicholas's body. He was not snoring, but he was not silent either. His body rose and fell as he breathed slowly — peacefully. Hunter was riding the wave and enjoying the comfort and serenity he felt in Nicholas's arms.

The moment was disrupted abruptly as Nicholas woke from a nightmare. Hunter pretended to still be asleep as Nicholas untangled himself from the sheets, and Hunter. He stepped onto the cold wooden floor and marched across the room toward the bathroom. The room was partially lit from the rising sun outside so as Nicholas paraded away Hunter watched as the tight-assed, sculptured, naked Nicholas made his way to bathroom. Nicholas did not close the door or turn any light on. Instead, he stood naked in the dark peeing. Hunter could still see the backside of Nicholas — part of his ass reflecting in the mirror. When Nicholas finished and came out from the bathroom Hunter was still staring, smiling. He could see Nicholas was a little aroused as he slipped back to bed with the confidence of a man who was about to get exactly what he wanted.

Hours later Hunter woke again. The morning sex had worn them both out, sending them into another blissful sleep. This time however, Hunter realized that he was alone. The sheets still smelled of Nicholas, but he was gone. Hunter jumped out of bed, his body still naked and sticky, and he called out to Nicholas, hoping that he was still in the apartment. No one answered and as he walked through his apartment, realizing that he was alone, he hoped for a note—something left behind by Nicholas to indicate that the night, and the morning, were fun—something Nicholas enjoyed as much as Hunter. When he was done looking, Hunter collapsed on the couch—the leather felt very cold against his naked body. He was trying to accept that maybe Nicholas was just another one-night stand, and at the sad realization, he began to quietly cry for letting himself get so emotionally attached too quickly for so little return—again.

CHAPTER TWELVE

More than two weeks had passed since the night Oliver saw Nicholas at the bar. In that time Hunter had decided that he was going to stop sleeping with men until he found a real boyfriend. He was still having a rough time processing the fact that Nicholas had left him alone. Nicholas, meanwhile, had been cleared of any involvement in the death of his father. For Oliver, however, it was a tough two weeks. His mother dropped a bomb on him about his father.

For the past two decades Oliver grew up loving his mother and father, like any child would. They had their differences, but love was the one truth keeping them together—or so Oliver thought. His paternal father had died a few years earlier. He went to his grave never knowing the truth about Oliver, and it was time, his mother believed, that Oliver did know the truth. She decided to start with another funeral. Oliver was trying to understand why his mother was so interested in the funeral of a man Oliver never knew. Peter had never come up in any conversation, and to his recollection, Oliver had never seen a photo of Peter with his mother.

On the day of the funeral Oliver arrived with his mother hoping to see a familiar face — someone who could make sense of why he was there — why his mother was so determined to be there. They sat near the front of the cathedral at his mother's request. Aside from the quiet choral music playing at a low volume, the only other noises were the loud clash of shoe to tile as people made their way in. Periodically Oliver would turn around to see if he could recognize anyone, but he did not — until just before the service was about to start, when Nicholas walked in. Even though Nicholas was wearing sunglasses Oliver felt that he looked familiar, but he could not place him. The two stared at each other as Nicholas made his way down the aisle to sit as near to the front as Oliver, but on the opposite side.

As soon as Nicholas sat down next to Melissa the priest come out to start the service. Melissa gave Nicholas a look as if to say, "Nice of you to finally show up, you spoiled brat." Melissa was trying to give off emotions of someone who lost the love of their life, but it was coming off more as desperate and nervous — not only to Nicholas, but anyone who knew her, and it certainly would have to Peter, too. The service went by more quickly than Nicholas expected, but still not fast enough for his liking. He liked killing but did not care for funerals. He would look over toward Oliver every so often. He was pleased that no one gave a eulogy, least of all Melissa. She tends to ramble. She had no clue what Peter left her in his will and that made her very nervous. Nicholas, on the other hand, knew everything—what she was getting, and he was letting Melissa sweat it out until the reading of the will scheduled for next week. While he did not let Peter suffer, he was okay letting Melissa suffer—a lot.

As the service ended, and everyone followed the casket outside, Oliver was surprised to see no hearse. This cathedral sat firmly in front of its own cemetery—one that had existed for more than 100 years. The casket was carried just a few dozen feet, out the front door and around to a corner lot behind the old building where another, shorter service proceeded Peter's body being lowered into the ground. Through it all Oliver's mother cried. Oliver noticed that she was more upset over Peter's death than she had been about her own husband's funeral.

As Oliver and his mother were leaving the cemetery Oliver turned to look at Nicholas and Melissa standing over Peter's grave. He never interacted with either of them. Neither did his mother. They were dark silhouettes with their heads down. As he stood there watching he was surprised when Nicholas turned around and looked back at Oliver and smiled. Oliver could not see the green eyes behind the sunglasses. Oliver turned and got into the car where his mother was waiting. He still could not figure out why Nicholas looked so familiar. Without seeing the green eyes Nicholas was just another pretty boy to Oliver.

"Are you going to tell me why we were here?" Oliver asked bluntly. "You spring this funeral on me last minute, we sit through this whole sad ordeal, and I have no idea why, or who we were grieving."

"Your father," his mother said in almost a whisper as tears rolled down her face, taking some of the heavy mascara with them.

"I'm sorry — what?"

His mother wiped the tears from her face and before looking Oliver in the eye and telling him all about her affair with Peter decades earlier. Once she started talking about the past, she could hardly stop. She told him all about Peter, the troubles she was having with her husband, and of course about Catherine. She told Oliver that she wanted to tell him this story so many times before, but never had the courage. She certainly could not do it while her husband was alive since he was clueless about the affair, and the fact that Oliver really was not his son.

Oliver was speechless. He turned from his mother and looked out the window as the world whipped past. Houses, trees, people—all coming into and then out of sight at great speed. He felt his life was moving at the same pace—that everything was happening so fast—everything he knew was changing as quickly as his view of the world through the window. A million thoughts were rushing in every direction, making it hard to follow any one thought in his head.

His mother sat silent for some time to let Oliver take in the news—really let it sink in. Then she began peppering him with questions. Oliver and his mother always had an open line of communication—or so he thought—clearly, she could keep some secrets. But sitting there in the car, unable to go anywhere but forward, Oliver was trapped — and she knew that. He had little to say back to her — he was still stunned. By the time they arrived home Oliver had accepted his mother's news — mostly to put her at ease. He said that it did not change anything for him or how he felt about the dad he grew up loving. It also did not mean that he was going to spread the word that he really had two dads. That was a secret he was hoping to take to his grave, much like his mother thought that she would have done.

CHAPTER THIRTEEN

Nicholas and Melissa sat in the waiting room of the lawyer's office. Melissa had wanted to have the meeting in her own living room where she would be more comfortable but given that Peter's brain had been splattered across the bedroom directly above the living room just three weeks earlier, they had no choice but to meet elsewhere. The lawyer then told Melissa and Nicholas that Peter had fathered a child out of wedlock more than two decades ago, and that child was due to receive a portion of the estate. Melissa was confused. She wondered how someone she never met, and Peter never mentioned, was going to hold up a reading she had been waiting for — the winning lottery ticket she had been holding on to all these years.

At that moment it all made sense to Nicholas why Oliver and his mother were at the funeral. At that moment it became clear that the boy he had fantasied about for years — the boy, now man he watched and wanted, and who might now know who Nicholas is, was in fact related to him. He smiled at the thought, and Melissa scolded him for smiling. The lawyer said that the child was not coming to the reading, and that per the orders from Peter, that child would be addressed separately. Peter wanted Nicholas and Melissa to know of the child—not his name, but that he existed and that he was going to be given some money. With that news the lawyer proceeded to read Peter's will to Melissa, Nicholas and the witness in the room, the lawyer's secretary.

"That's it?" Melissa yelled. "That is all I get for being married to that old man for all those years, and for putting up with this brat?"

Melissa was furious that she was only getting the small trust. The insurance company concluded that Peter had shot himself to end his pain and suffering. This classification of suicide voided the $2M payout that Melissa was to receive, which drastically reduced her winning total. Nicholas also lost out on the insurance payout, but he was not worried about it. He did not really care about the money, and even if he did, his trust was large enough to him to live very comfortably for the rest of his life.

Melissa did not care that most of Nicholas' money came from Catherine, and had been held, and invested for this very occasion. She still wanted more. She was equally as irritated to learn that an unnamed child was getting money from her dead husband. She grabbed the check from the lawyer's hand, furious that all she had to show for her marriage was a single piece of paper with a couple of commas in the dollar field and stormed out of the office. Her performance convinced Nicholas that she was married to Peter for his money the whole time, and that infuriated him. He was going to make her pay — later. Nicholas was dumbfounded that Peter went through all the drama about letting him know in advance about all the money he would inherit, and what little Melissa would get. Peter, it appeared to Nicholas, had gone to great lengths to show all his cards to Nicholas, but Nicholas was wrong. Peter had taken the secret about Oliver to the grave.

With Melissa gone, Nicholas wanted to get out of the office to get some air. He also wanted to go kill Melissa, but he thought that might have to wait a little while, so he headed back to Peter's house. He was expecting to find Melissa there — pouting over the small amount of money she received—a sum that most middle-class widows would be very excited to enjoy for the rest of their lives. The money was enough for Melissa to live a comfortable life—not necessarily a lavish life. Yet somehow that was not enough for her, which Nicholas found interesting considering she and Peter did not live that a flashy of a lifestyle. Peter drove a ten-year-old Honda Accord. He wanted to live well, but not bring unwanted attention to himself.

A week later Nicholas went to Peter's house to he found the front door wide open. Melissa's BMW convertible was parked in the driveway instead of the garage, which he found odd. He called out to her as he walked through the open door. She yelled back from upstairs. A few suitcases were already packed and resting by the front door ready to leave. Nicholas closed the door and sat on the couch closest to the front door, waiting for Melissa to come downstairs. A few minutes later she came down the stairs dragging two more suitcases.

"Going somewhere?" Nicholas asked with a strong hint of sarcasm. "Looks like you will be gone awhile."

"I am getting the hell out of here," she spat back at Nicholas with total disdain in her voice. Your father cheated me out of what was rightfully mine. I am done."

"Rightfully yours? Who the fuck do you think you are? "You should be fucking grateful he left you anything. The investments all come from my mother and her family money — something you have zero rights to so get off your fucking high horse."

"You would say that you spoiled fucking brat," Melissa shot back. "You have never worked a day in your life, and Peter spoiled you every day."

Nicholas laughed at the absurdity of Melissa's claim. Sure, there was some truth to him never working, and Peter always making sure that Nicholas had what he needed. He did not come over to argue with Melissa. His goal was to make sure she was leaving town like she had been threatening to for a week. He wanted her gone, and as much as he wanted to kill her — take her last breath away from her, he was not passionate enough about killing Melissa to waste his time. He was focused on Oliver, more now than ever.

Melissa ran around the house gathering things to throw in her car. She continued to yell at Nicholas — her voice fading in and out as she travelled from room to room and out to her car. A few neighbors walking their dogs stopped to hear the yelling. To speed up the process, Nicholas helped by carrying all the large suitcases to the car and throwing them in the trunk or back seat. He was not being neat about it but was making sure all her shit was out of his house.

With her car packed, Melissa yelled at Nicholas one more time as she walked out the front door, slamming it behind her. She got into her car, reversed out of the driveway and sped down the road, into the sunset. Nicholas hoped that it would be the last time he would have to see her. He could ensure that, but he decided to just let her go.

Three months later Nicholas saw the headline in the local paper when he was hanging out at the coffee shop enjoying a tea with Hunter. It was not a date. Hunter happened to be sitting in the coffee shop when Nicholas walked in. It was the first time the two had seen each other since the night Peter died. And now here they were, Hunter and Nicholas together again on the night that Melissa's death was in the newspaper. He only noticed it because Melissa was referred to as the widow of Peter Lawson. The headline read "Widow's death mirrored husbands." Melissa had died by gunshot to the head, just as Peter had, but this time Nicholas did not have his hand on the trigger.

Nicholas felt certain that she would fade out of his life, and he would never have to deal with her again. They had no real connection—they never bonded while she held the title of stepmother, and with Peter gone there was no reason for her to remain a part of Nicholas's life. He liked it that way and hoped it would stay that way. Another part of him wondered from time to time if he needed to tie up that loose end as he had tied up so many others in the past. For all his charm and good looks—for all this murders and misbehaving, Nicholas always ensured that no one could ever speak of anything they saw or thought they saw him do. He was excellent at clearing the tracks, ensuring that none were ever left behind—just like Adam. Nicholas found Melissa so annoying and ungrateful that he might get a kick out of making her suffer—letting her know the true Nicholas before taking her life too. But for all his pondering and procrastinating

Nicholas never got the chance to make that decision. It was made for him.

Days earlier Nicholas got the call that he assumed so many of his victims' survivors got — the call from the police that someone had died. So when the police called, Nicholas found it both intriguing and alarming. He felt quite confident that he left no tracks behind any of his recent kills, including Peter, so he could not imagine why they would be calling him, and on all things, his cell phone. He would learn that his number was found in Melissa's phone, and surprisingly his contact file was listed as "stepson." Nicholas found that interesting considering she never wanted to be thought of as a mother, given how close they were in age.

When he answered the phone and acknowledged that he was who they needed him to be the officer on the other end of the line asked if Nicholas knew Melissa and let him know there had been an incident — not a murder or brutal killing, just an incident, and asked that he come to the police station. Part of him feared this was some trap — maybe he did forget to cover a track — there was that one guy in the alley so long ago — the submissive and abused one who Nicholas sent home in a cab after watching his boyfriend beat up that homeless man … but he never saw Nicholas hurt his lover. Then there was the lover himself. Nicholas did give him a good beating but did not kill him—maybe that was the mistake. He pondered these and other cases where he let someone go—as he thought about them all he realized that there were quite a few people he saved or hurt but released. Maybe he was not as much of a monster as Adam after all. There was a long silence before the officer started to repeat herself. In mid-sentence Nicholas interrupted her and said that he could be at the station within the hour.

When Nicholas arrived at the police station, he immediately felt like he made a mistake—all eyes were on him as he walked through the glass doors into the precinct. Maybe he was the monster he feared. Maybe he was about to go down like his real father. His armpits were suddenly very damp, and he felt warm all over. He slowed his excited pace as he walked through the doors and toward the reception window.

"Nicholas Lawson to see Sergeant Jacobson," he said to the young cadet behind the thick, scratched plexiglass window. "She is expecting me."

The cadet asked Nicholas to have a seat on the bench to the right of the window, and he called Sergeant Jacobson's direct line. Within minutes the cadet issued directions to Nicholas to head into the maze of corridors to where the sergeant was waiting. Once again, thoughts filled his mind about the mistake he might be making—walking into a trap. Nicholas avoided police stations for several reasons and being cornered into an office to be arrested was certainly high on that list. More thoughts of the people he let live over the years—certainly the ones he hurt—flashed through his mind, but no one name, or face came into focus as someone who might remotely know who Nicholas really was.

When he did finally reach the end of the directions from the cadet, he found himself standing in front of a windowless door to a windowless room. He knocked and was instructed to enter. Once inside instead of finding a herd of police officers ready to cuff him for any number of reasons for which he should be cuffed, tried and hung, he found Sergeant Jacobson and two junior officers going over notes and reports.

"Thank you for coming in Mr. Lawson," the sergeant said as she pointed to a chair. "You might want to sit down to hear what we have to say."

Nicholas sat, almost reluctantly, and then as he looked at the desk, he saw some horrific black and white photos—well, horrific to most but fascinating to him. Because of the poor-quality Nicholas could not make out who was in them, just that the person was covered in blood. Again, his mind started racing.

"Mr. Lawson, do you know a Melissa Lawson?" asked one of the junior officers.

"Yes, as I said on the phone, she was, I mean is my stepmother."

"Was?"

"What I mean is that she married my father a decade ago, and never really had any connection with me. My father died recently and once he did, she bolted. So, yes, she is still my stepmother, but neither of us thinks that really means anything, now more than ever."

"Well, I am sorry to hear that you and your stepmother did not have a good relationship. And as a result, you might take this news more differently than we expected," the officer continued.

"Melissa Lawson was found dead in a motel room the other day. It has taken us this long to find any next of kin to inform."

"I'm sorry," Nicholas said. "But did you say she was found dead in a motel room? Are you sure you have the right Melissa Lawson? She was a bit of a snobbish bimbo, so I cannot begin to imagine how she could have ended up in a motel, especially with all the money she got as a result of my father's death. Sorry if that sounds harsh, but it's true."

Nicholas realized that for someone who walked into the police station less then 30 minutes earlier somewhat frightened that he was finally caught, he was spewing a lot of dirty laundry about Melissa as if trying to throw her or her killer into the laps of the police. He was so overly relieved that he was not being arrested that he found himself being overly verbose airing too much of the Lawson family dirty laundry.

The officers, intrigued by the relationship between Melissa and Nicholas, proceeded to give Nicholas some of the details—what they knew so far. Melissa was found in a motel not too far off the highway. Based on the condition of the room and conversations with the motel front desk, Melissa had been staying in the motel for a couple of weeks leading up to her death. Security cameras showed several men coming and going from her room at all hours of the night, and in fact the main reason the police were called was because the motel manager went to Melissa's room to speak with her about all her late-night guests. When she would not answer the door, the manager used his master key to enter and found Melissa—her body mangled, straddling the space between the two beds. He called the police immediately.

Forensics concluded that Melissa had been dead for less than six hours when she was found, and that the cause of death was drug overdose. While she had clearly been beaten to within an inch of her life, and left for dead, it was the large sums of heroin that had been shot into her arm that killed her. In fact, there were more than half a dozen needles still stuck in her arms and ass when the police arrived. Her killer wanted her to suffer and wanted her to die a slow death. None of the motives made sense for a typical robbery, and it did not appear that Melissa had any valuable possessions in the room. In addition to all the needles, she had a bullet hole in her head. Forensics determined that she was already dead when she was shot.

The only lead was a video of the last man to leave the motel room. While the image was grainy, it was clear enough to see the man enter the room, and then leave the room a couple of hours later. He walked away from the camera both times, which lead the police to believe that the man knew that the cameras were watching. There were not a lot of cameras on the motel grounds so where the man went after walking out of the camera's view was still undetermined. The police questioned all the motel guests, and no one recognized the man in the video, and for that matter no one recognized Melissa either.

Nicholas questioned the police about the timing — restating that Melissa had left with her money only three months earlier. It appeared that Melissa went straight to the motel after leaving Peter's house, and not to New York City or someplace more fabulous. He was puzzled why she would make such a move.

This was a lot of information for Nicholas to take in, and he was grateful that the police were so forthcoming. They indicated that they shared all the information in hopes that Nicholas might know something, or maybe even be able to recognize the man leaving the motel room. He did not. He was, however, more interested in what happened to all the money Peter left Melissa. He knew she could not have spent it all that quickly. Nicholas was interested enough in this case to want to be in the loop, but not interested enough to want to do anything about it. Melissa was dead, and as far as he was concerned that was the end of it for him. With her out of the picture Nicholas had one less obstacle in his life. He half-heartedly wished he had followed through with killing her. He probably would not have been so brutal—maybe he would. His most brutal kills were often not thought out in advance, and simply take advantage of the surroundings in the heat of the moment. From what the police shared; this killing seemed more "heat of the moment."

The police did give Nicholas what few personal possessions of Melissa's they found at the scene—a set of keys, a wallet with credit cards and a driver's license, and one suitcase of clothing. Nicholas found it odd that Melissa has so little clothing at the motel given how much she liked to shop and just how much clothing she owned. He wondered where the rest of Melissa's clothes were. He did notice that one of the keys was for a storage unit. He did not point that out to the police, but rather decided he would enjoy uncovering that mystery on his own.

CHAPTER FOURTEEN

Six months had passed since Oliver learned about Peter's affair, and he was still grappling with the reality that a man he never met had taken the time to create a trust fund for him. But it was not the money that Oliver found so amazing. It was the envelope that came with the money, and more specifically, the book inside. Oliver was surprised to learn that Peter had kept a journal for more than two decades—for Oliver. What Oliver and his mother did not know was that Peter had been following Oliver his whole life. The journal was packed with passages to Oliver as if he were the journal and Peter was sharing his deepest secrets and daily mundane activities. Page after page was filled with words of regret, of sorrow—and a lot of apologies. Every so often Oliver would come across a page with a picture of Peter and a much younger Nicholas on some adventure—Disney World, the Eiffel Tower, the Golden Gate Bridge, Tower Bridge—the images were scattered throughout the journal but showed how Peter and Nicholas aged and were accompanied by regrets about how Oliver should have been there too. The pictures stopped at around age 14, so Nicholas was still young and completely unrecognizable today.

Oliver shared the journal with his mother that first day in the lawyer's office, but never again. She got to feel the smooth black leather binding and get a good grip of its huge size, but aside from a quick flip through the first couple of pages she never read the words or saw the images — never got to see the wonderful life Oliver could have had with Peter. She had loved Peter a very long time ago — at the wrong time in her life. Had they met later, or maybe earlier, life might have been so different for both — and for Oliver.

Eventually Oliver shared the details of the journal with Camilla and Howard. Early in the book the name Nicholas meant nothing, and the childhood pictures were cute — adorable even. It was not until the end of the journal when they saw a picture of an older Nicholas — but still a teenager. He was set back in the photo wearing a sun hat and Bermuda shorts. He had sunscreen on his nose, and he was squinting, trying to keep the sun out. You could not see his green eyes. The picture could have been anyone as far as Oliver was concerned.

"I dated him," Camila said, poking the picture forcefully with her middle finger.

"Stop that!" Oliver said. "There's no way you ever dated this guy." First, he is clearly a teenager in this photo, and secondly, he looks like any generic Joe in a picture."

"How are you making any connection between this teenager and an adult man," Oliver continued. His voice was cracked with frustration. "If the kid in this picture is my... sibling in some way, there is no way that same person dated Camilla. It just doesn't happen like that, except in the movies."

Without skipping a beat, Camilla started telling Oliver and Howard about dating a man named Simon. She shared that he was a very smooth operator—said all the right things, did all the right things to impress her. She shared how he loved and left her. They were having a great time, and then they weren't. Camilla started crying a little as she told Oliver and Howard how she thought Simon could have been "the one" for her. When she looks back on that time in her life, she realized how little she really meant to him. He popped into her life, and then back out almost as quickly. She got wrapped up in the mystery and thrill of it all, but admitted that it all happened so fast, and was over almost before it began. She would never forget his bright green eyes.

She told them about the one and only time Simon came to her apartment. She was cooking dinner. They were going to have a romantic evening in. They did — dinner, drinking, wild and insanely sweaty sex. When she woke the next morning Simon was gone. No note. No clothes left behind. Just gone. She tried sending him a text, but it was undeliverable. She tried calling, but the number had been disconnected. As quickly has Simon had come into her life, he was gone without a trace.

She had no pictures of them together. She had no text threads — for as often as she would text him during their brief encounter, he never texted back — instead he would call her. No voicemails either. They had "dated" for less than two weeks — so some might question if it was really dating, or just a hook up — and in that entire time Simon never met any of her friends, and she never met any of his. She didn't even know his last name, if Simon was his real name, or if he even went to her college as he claimed.

Camilla had gotten so wrapped up in the passion of the moment—the excitement that someone as handsome, and nice, and sweet and considerate and … perfect would be attracted to her and want her as badly as it appeared Simon—Nicholas wanted her.

She never forgot Simon—never forgave him either. Through her story telling she also indicated that the night she met Simon was the night that she, Oliver, and Howard went to a little dive bar—the name she could not recall—but that it was the night Oliver introduced Howard and Camilla to one another. It was the night that Howard met Reed for the first time, and it was one of many nights when Nicholas was in the dark corner watching Oliver. Of course, Oliver never saw Nicholas that night—in fact he barely remembered the night. Camilla and Howard remembered it well—they both met people who changed their lives forever.

"I need to tell you both something," Oliver started. "And you cannot freak out. Promise me that you will not freak out." They both nodded.

"Peter's son, Nicholas was at the funeral, and he sort of resembles a guy that Howard and I saw at a bar weeks earlier. And now I think I remember where I saw him even before that. I am not 100%

positive, but as I think more about hit, I think I saw him when I was in London," he continued. "I was walking through a cemetery, and—"

"Wait. What?" Camilla interrupted.

"Let me finish. Yes, I was in a cemetery. There is one not far from where I was staying. It is historic—goes back 600 years or something. Very old. Very beautiful. It's even in tour guides as being a place to visit. Anyway, that's not the point."

Oliver continued to tell Camilla and Howard how he visited the cemetery, and how he ended up being witness to a plethora of sexual activity. He talked about the straight couple he saw having sex, and then the lesbian couple—or was it a throuple? He could not remember. He could see that he was holding their attention, but it was waning. He told them how he watched someone who looked just like the guy Howard and Oliver saw with Hunter having oral sex with another guy in the cemetery. On a roll, and leading up to the big finale, Oliver told Camilla and Howard about the green eyes—how they were looking right at him while the one guy was having sex with the other guy—that as Nicholas was climaxing—while Nicholas bit his knuckle to keep from screaming out in ecstasy, he was looking right at Oliver as if nothing else—no one else mattered or was present except Nicholas and Oliver. He ended the story there—he left out the part where he discovered the dead body, and that he was convinced Nicholas had something to do with it but had no evidence.

"And that was the first time I saw Nicholas, assuming it was even Nicholas," Oliver finished. "At least that is the first time I remember seeing him—I don't think I could ever forget those eyes. Oh, yeah, and by the way," he continued, finally ready to come out to his best friends, "I'm gay."

There as absolute silence for a sold five seconds. The three of them sat on the couch with the hum of music vibrating throughout the room. A few more empty wine bottles were now on the coffee table, and the pizza they made earlier—what remained of it was getting cold, but the delicious smell still filled the air. Oliver sat silent trying to determine if Camilla and Howard were stunned into silence because he came out or because of his Nicholas story—or both. The silence had him second-guessing his decision to come out, and he was about to make a joke about it when Camilla and Howard both stood up and hugged Oliver tightly.

When they finally released him, he was able to take a long, deep breath.

Camilla spoke first. "I love you, and I am so happy you finally came out. I have been dying to set you up with someone hot but was biting my tongue until you came out. I cannot tell you how long we have known."

"Girlfriend is spot on," Howard said. "I am so happy for you, but at the same time I am freaking out about old green eyes. What did you do while he raped you with his eyes that day? Man, I would have been freaking out. "

Oliver told them that he did freak out. He told them that he didn't share at the time because it seemed so isolated—he chalked it up to a vacation story, and nothing more, until he saw the man with green eyes at the bar the night he and Howard were talking with Hunter. And now to hear the story of Simon and his green eyes. Too many connected characters with green eyes were appearing in their lives. Oliver wondered if the boy in the pictures, the man Camilla dated and the man at the bar were somehow the same person. Only in the movies, he thought to himself.

CHAPTER FIFTEEN

A few weeks had passed since Oliver came out to his friends. Next on his list was his mother. He did not want to tell her, but felt it had to be done now that he was out. He did not want her learning about his lifestyle choice from a third party — that somehow it would get back to the old ladies in her bridge club, and one of them would console his mother for her shame. Oliver and his mother had some estate planning business to discuss over lunch, and he thought that was a good time to put everything on the table. Somewhere between the third and fourth martini for his mother, and after the two decided what to do with the funds left for Oliver by Peter, Oliver told his mother he was gay. With her martini glass in her left hand, she raised the mostly empty glass to get the attention of the waiter, signaling that she needed a fifth one. With that ritual behind her she put down the now empty glass and laughed.

"My sweet, sweet Oliver," she slurred a little. "You are the most wonderful person to ever come into my life, and I know I am not the best at showing it all the time. Thank you for telling me that you are gay. I could have told you that a decade ago, but you needed to be ready to realize it on your own. Your father never believed me — was mortified at the thought, to be honest. It brought up memories of his uncle Samuel. I am glad he is dead because he would have been awful to you if you told him, and I never wanted that for you."

She continued to ramble on about how bad his paternal father had been and how maybe she should have given Peter more of a chance. And before anyone knew it, Oliver's mother had taken his moment — his coming out and turned the conversation to be all about her. She was sucking the life out of what Oliver hoped was going to be as accepting and wonderful as it was when he came out to Camilla and Howard.

Before she could get both feet on her soapbox the waiter brought the drinks. He brought two — one for each of them — and signaled to Oliver that from a distance it looked like he could use a drink, and this one — his first — was on the house. He smiled, thanked the waiter and dropped the "Mother!" bomb to get her to shut up. Oliver was able to take control of the conversation again and asked about Nicholas. He did not share Camilla's story, or his own possible Nicholas tale. Instead, he wanted to hear what his mother knew about Nicholas, and when he thought they could meet, or if they should meet at all.

His mother shared a few stories about the times she and Peter had together and somewhere around her sixth martini she revealed that Nicholas was born on the same day as Oliver, and that he was a bastard child—not blood related to Peter. By this time her words were too slurred, and she was too tired to continue talking about Peter, so she never told Oliver about how Nicholas was conceived. She only got parts of the story from Peter anyway, and it was so long ago—she decided that required a clear head.

She paid the tab, as she always did when they got together. Outside the restaurant Oliver kissed his mother and put her in a cab—giving the driver clear instructions on where to take his mother, and how to help her into her house. He gave the driver a generous tip and watched the old yellow car sputter down the street away from him. He watched until the car turned the corner and was finally out of sight. Oliver was exhausted. He got more information out of his mother than he expected and was more curious about Nicholas now. He needed to figure out a way to casually run into Nicholas, but first he needed to know where he might be hanging out, so as he walked home, he sent a text to Hunter.

The last person he expected to hear from was Oliver — okay, maybe Nicholas, but when he got the text from Oliver to "hang out," Hunter was pleasantly surprised. He did not follow any of the "smooth operator text code" of waiting hours or days to respond. No sooner did he send the text did Oliver see the three little dots, then nothing, then dots again for a long time before he got the novella text back from Hunter. It was much more than he expected, and in hindsight, it was much more than Hunter felt he should have written, but you cannot take a text back — it was out there. Oliver now knew that Hunter was smitten with him, and keen to meet up now, later — whenever Oliver wanted to meet up. Oliver thought it was cute — adorable even. He remembered having a good time the night he spent with Hunter, and now that he was out — at least out to some and working it into the conversation when it made sense, he was looking forward to catching up with Hunter, but even more so he was interested in learning more about what Hunter knew about Nicholas.

With all the texting back and forth, Oliver felt certain that he and Hunter would be meeting up right away, but after 30 minutes of back-and-forth SMS foreplay Hunter stopped responding. Oliver kept texting, starting to look desperate, but eventually he stopped, too. Furious at Hunter for all the wrong reasons, Oliver sent a text to Camilla and Howard asking them to clear their evening — the three of them had some investigating to do.

CHAPTER SIXTEEN

When Hunter sent his last text to Oliver, he contemplated sending it with a heart emoji—was that too smitten? He thought the eggplant emoji would make the text come off like a booty call. Hunter did not want to come off as that kind of guy—even though he knew he was that kind of guy. Oliver knew it too. They did hook up the first night they met. But, before Hunter could decide what emoji was the appropriate one to send, there was a knock on his front door.

Hunter opened the door to find Nicholas standing there, fist in the air halfway toward the door aiming to knock again. He dropped his fist, his whole arm, and replaced it with a huge smile and held up his other hand—a travel tray holding two coffees.

"Did you order some coffee?" Nicholas asked, trying not to laugh as he pretended to be a delivery boy—as if he were living out a fantasy one of them desired. Hunter stood in the doorway trying to comprehend the moment. He was just texting with one guy he secretly wanted as a boyfriend while another guy in the running for the same title stood before him now.

Hunter let a string of mumbled words fall out of his mouth as he signaled Nicholas to enter the apartment. By the time he closed the door Hunter once again had control of his thoughts and words. He was stunned and excited to see Nicholas, especially with no notice. The two sat down on the couch—it was a small couch to go with the small apartment. The kitchen, dining room, and living room were contained in a single space that was connected to a separate bedroom with a bathroom ensuite. Any guest would have to walk through Hunter's room to pee, but Nicholas already knew that. He had been here before—been naked on the very couch they sat upon now, so he was comfortable with the layout—the small footprint. The windows in this open space all looked out toward a wooded area on the edge of a park making the apartment very private, even with the curtains open or lights on at night. Nicholas already knew that too.

Nicholas put the tray on the coffee table then pulled out one cup and handed it to Hunter then grabbed the other for himself. They sat in silent for a moment, each holding their cups of not-so-hot coffee. It was Nicholas who broke the silence.

"I hope you don't mind me stopping by so unexpectedly," Nicholas said as he put his coffee cup on the table. "I was hoping that we could—"

Nicholas was interrupted by Hunter who also put down his cup then leaned into Nicholas, and tackled Nicholas' words with his lips. It was a bold move for Hunter—one that he would not have been so brave to take just a few months ago—but today, this day, in his apartment he felt he had the confidence to take a chance. He was thrilled that Nicholas came back, and before he let Nicholas say anything about "just being friends" or any bullshit like that, Hunter wanted to put it out there about how he felt—about what he wanted, right now. The kiss went on longer than Hunter intended, but mostly because Nicholas reciprocated, exciting Hunter more. The kissing got more intense, deeper, more lustful, and as Hunter swung himself off the couch to get a better position over Nicholas, he kicked both cups of coffee over, sending dark, lukewarm water flowing all over the coffee table. Hunter freaked out and jumped up for a towel from the kitchen before any liquid could cascade over the sides of the table and all over the floor. By the time he had finished cleaning up the mess he was certain that the moment had been lost, so he sat back down on the couch as if nothing had just happened and struggled to find a topic for small talk.

Nicholas was not interested in the small talk. He was not here to talk, not really. He was not here for a booty call either. It was Hunter's turn to die. Nicholas had realized that he was weaving a wider web which meant more characters were coming into his life, even peripherally, and he needed to stop it. There were too many people in his life—too many who knew him, or who could possibly identify him if asked by the police. He liked Hunter—he really did, and not just for sex. He liked his personality, his charm, and the innocence of his character. But none of that mattered when it came to Nicholas's ultimate survival.

As Hunter rambled on about almost anything that came into his mind, just to keep from talking about the disastrous mess he made trying to make out, Nicholas was looking at the coffee table and the soaked towel that was balled up, saturated. Both cups of coffee had spilled out leaving nothing in either cup to drink. All Nicholas could think about was how $450 worth of tetrodotoxin was just wasted. That was the last of his supply, and he was expecting that poison to be the quickest, easiest, and least painful way to get rid of Hunter. Nicholas hadn't brought anything else — no weapons, nothing to clean up any mess, and certainly no back up plan. He just sat staring at where the dark liquid had once flowed across the table. Hunter could tell that Nicholas was not really paying attention to the rambling so he did the next best thing he could think of — he reached over and pulled Nicholas toward him and started kissing him again.

"Let's move this into the bedroom," Nicholas suggested as he sat half on the couch and half on Hunter. The couch was much too small for two grown men to be having sex on it. Hunter was all too happy to move. He jumped up, grabbed Nicholas by the arm and they ran into the bedroom. Once in the room Hunter was pulling off his own clothes, trying to get naked as fast as he could. He was more excited than he wanted to be this early into the action, and Nicholas could see Hunter's soldier flap up and down as Hunter bounced out of his clothes. Nicholas, on the other hand, was moving quite slowly, almost methodically, with his undressing—as if he really did not want to get naked. He had plans for the night, and they included crossing Hunter off his kill list, not fucking him.

Nicholas was not prepared to kill Hunter now that the poison had been wasted. He started thinking about whether he saw anyone in the halls when he arrived, or if anyone would notice him if he slipped out soon. Nicholas wondered if he could jump off the balcony and get lost in the woods behind the apartment building without being seen—probably not in the daylight. Sunset was still a couple of hours away. Nicholas never had a kill go wrong before. The planned ones were very well planned out. The impromptu ones always seemed to present Nicholas with the ways, means, and exit he needed—but then those were always people he just met—not someone he knew, and who knew him. He was overthinking the situation. Nicholas knew that he had two options: fake a headache and get out the apartment now and regroup for a second shot later, or give in to the lustful moment, have some earth-shattering sex, kill Hunter with whatever he could muster up, and slip out through the woods.

When he finally decided what he was going to do Nicholas refocused on the bedroom and realized that Hunter had been standing very close to him, naked, stroking himself trying to get Nicholas to pay attention. Nicholas was at full attention now. Hunter helped Nicholas out of his clothes and the two naked bodies twisted and turned, thrusted and twitched for hours. The two guys took a break at one point — they were both sweating a lot, and they were parched. When Hunter came back into the bedroom with two glasses of water, he was carrying the towel that he had used to clean up the coffee spill earlier. His intention was to use the same towel to clean up a new liquid spill he left on the sheets. Hunter put the two glasses of water down on the nightstand and before he used the towel to wipe his bedsheets he wiped his own sweaty body — his chest, his crotch and his neck and face. Nicholas watched and wondered — hoped — that Hunter was inhaling the poison from the towel. Was that even possible, wondered Nicholas. Any amount left would not be as potent, but Nicholas was hopeful that it would still work, albeit it might take a little longer to do the job.

When Hunter finished with the towel, he offered it to Nicholas before wiping up the sheets. Nicholas declined, and instead headed to the bathroom to clean up. Through all their activity, Nicholas had not climaxed. While in the bathroom Nicholas contemplated his next move. He enjoyed the sex but wanted to get out of the apartment quickly. He had other things he needed to get done. He sat on the toilet, naked, thinking about how good the sex was with Hunter. After sitting long enough Nicholas eventually peed. He flushed, washed his hands, and dried his body of all the sweat and bodily fluids. Hunter's odor was hugging Nicholas. He could smell him so fragrantly—he had to get home and shower him off. When Nicholas came out of the bathroom, he found Hunter spread out on the bed, limp dick side up. He was no longer breathing. Nicholas had not realized that he had been in the bathroom that long but was pleased with how the evening had turned out.

Nicholas did not assume that Hunter was sleeping—recovering from all the sex. He knew— hoped that what little poison that had been soaked up in the towel that Hunter rubbed all over his body—his face, had managed to get absorbed into his skin. He assumed that if it had, it would be many hours before Hunter would be dead. To see that it all worked faster pleased Nicholas very much. He collected his clothes, got dressed and freshened up. He did not touch Hunter's body. He wanted it to be found in the exact way it died. In fact, he touched nothing more in the room other than his clothes. Then, as planned earlier, Nicholas walked out onto the balcony, closed the door behind him and climbed down to the balcony below — the apartment was occupied, but no one was home. From there Nicholas jumped down to a patio. Once on the ground Nicholas brushed himself off and walked into the woods knowing he would emerge from the other side, in the park, lost among the crowd.

Nicholas looked back once just before being swallowed by the trees. He could see the bedroom light on in Hunter's apartment. He thought about how long it would take for someone to notice that Hunter was dead, or even missing.

* * * * *

Oliver, Camilla, and Howard were sitting in a booth reading over a menu they had memorized months earlier. They could not decide if this was a wine night or cocktail night. So much had happened over the last few weeks that they were having trouble processing it all. They opted for dirty martinis all around.

"You guys remember Hunter, right?" Oliver asked as he took his first sip. The other two nodded as Camilla took a sip and Howard pulled an olive off a toothpick with his teeth.

"We slept together," Oliver blurted out because he felt that the conversation, he was about to start needed context, and that was the best, most direct context he could muster up.

"What the ..." Camilla squealed. But before she could go on Oliver cut her off. That adventure was a story for another day. Oliver wanted to focus on different details about Hunter — more specifically that a green-eyed man and Hunter knew each other. Hunter could be the key to them finding out if this man was Nicholas.

"Damn, that hot-ass boy gets around," Howard said, chomping on his third olive. "They were meeting up at the bar that night we ran into them — drinks before a booty call, maybe."

"Is your mind always in the gutter?" Camilla asked. "All you boys think about is sex. There is more to a relationship—friends, co-workers—so many other reasons two guys might meet up other than sex."

Oliver and Howard looked at Camilla with an expression that told her she was right, and wrong—and wrong when it came to Hunter, in particular. As the next round of drinks came, and they still had not ordered any food, Oliver told his friends that he thought Hunter could have been a link to learning more about the green-eyed man, assuming, of course that the man they all thought was Nicholas was Nicholas.

"Could have been?" Camilla asked.

"The little fuck totally ghosted me," Oliver said as the waiter arrived to take their order.

"Sorry but are you all talking about Hunter Stephenson?" the waiter asked. And when the three looked at him oddly, mostly because none of them knew Hunter's last name, the waiter got more descriptive. "Handsome, tall, broad shoulders … looks really good shirtless." Camilla was still in the dark, but Oliver and Howard nodded as the waiter described Hunter like he was describing the specials of the evening.

"He's dead," the waiter said. "It's all over the news right now." The three of them pulled out their phones and started searching for anything on Hunter—now that they had a last name.

"How is this possible?" Oliver asked no one in particular, least of all the waiter. "We were texting just a couple of days ago."

The waiter went on to share what he knew, which included him knowing Hunter's neighbor who called the police because of too much noise coming from Hunter's apartment. Hunter had a very nosy neighbor—a retired schoolteacher—who had nothing more to do with her days and nights but watch her neighbors. Most of the time the residents of the apartment building did not mind the old woman—some even ran errands for her on occasion or brought her a hot meal now and again. She was not a stranger to the other residents—just an annoyance sometimes—well, when they wanted their privacy. The waiter, Mike, was once a student of the old woman—she helped him get his shit together in school. If it weren't for her, Mike would probably be face down in a dark alley with his face in a puddle of water, strung out on whatever drug cocktail he could have sold his body for that day. Instead, Mike was clean—had been clean for a long time, and he repaid his old teacher with an occasional surprise visit of sweets, or a hot plate.

Mike had stopped by the apartment on his way to work tonight. There was yellow police tape everywhere, and the sky was flashing blue. The police had evacuated the building and were searching the grounds for any clues. The old woman sat in a chair in the front yard—out of the way of the police—watching all the excitement as if she were watching Chicago Blue. When Mike found her and gave her a bag full of hard candies from a local shop owned by another, older student she grabbed his arm, and without being asked, proceeded to give Mike all the details he never wanted. He had seen Hunter often on his visits—and Hunter was often shirtless.

Oliver kept interrupting Mike with questions while Mike was trying to share what little information he did have, which stretched out a particularly short story into one long enough that Mike's boss had to yell at him twice to stop talking and get back to waiting on his other tables. Oliver purposely ordered another round of drinks so Mike would have to return and share the rest of the details. Through it all, Mike shared that the old woman watched as a very handsome man with two cups of coffee entered the building—but he never came out or she never saw him leave the building.

The old woman described this mystery man as tall, young, and very handsome. Clearly not enough to help the police in anyway, except that they did confirm that two coffee cups were found on a table in Hunter's apartment. They revealed that information to the old woman in hopes of jogging her memory some more to get a better description of the man she saw walk in. She admitted that it was not his first visit to see Hunter, and in fact she had seem them kiss one night when they came stumbling in at 3 a.m. She did not sleep much, so she really did see everything.

As Oliver, Camilla and Howard listened to Mike, Oliver wondered if this mystery man could be Nicholas. Given what he knew about his visit to the cemetery in London, and what Camilla had said about dating who she believed was Nicholas, Oliver was beginning to paint a picture in his mind of Nicholas being quite a bad guy. But he had no evidence, and nothing connecting any dots, so he was not about to jump to any conclusions. Oliver was confident that he was on to something, and he was going to make it his mission to solve this mystery. With his newly acquired trust he would have the time, and resources, to dedicate hunting down the green-eyed man.

Oliver knew that Mike was skipping details—just giving them highlights—but Oliver wanted more. Oliver was convinced that given more time Mike would reveal a wealth of information about Hunter's death, and the mystery man his teacher was convinced she saw that night. As the three were leaving the bar Oliver sought out Mike and exchanged numbers. They agreed to get together in a couple of days.

CHAPTER SEVENTEEN

Days had gone by, and Oliver still had not heard from Mike. While he was able to find out some information online about Hunter, it was all superficial —nothing substantial. Nothing that would really help Oliver determine if Nicholas was involved in Hunter's death or not. He needed Mike—or at least the old woman. Just when he had given up all hope, Oliver received a text from Mike asking to meet up. Mike suggested the park, which was on the other side of the woods from Hunter's apartment building, although Oliver did not know that at the time. When Oliver told Camilla and Howard what he was doing—meeting Mike in the park—they were against the idea. They did not think that Oliver should meet a near-stranger in the park. Howard suggested that he tag along, but Oliver told his two best friends not to worry about him. They all knew where Mike worked, so if Oliver went missing for any reason, Camilla and Howard would know where to find him, or at least someone who knew him.

The night after sharing the old woman's story with Oliver and his friends Mike found himself back at Hunter's apartment building hoping to talk with his old teacher again. Instead of sweets he'd brought a hot meal in hopes of enjoying it with his teacher. Since the murder was still fresh, the police were still canvassing the property and the apartment. The old woman continued to watch the police, paying attention to everyone who came and went. She remembered Hunter being very kind to her. He hadn't necessarily gone out of his way for her like Mike did, but Hunter was polite to her, and helped her when it looked like she needed help— getting mail, taking out the trash, holding the door. She was an old woman after all, and to a young man in his early 20s, someone in their 70s only reminded him of his grandparents—and they needed a lot of help every day.

Mike saw a young cop standing outside. It did not look like he was doing much, but he was keeping watch, tracking everyone who went into the building—questioning the ones who attempted to get in but did not live there. Mike saw this officer looking somewhat bored—not a lot of people were coming and going, so he stopped and struck up a conversation. Had Mike not found the officer attractive he probably would have walked right past him but given his love for a young man in uniform, Mike stopped, and after answering the officers' questions, started rattling off a list of his own. At first the officer was hesitant and selective with how he was answering the questions. He was, after all, a man of the law, and this was an ongoing case. He was not supposed to be revealing details that the police wanted to keep under wraps so as not to give the murderer, or any copycats, any ammunition.

Eventually the officer warmed up to Mike — they even exchanged numbers to get together for a drink later in the week. Mike was able to learn what the police assumed — Hunter was poisoned — the murderer escaped out through the balcony — that Hunter knew the murderer well. What Mike did not learn from the officer, mostly because he did not know, was that Nicholas was watching. Nicholas has been watching since before he left the scene. The security cameras at the entrance of the building were not working very well — the image of Nicholas and his coffee cups that was recorded was so grainy that no one could identify if the figure was tall or short, male or female, black or white, or something else entirely.

Nicholas, on the other hand, had placed a remote camera in a tree in the front yard of the apartment building. No one would think to look in the tree, and if they did, they would not see the concealed wireless camera, but Nicholas had a clear, bird's-eye view of all the comings and goings—all the police activity, and the conversations between Mike and the old woman. There was no audio capability in the camera in the tree, but Nicholas did not need to hear what was happening. He was more interested in seeing who was there—who he might need to worry about. The residents who talked with the police once and then went back to their lives—they were of no interest to Nicholas. Those who talked repeatedly with the police, or those who did not even live there, but kept coming back and talking with the police and the residents—those were the people who interested Nicholas most. Mike interested Nicholas.

* * * * *

When Mike and Oliver finally met up later in the week Mike had a wealth of new information thanks to a long, sweaty night dancing naked under the sheets with the officer. While Mike did not know Oliver that well—serving him and his friends one time at the bar, he felt obligated to share information with Oliver—to help solve a mystery with him. He also thought Oliver was handsome and hoped this was a way to get a date with him.

Oliver was sitting on the park bench as instructed by Mike. The weather had warmed. The weather was not warm enough for shorts, but certainly warm enough to forego the jacket, or sweater. With the sun shining brightly and the rising temperature, the park was a chaos of activity— families, dates, dogs, frisbees, picnic lunches— everywhere you looked in the park there was activity. This put Oliver at ease a little, not that Camilla and Howard had convinced Oliver that Mike was bad, but with all that had been happening, Oliver liked the idea of a public meeting. He watched couples walk by—some being pulled by their dogs and others with earphones listening to music, or a podcast—lost in their own space while surrounded by so many. While there was a lot of activity Oliver took solace in the peace of it all—everyone appeared to be happy. Everyone was enjoying the weather, the company, the companionship around them. Everyone was oblivious to the world around them, or the death that surrounded them—that always surrounded them.

When Mike arrived, Oliver rose and they hugged a little longer than Oliver expected, but he liked it. Mike was a larger guy—meatier—so his hugs were stronger, more engulfing—warmer. The two opted to sit on the bench and talk rather than walk. They both peppered the other with questions about themselves—where they were from—when they came out. They talked about the small town, and the neighboring big city. They spent an hour talking about their past before they dove into the present, and the murder at hand. Through it all they were focused on each other. Oliver stopped noticing the people passing by—what they were doing or wearing or saying. He was focused on what Mike had to say. The two were so engrossed in the conversation that neither noticed the man in the distance watching them. Mike wouldn't have noticed him—or at least identified him. Oliver might have recognized Nicholas; had he been looking. From the camera in the tree outside the apartment building, Nicholas knew Mike's role in all of this— just collateral damage if it got to that point. Nicholas knew that Oliver and Mike were not close—they'd just met, thanks to Nicholas, in a way. But Nicholas knew, or assumed with a great deal of accuracy, that Mike was filling Oliver's mind with a version of Hunter's death that was riddled with false assumptions.

CHAPTER EIGHTEEN

Reed hadn't been to the gym in months—not that he needed to go regularly. He was well toned and had the metabolism of an athlete. No matter what he ate, or drank, he never got fat. Howard was a little jealous at times because he felt like he was always at the gym trying to maintain his figure—but his boyfriend's body was like that of Roman statue—it never changed and was rock solid. Reed checked in at the front desk, chatting up the front desk clerk a little longer than most. She was cute—funny. They had gone to school together, so catching up made sense. He was surprised that she was stuck in a front desk job at a gym—until she told him that she was a physical therapist filling in while the regular girl was a lunch. They had some classes together in school—and they were both going to be doctors, which was more of their respective parents' dreams, and less of their own. In the end she listened to her parents, a little. Reed, on the other hand, did not. He choose the path of quick money and went into finance.

In the locker room Reed was impressed with the plethora of bare skin—men of all sizes just walking around as if towels didn't exist. Some really toned guys with large, flaccid members resting in a well-trimmed fluff of pubic hair were intermixed with several less toned guys with average ones hiding in thick bushes of hair. Reed believed that how a man kept his junk trimmed spoke volumes about the type of person he was. It was easy to tell the straight guys from the gay ones—even the curious ones took the time to keep things trimmed. Of course, he did not stare at the room full of dicks the whole time he was getting changed—he looked up and saw faces. Some guys were looking down, away from the rest of the room while others looked straight at you—confidently standing naked in a room full of naked men—and wearing an expression of interest—a smirk or smile as if to say, 'yeah, it's that big, and I think you are cute.'

Reed enjoyed the view but was not interested in sampling any of the goods. He was loyal to Howard, as he expected Howard was in return, and while he enjoyed looking in the window, he rarely engaged. Today, however, was different. As he stood naked, sorting through his gym bag for his workout clothes a man approached the locker next to Reed. The man, still fully dressed, looked Reed right in the eyes, and then let his own eyes move down Reed's body—right down to the bare toes, and then back up to Reed's eyes—Reed was held in a trance by the green eyes that looked back at him. There was something about this guy, and his silent stare that got Reed a little excited. He felt the blood flowing to his crotch and quickly picked up a towel and wrapped it around his waist.

"You shouldn't be embarrassed and cover up. You have a very sexy body."

Reed was not embarrassed as much as taken aback by the idea that someone—other than Howard—could so easily get him aroused. He smiled at the green-eyed man and thanked him for the compliment as he continued to get changed to start his workout. All the other guys around him—both naked and clothed—continued their routine without skipping a beat. No one paid any attention to Reed's slight erection other than Reed, and well—Nicholas. After all, he was the one who caused the blood to rush.

Nicholas tried striking up small talk with Reed, but Reed was too focused on getting ready for his workout. Within minutes he was flaccid again and refocusing on today's routine — chest and arms. He put his ear pods in his ears, tapped his watch a few times, and nodded to Nicholas as he headed out of the locker room. Nicholas was not used to being ignored, and certainly not in a room full of naked men. He was approached by a few guys while he was changing but paid no attention to them. He was here for Reed.

On the gym floor Nicholas was trying to keep tabs on Reed. He even tried to work in a rotation on one of the machines Reed was using. Reed let Nicholas work in the rotation but did not engage with him. When Reed worked out, he tended to stay in a zone — not get distracted with chatter. He had seen so many guys, and girls, "work out" when really all they were doing was lifting a few weights and gossiping for 20 minutes, then calling it a day. Reed was not like that at all. He would not exercise with Howard anymore because Howard loved to talk gossip about the other guys in the gym — there was not a lot of intense physical activity, so Reed tended to go to the gym alone. He could get in and out without any distractions. And he had the body that proved his method was working. Today, however, Nicholas kept popping into Reed's line of sight—being very passive aggressive in his approach—which was very unlike Nicholas. But then as of late Nicholas had been quite off his game. It has been weeks since he killed Hunter, and since that did not go as cleanly and quietly as he had hoped, Nicholas was feeling a little off his game—like maybe the police were finally catching up to him. Now more than ever, he was remembering the story his dad told him about how Adam had finally been caught. Nicholas knew that statistically the police would catch up to him at some point. He had lost count of the number of people he had killed, and he was usually very good about keeping his cool and staying ahead of the law. But that has not been the case for the past few weeks.

Reed continued to ignore Nicholas, and when he finished his workout, he retreated to the sauna to relax before hitting the showers. Nicholas gave up and left the gym furious that he was unable to keep his focus—that he'd gotten so close to Reed so quickly but failed to execute any plan. Nicholas was getting sloppy.

CHAPTER NINETEEN

Camilla was planning to meet Miles at the coffee shop where Imani worked. They had not seen each other in a few weeks so Miles was completely in the dark about everything that had been happening. Miles had been visiting his sick grandmother, and while there his grandfather passed away so there was not a lot of down time to even chat with each other, at least that is what Miles kept telling Camilla. They had that kind of relationship—one where they could go days without talking or even seeing each other and almost pick up right where they left off when they got together again … usually. Not this time.

Sitting alone at a table in the corner, Camilla pondered how she was going to tell Miles. Imani delivered a cup of green tea and a scone to the table and gave Camilla a hug—but not for the reason Camilla thought. She knew what Camilla was going to do, and Imani knew that it was never easy delivering bad news—but then she also knew what Miles had been up to and was not sure who was going to get the bigger shock—Camilla or Miles. Alone at the table Camilla enjoyed the warm scone and looked up each time the bell connected to the top of the door frame chimed as the door opened. Miles was already twenty minutes late and not answering his phone. By the time Camilla finished her tea and scone Miles was close to an hour late and there was still no sign of him. The doorbell kept chiming, and people kept coming and going, but none of them were Miles.

Imani picked up the empty plate, cup, and saucer from Camilla's table after giving her one more hug. She could tell Camilla was giving up on Miles and was going to head out. As she walked away from Camilla and the table, the bell chimed again. When Camilla looked up, she thought she recognized the man walking in, but it wasn't Miles. She froze in the chair, and quickly looked away hoping that she had not been noticed, but within seconds she heard his voice.

"Camilla?" he asked, already knowing that it was her. "How are you?"

Speechless for a few seconds, she finally responded that she was well, but that she was just leaving. She stood, but by now he was blocking her in the corner. They did a little dance as each tried to move out of the way of the other, and eventually she got around him. Once past him Camilla turned around and looked right into the bright green eyes before her.

"You really hurt me!" she said as she wiped away a tear, turned and walked out of the coffee shop.

Nicholas did not follow her. He had not expected to run into her, and only spoke to her because she had seen him. He was still preoccupied with having just been rejected by Reed at the gym. He was frustrated, and now flustered. If Nicholas could have gotten in and out of the coffee shop without being seen, that would have been his preference. He had been trying on stay below the radar so running into Camilla, of all people, was not ideal — not now, and probably not ever.

As Camilla walked out of the coffee shop, she bumped right into Miles as he was walking by — not in. He had ghosted Camilla so he could hang with a new friend, Russell, who he met at the gym before he went away. Miles had completely forgotten that he agreed to meet Camilla, so he claimed. Under normal circumstances he would have been able to talk his way out of the situation, but because Camilla found him holding hands with this Russell, Miles knew that there was nothing that he could say that would help his case. Camilla smiled at them both—even shook the new guy's hand—and gave Miles a hug as if to console him for the loss of this grandfather. As she pulled him in tight for the hug, she whispered into his ear, "You fuck!" She released him and walked away.

As Camilla walked down the street away from the coffee shop, and in the opposite direction of Miles and his new man, she found herself crying but did not understand why. She was going to break up with Miles in the coffee shop—that was the reason she wanted then to get together. She knew that Miles was bisexual and assumed that he fooled around. All boys do. Their relationship was not serious—or was it open? She could never remember. She knew that she did not have feelings for Miles like Howard had for Reed, and she was confident in her decision to officially end the relationship that day, so the tears were confusing her. Maybe, she thought, the tears were because she saw Carter.

If Miles were to come crawling back to Camilla anytime soon, she thought, she would be reminding him of this day, and then probably kick him in the balls. Clear eyed and a little more composed now, Camilla's walk turned into a confident stride as she turned the corner, putting this chapter of her life behind her. She told two old flames to fuck off, sort of, and she was feeling good about herself. But at the same time, seeing the green eyes as Carter said hello was still frightening her a little.

An hour later Camilla was still walking around the park trying to clear her head of—well everything— when her purse buzzed. She looked at the screen and did not recognize the number, so she let it buzz as it fell back into her purse. It stopped. Then started again. Then stopped again. Then by the third buzz, tired of all the "unknown caller" calls she gets Camilla answered her phone. By the time Camilla hung up her phone she was sitting on a park bench, crying again. The news she received had been more than she could handle standing up. She took a minute to compose herself, and then she called Oliver.

Oliver met Camilla at the hospital. He was there, waiting for her, when she walked in. She wondered how he got there before her, but really, those details did not matter right now—probably ever. More importantly, she wanted to know how Miles was doing. Oliver grabbed and hugged Camilla as tightly as he could without cutting off her circulation. She hugged back just as tightly and started crying again. She sobbed into Oliver's shoulder trying to talk, but all her words were inaudible. He thought she said something about just seeing him but was not sure. He needed Camilla to calm down long enough to understand her and bring him up to speed on what she knew. They went to the nurse's station to ask about Miles.

After explaining to the nurse that she'd received a call from the hospital—something about Camilla being listed as Miles's emergency contact—and what their relationship was, Camilla went on to explain that Miles's parents were on the West Coast. Camilla remembered being taken aback when Miles asked if she would mind being his emergency contact—it was not something she was used to being asked on the second date. She liked Miles almost immediately, and though she could not predict the future, she agreed. She just never expected she would be needed, and certainly not in this way.

Camilla and Oliver were finally given some details. Miles and his friend—the one Camilla saw holding Miles' hand outside the coffee shop—were pushed into oncoming traffic. The guy, whose name Camilla, and Oliver still did not know—and who was currently a John Doe in the morgue because he had no identification on him, had died on impact. The semi-truck that was barreling down the road, going faster than it should have been, never had a chance to stop in time. The driver watched from above as John Doe kissed the large, filthy, metal grill with such force before falling to the ground and being run over by the four back right tires. The driver had told the police that it was as if the guy had jumped in front of the truck.

John Doe was almost unrecognizable by the time the paramedics arrived. Miles, on the other hand, who was on the inside of the sidewalk when the two were attacked, smacked his head on the side of the truck and was thrown back toward the sidewalk. Miles was in critical condition and the doctors did not have much hope of him making it through the night. He had lost a lot of blood, and so many of his bones were shattered. There was a lot of blood and fluid in Miles' skull, and he was not responsive to anything. He was alive, but in a coma.

Camilla was still crying and had a look of fright in her eyes. The nurse came from around the counter and held Camilla by the arm and led her to a chair to sit. Camilla was shaking violently. A second nurse came over, and the two nurses talked about sedating Camilla to calm her down. They looked at Oliver as if to ask permission. He was standing alone, helpless, watching his best friend freak out—he begged the nurses to do anything they could to help. Within seconds a third nurse arrived with a small needle. It took the three of them, but a few seconds later Camilla was much more mellow—not completely knocked out but relaxed enough to start making some sense.

Oliver sat beside her after the nurses led them both into a room across from the nurses' station—out of the hall, but still within view of the nurses. He hugged Camilla as she nestled against his shoulder, wrapped in the warmth of his strong arm. She continued to sob, but quietly now. When he felt she was ready, Oliver asked Camilla to repeat some of the gibberish she spouted earlier. It took longer than she wanted, but Camilla was able to recap her encounter with Miles and his boyfriend outside the coffee shop not long before the accident. It all sounded rather mundane and uneventful to Oliver until Camilla got to the point of who she left behind in the coffee shop — Nicholas. To anyone else, that part of the story would have no more value or interest than the rest of the it, but given what Camilla, Oliver, and Howard had discovered, or assumed about Nicholas, they both thought that it was too much of a coincidence. Instantly they both assumed that Nicholas was somehow involved in yet another death, and possibly one more, if Miles did not come out of his coma.

CHAPTER TWENTY

Weeks had gone by, and Miles was no closer to recovery. His parents had flown in and were staying in the only B&B in town. His mother was not a fan of big chain hotels—never trusted them. She was convinced that because her family was black, they were treated poorly. Back when the family would stay at national hotel chains Miles' mother was convinced that they always got the worst room in the building; were always given the worst service; and were always overlooked if a white family was in the vicinity. Miles could share horror stories about how his mother would embarrass the whole family with her crazy notions of ramped up racism across the hotels. After a few months of feeling segregated at the hotels Miles' mother moved the whole family to locally owned—black owned, B&Bs whenever they traveled.

With his family in town now, Miles was surrounded by people who loved him. This freed Camilla up to share her conspiracy theory about Nicholas with Oliver. The two of them, along with

Howard, were becoming more and more convinced that the death around them might all stem from the same source. They still had no evidence to prove their theory, and nothing linking Carter the green-eyed man in London and Nicholas as the same person, but that did not stop them from playing Nancy Drew and the Hardy Boys. They began with Miles and worked backward. John Doe was added to the list, and the only connection those two had were that they were on the same block as Nicholas the day of the accident.

Then there was Hunter. Oliver felt confident that this one might be a stretch, but the last time he had seen Hunter was when the green-eyed man was in the room. It was plausible, or could be in order to form a pattern, but trying to connect those dots was proving tough. The stories from Mike sounded very believable, at least to people trying to make a connection. Of course, Mike was no longer responding to Oliver's text messages, so trying to get more information from him was impossible. Camilla even theorized that Mike might be missing for a reason—another piece to their puzzle. Then there was Peter who supposedly had taken his own life while his wife was out of town. Plausible?

Maybe. But likely? The three were not so sure anymore. Considering that Oliver did not even know about Peter until his death, the fact that Peter raised Nicholas, and Nicholas might have been the green-eyed man Oliver saw in London with a man who only minutes later was found dead in a cemetery had Oliver convinced that Nicholas might be a serial killer.

Again, still no proof.

As Camilla, Oliver and Howard worked on their list—a list they were planning to take to the police once they felt the list made sense—included all the "facts" as they believed them to be, they struggled with how much they began to conclude that Nicholas had been part of their lives for so much longer than any of them had assumed. Oliver even took it so far as to think that Nicholas might have had something to do with Elizabeth's death. He half-expected Camilla or Howard to argue that connection, but the more he talked out loud, the more the three of them were believing their theory.

The belief that Nicholas was somehow behind all these murders was so strong in the three of them that they had gone so far as to create a murder wall in their dining room. They had no adult pictures of Nicholas so at the center of it all was the photo of teen Nicholas from the book Peter left Oliver. They found pictures of all the victims online. After hours of work one of the walls in the dining room looked like a scene out of a serial killer movie, or police detective's white board. Post-It notes and photographs were taped to the wall and colored yarn was strung from one pin to another showing assumed timelines and connections between victims and Nicholas. There were a lot of gaps, of course. None of them knew Hunter that well, and had never met Peter, but that did not stop them from making uneducated guesses about the timeline.

As Camilla, Oliver and Howard sat in the dining room, sipping on a lovely Cabernet that Oliver's mother had sent over some weeks ago, the three looked at the wall and wondered what was missing—who was missing, and what would come next. The three looked up at Reed as he walked into the room. Knowing that none of his friends were criminal justice majors—and none were now or ever before employed by the police department, he was stumped at the new artwork covering the only solid wall in the dining room. He had not seen any of them in weeks—he had been busy traveling for work. He had talked and video chatted with Howard, of course. They even managed to figure out how to have sex through FaceTime while apart. In all the conversations Howard never really mentioned the infatuation that he, Camilla and Oliver were experiencing now—mostly because he felt it would be too much to try to explain on the phone or video. This was something that required some wine and time to digest in person, as most conspiracy theories do.

Reed kissed Howard forcefully on the lips, showing his affection in a way that still made Camilla uncomfortable. When he pulled back for air, Reed got a good look at the dining room wall. His perplexed facial expression was enough to make Howard start talking. He rambled on about a green-eyed man, Carter, Nicholas, and Hunter, and Peter, and other people Reed knew nothing about, and was jumping all over the story—not following any logical path or making much sense so Oliver interrupted and took over the story. Oliver paused and took the story back to the beginning, summing up the whole wall in a few short sentences. By the time Oliver stopped talking Reed was close to the wall studying the images and readying the various pieces of paper, and post-It notes stuck to the wall.

"What is this about a green-eyed man?" Reed asked without turning around to face the others. As he asked the question, he was hoping to get an answer that would explain his recent gym experience, but he was not ready to share any of that with any of them just yet.

"Do you know him?" Howard asked. He was in no mood to play any games, and if Reed knew anything Howard wanted to know. Before Reed could answer Oliver chimed in that the man at the center of this theory — this wall, was a man with stunning green eyes — mesmerizing green eyes that could seduce anyone.

"He was stalking me at the gym a few weeks ago," Reed said as he turned around to face Howard. "A good-looking guy with beautiful green eyes came out of nowhere. I was in the locker room, and he was there, naked, talking to me like we were besties. I left him to go work out, and when I turned around from one machine he was there trying to work in a set. I left for the sauna, and within a few minutes he was sitting across from me. It was weird — like creepy weird. He was following me around. He never said what he wanted — never got physical or threatening to me. I was finally able to ditch him, but it was creepy as fuck."

"And you haven't seen him since?" Camilla asked. Reed shook his head and crossed the room to hug Howard. He whispered into his ear that he was sorry for not saying anything sooner, but that he just thought it was an unrelated gym stalker. For all he knew, it could still be totally unrelated, but Reed kept quiet and let his friends continue fueling their conspiracy theory.

Oliver was pacing the room, cussing to no one, then shared his fear with the rest of the room. Oliver was convinced that if it was Nicholas at the gym stalking Reed, and at this point they all felt certain that it was, then none of them were safe, and clearly Nicholas was working his way into all their lives. For what reason Oliver was still not clear, but now more than ever, he felt like he needed to meet Nicholas — in a public place — to try to get to know him or try to understand if he and his friends were just being conspiracy theorists, or if Nicholas was coming after them, one at a time. He was aware of the one flaw in all of this... he still did not know Nicholas, and no two sightings were by any two of them to even remotely connect any of their theories together.

* * * * *

As much as Oliver wanted to find and meet Nicholas, every time he thought about it over the next few days, he felt his heart race. He had convinced himself that Nicholas was a bad person — but he knew nothing about the man — other than what his mother told him, and none of that was bad. Camilla had dated Nicholas, or at least a man who resembled Nicholas, named Carter, and none of them knew much about the guy and were jumping to crazy conclusions — that is what Oliver finally convinced himself. Oliver was becoming convinced that he and his friends were creating a conspiracy theory so big and believable that it had to be true. By virtue of believing it, he was more convinced now that it had to stop. There were lots of handsome green-eyed guys in the world, after all, 9% of the US population has green eyes. Oliver had to do something so he could get on with his life. Especially now that Miles had passed away.

His parents had kept Miles alive by machine for as long as they could. The doctors were not giving any new hope, and Miles had made no changes toward recovery. In fact, his body was slowing giving up, and the machines were working harder and harder to keep him alive. Camilla was at the hospital when Miles's father signed the paperwork, and she was in the room with Miles's parents, consoling them when the last machine stopped making any noise. The three of them sat in silence for almost another two hours before Miles was pronounced dead.

The room was silent once the machines stopped. Phones, machines and mumbled voices were heard outside the room, but they were faint. The silence was joined by odd smells—Camilla never put her finger on the combination. She could make out the urine smell—could see the urine saturating the bed and blankets covering Miles. His catheter came disconnected and he was pissing himself one last time. She was convinced he shat himself too. The room smelled of death—or what she thought death should smell like. She cried as little as she could manage because she wanted to stay strong for his parents. Camilla tried to think about how her parents would feel if it were she who was in Miles's position, and that only made her want to cry more. She could not imagine how parents cope with losing a child, especially one so young.

Camilla hugged Miles's parents, and in a very soft-spoken voice, told them that it was time to go. The nurses had returned and had been removing all the remaining tubes from Miles and began cleaning him up. She wanted to scream at them for being so disrespectful and orderly in moving Miles out to make room for the next patient but knew they were just doing their job. They had to keep things moving along—the dead needed to make way for another life they could hope to save.

As Camilla stood outside Miles's room hugging and saying her good-byes to his parents, she looked up from hugging his mother and at the end of the hall—less than 15 feet away, she saw an orderly heading her way—or at least someone dressed like an orderly. He was tall with dark hair. He had the evilest of smirks on his face, which pissed her off, but it was his bright green eyes that made her heart start pounding. It was pounding so hard that Miles's mother felt the immediate change as she hugged Camilla. Of course, Miles's mother thought it was because of the loss of Miles. She was clueless that the man Camilla believed killed Miles was fast approaching them. Camilla held Miles's mother tight, hoping that she was going to protect Camilla from whatever was about to happen as she stared right into the green eyes. She recognized them. This man coming toward her was Nicholas — she was certain now that Carter was a fake name. She was convinced he was behind everything she and Oliver and Howard, and now Reed was blaming him for — for the artwork on her dining room wall. Nicholas never stopped grinning, and never stopped looking directly at Camilla until he passed her then kept on walking as if he never intended to speak to or acknowledge her in any way other than to stare at her as he passed. She waited a moment and then released herself from the hug and turned around. He was gone.

"I've got to go!" Camilla shouted at Miles's parents as she ran down the hall in the same direction Nicholas went. She never did see Nicholas again that day, but then she was not looking for him when she ran off — she was rushing to get to Oliver — to warn him.

CHAPTER TWENTY-ONE

Oliver was sitting alone on a bench in the park when Nicholas sat down beside him. Oliver had been deep in thought, watching people go by without really paying much attention to who they were or what they were doing, which would explain how Nicholas managed to get so close. When he sat down, the movement of the bench startled Oliver just enough for him to look to his left and notice the stunning young man next to him—the man was wearing sunglasses. Oliver did not recognize this man wearing sunglasses and sporting a full head of white hair—such a bleached dye job, and a barcode tattoo on his neck. That spoke volumes to what little Oliver knew about Nicholas, and how, no matter how much time Oliver thought that he had stared at or watched someone he believed to be Nicholas in the cemetery or the bar, or even at the funeral, he really had no idea what Nicholas looked like without the green eyes to give him away. Sure, he had the photos from the journal, but the last photo in the journal was more than eight years old.

Nicholas had matured a lot in those six years. The boy in the photos was not the man sitting next to Oliver now.

The two sat in silence for a few minutes—although it felt like an eternity to Oliver before Nicholas finally spoke. His voice was low and deep—he could have been a radio announcer. It was soothing to hear. Oliver turned to look at Nicholas as he spoke because he could not believe that such a deep, clear voice was coming from such a young man—Oliver assumed that the man sitting next to him was much older because he noticed the white hair, thinking it was grey until he realized it was a dye job. Oliver's voice was deep—manly—but suddenly felt pubescent now next to this man. Nicholas was making small talk—throwing out random sentences to get Oliver to bite. The weather conversation fizzled after a few seconds. A couple across from the bench having a picnic looked like a good next topic—they were arguing, or so it appeared. They were far enough away so the boys could not hear the couple, but could see the facial expressions, and hand gestures. The two shared a few scenarios and laughs, but then they were, once again, silent. Oliver wanted this man to stop talking—he was trying to have a quiet, peaceful moment. But at the same time, the few glances he made toward Nicholas had him wanting the conversation to never end. From his flawless skin tone to his angular bone structure Oliver was getting sexually aroused. The man's hands were large, smooth, and he had well-manicured nails at the end of long fingers. And his smell. Oliver wanted to bottle him up so he could go on enjoying that smell forever. It was like nothing he had ever smelled before—rustic, and regal at the same time. He was having trouble identifying it, but he liked it all the same.

Oliver's phone broke the silence with a loud buzzing sound as it vibrated against the park bench, through his jeans. He ignored it. There was no one he wanted to talk with right now other than the guy sitting next to him.

Eventually the two found some topics to keep their conversation moving along. They jumped from topic to topic as if they were discussing newspaper headlines. No one topic was deep enough for much personal information to be shared, but Oliver was certainly enjoying the conversation. The ease and flow reminded him of when he and

Howard first met, and how natural the conversation went. Sitting on the park bench admiring the vibrant landscape of color around them under the bright blue sky, Oliver started to wonder if anyone ever met "the one" on a park bench on a spring day.

The cynic in him started thinking that maybe he was being pranked. He looked around for cameras, but he did not see any. Then he started thinking that this guy had to be a creep—had to have some baggage that would only surface when they were alone, in some motel or poorly furnished apartment—signs that the guy was transient—only to have two or three more guys coming out of another room to gang-rape Oliver, or beat the shit out of him and steal his clothes and money, or worse—skin him alive so that he died a slow and very painful death. His imagination was getting ahead of the conversation and began to scare Oliver. He remembered reading a news article online, or maybe he saw the news video on social media where that happened—a girl was lured back into a motel and raped, beaten and left for dead—many girls, at many motels up and down the California coast. They were all young, attractive girls, all traveling alone, and all suckers for a cute guy who chatted them up in a park, or a bar — those details were not clear to Oliver now, but the story was fresh in his mind as he sat there on the park bench talking with this cute stranger.

Oliver's phone buzzed again, shaking him out of his daydream. This time it buzzed and buzzed, then stopped, and buzzed more. He never pulled his phone out of his pocket because he did not know if one person was calling him nonstop or suddenly, he was mister popular, and everyone wanted to speak with him.

By the time Oliver refocused on the conversation and stopped dreaming up ways that this guy was going to hurt him, he realized that the guy had put his hand on Oliver's, caressing it ever so gently as if to put all those dreams, and nightmare scenarios to rest. His hand was so soft and warm. Oliver did not pull his hand away — he left it there on the park bench to be smothered with warmth. He bushed a little as he looked over at the guy who was now looking at him, but still through his dark sunglasses. With his free hand, the guy slowly pulled the sunglasses off his face so he could look Oliver right in the eye. When Oliver looked up, he was met with the most vibrant and beautiful eyes shining as bright as the blue sky. Oliver felt his chest relax as if part of him was expecting green eyes — expecting to be face to face, finally, with the monster he had become so obsessed with thanks to Camila and Howard.

"Your eyes are so beautiful," Oliver heard himself say out loud while he verbally slapped himself in his own head for saying something that sounded so lame.

"Thanks. My name is Eric," Nicholas said as he removed his hand from the top of Oliver's and extended it for a formal handshake. "Without sounding too forward, you are very cute. Would you like to grab a coffee or dinner with me sometime?"

"Oliver," he managed to spit out. "I mean, my name is Oliver, and yes that would be nice."

The two shook hands sealing a conversation that had gone on for more than an hour already and agreed to meet for dinner the next night. Eric gave Oliver a phone number, and said that he had to be somewhere, but that he was looking forward to dinner and continuing their conversation. Nicholas stood up and walked away. Thirty minutes later Oliver sent a text to the number Eric gave him. The text was longer than Oliver intended for it to be.

After sending it, and rereading it a dozen times, Oliver realized that he had rambled in the text like a nervous schoolboy. The gist of the text indicated his excitement for dinner and seeing Eric again—but in a very long-winded way. He waited for a reply, but none came. He wanted to text again but knew that would look desperate. He got up and headed home.

* * * * *

"Where the hell have you been?" Howard heard Camilla yell at Oliver as Howard emerged from his bedroom, leaving Reed snug under the sheets, still sound asleep. "I have been looking everywhere for you since yesterday. You were not answering your phone, or texts, and you never came home last night."

When Howard came into the kitchen, he saw Oliver sitting at the kitchen table looking exhausted with Camilla standing above him like a scolding mother. "What are you two on about so early this morning?" Howard asked.

Frustrated, Camilla started to fill Howard in, but the room was interrupted by the buzzing of Oliver's phone. Oliver finally got a reply from Eric.

Unlike Oliver's novella text, the reply was a smiling face emoji with the name of a restaurant—The King & Queen, and a time—7 p.m. Oliver smiled.

"Seriously? You jump all over your phone now, but yesterday you're ghosting me? You two have got to listen to me," Camilla continued. "And I am serious. There is a serial killer out there and only we know who it is."

"Think it is," Howard mumbled under his breath.

Camilla stopped, looked right at Howard, and gave him the same look her mother gave her when she was a child—that look that had no words, but if it did it would say "Don't fuck with me." Then she proceeded to tell them both about seeing Nicholas at the hospital. She told the whole story to them as if she were an investigative reporter on the six o'clock news—including all the extra juicy details you only get on those overly dramatized news programs. As sure as she was standing in the kitchen now, she was confident that she locked eyes with Nicholas. As she described the green eyes, and the way he looked at her—as if to say, "I see you, boo," she said that she tried to approach him, but he ran. She embellished. He did not run — she ran to try to follow him.

"I think it is time we went to the police," Camilla said. "I know you do not want to do that, Oliver. But we must tell them what we know — that Nicholas is the killer."

"Listen to yourself Camilla," Oliver said, finally looking up from his phone. He had spent no time at all replying to Eric with a smiling face emoji and a winking face emoji. "We do not have any facts. We have speculation, and the last time I checked, none of us are detectives, and nothing we have is concrete. We have a bunch of snippets of information that we are almost forcing together so we can blame Nicholas for something we think he might have done. We need to put this nonsense behind us and go one with our lives."

Camilla knew that Oliver was right. The three of them, and Reed now too, all had experiences with a green-eyed man. With an estimated 30 million people in America having green eyes that did not really narrow down their case — they all could have encountered different green-eyed men. Sure, the one in London looked a lot like the one in the bar where Oliver and Howard met Hunter, but everyone has a doppelgänger, and the more Oliver thought about it, the less convinced he was that the two were the same person—it was two different continents, after all. The more they all talked it through, the more they realized that maybe there were grasping at straws, and instead they should be out living their lives.

The decorated dining room wall made a good case for a television show, but they each knew that if they really thought about it hard enough, they would realize that they were grasping at straws. Oliver could put an end to it all by calling Peter's lawyer and asking for a meeting with Nicholas, but he did not. Camilla could put an end to it by accepting that maybe she was not entirely over the excitement Carter caused her so many years ago, and so she was wanting to see him more involved. The more she thought about it, she could not even be certain that Carter, who she did see at the coffee shop, was the person she saw in the hospital.

Oliver's phone buzzed again—another text from Eric. Oliver smiled at receiving a follow-up text so much faster this morning. He put his phone down and looked up to see Camilla and Howard staring at him.

"What's his name?" Howard asked.

Oliver gave a confused look as if he had no idea what his two best friends were doing, or talking about, but they did not buy it. They both knew Oliver well enough to know when he was smitten. They tried to grab his phone, but he shoved it in his pocket before they could, and rather than be tackled or tickled for information he came clean and told Camilla and Howard about Eric—about how they met in the park the day before, and how they were going to dinner soon.

Oliver described how handsome Eric looked, and how calm Oliver felt around him. He described his soft hands, and his beautiful blue eyes, and his deep, soothing voice—even his tattoo and silvery white hair. Howard started on his rehearsed lecture—one he had given Oliver many times before—about how Oliver gets in too deep, too fast, and then is too easily hurt. He was telling Oliver to slow down, keep it casual—he did not need to be thinking about wedding bells just yet.

Oliver shrugged them both off and said Eric was different. It was as if Eric knew just what Oliver needed yesterday on the park bench, and Oliver had a feeling about Eric that was hard to spell out, but only that he was not going to rush into this one, and that Camilla and Howard could take a step back, relax, and trust that Oliver knew what he was doing. The only problem was that he did not, and they knew it all too well.

* * * * *

Days later, in front of the King & Queen, Oliver stood alone — like lost a child looking for his parents. He had arrived early to ensure that he was not late, but he did not want to go in alone. He wanted to walk in with Eric. He watched couples walk by — some holding hands, and others arguing with each other about something unimportant, he was certain. Others walked by each talking on their phones, ignoring the person they were walking with, talking soft enough to keep their phone conversations somewhat private. As the various types of couples walked past Oliver he thought about his parents. He wondered which couple most represented them. He never remembered them being the loving type with each other. Their relationship always seemed cordial, almost transactional. That got him thinking about his own relationships – if you could call them relationships. He looked at an older couple, both sporting heads of gray hair. Her arm locked in his, almost as if each was helping the other stay upright. They shuffled along as if they had their whole lives ahead of them, even though it looked they were walking toward death. As Oliver watched them walk away, he felt so much peace, and love in the image they portrayed. There was a couple, who he assumed had been together for 60 years or more – still locked arm in arm – still clearly in love. He yearned for that level of happiness, and love and peace.

As Oliver watched the old couple shuffle along the sidewalk, getting smaller and smaller the further away they got, he was completely unaware of Eric approaching from the opposite direction. Eric, on the other hand, was completely aware of Oliver, and what he was doing. Eric had been lingering in the shadows, in the distance, watching Oliver for a little while – not because he was nervous about finally meeting up with him, but more so because he had been aware of Oliver for so many years – had watched him from afar for so long, but always through a different set of eyes. Tonight, he was watching Oliver, not as someone he resented, but as someone he longed to be with. Someone who he thought—hoped—could be half of an old couple walking arm in arm down the street with him one day.

Eric startled Oliver as he approached from behind, but Oliver was more pleased than he was startled. Oliver half expected to be stood up—to be forgotten, as he often had been in the past. As the two walked into the restaurant Oliver remained clueless to just how much Eric was smitten with him. Eventually the two would come to understand the mutual feelings, but for now—here, tonight, they continued the cat and mouse game of gay dating. At the table, with a bottle of wine already finished, the second bottle allowed Oliver to share more about himself. He had been debating all through the first bottle if he would start at the present and go backward or start as a child and come forward. He even thought about how crazy it was that he was spending energy thinking about how he was going to lay out his story to Eric while Eric slowly shared random bits of his life with Oliver.

When Oliver learned that both of Eric's parents had passed, and that he had no siblings, Oliver felt a little sad for him—having to be all alone in the world. At the same time, he felt a connection with Eric, being an only child himself. The details of Eric's parents' passing were left out for now, as Nicholas did not think that was a level of detail that needed to be shared on their first date. Nicholas knew, all along, that while he had a dark past, and while he spent a lot of time killing people—both random and people he loved, there was something about Oliver that made him want to be a different person—a better person. For more than a decade Nicholas had been aware of Oliver, and the more he learned about him over the years, the more connected he felt to him, and the more he wanted to be better, for him—for Oliver. In all his years of loving, and killing, Nicholas had never wanted something or someone as much as he wanted Oliver. The challenge was getting Oliver to want him back—the real him.

Before either would let the other order a third bottle of wine, they both decided that they should end the night on a high note. Through all the small talk they both learned some basic details about each other. Nicholas was learning just how great of a person Oliver was—evidence to support what he had already assumed and observed over the years.

And for Oliver, he was falling in love with the calm, peaceful, patient nature of Nicholas. He laughed at Oliver's lame jokes, and touched, or held Oliver's hand at just the right moment each time, with just the right amount of strength to let Oliver know that he cared, but not too strong that Oliver would feel threatened or dominated in any way.

When it came time to pay the bill Nicholas insisted that he pay—it was his treat—his way of saying thank you to Oliver for coming out with him tonight, as if Oliver was doing Nicholas a favor by accompanying him. Quite the opposite. Oliver was the one who felt lucky to have such a good-looking guy want to have dinner with him and say and do all the right things at all the right times. A few times through the date Oliver felt like he might need to pinch himself to be sure he was not dreaming—his dreams felt real sometimes.

In the end, Oliver gave in and let Nicholas pay with the promise to let Oliver pay the next time. Nicholas liked that Oliver was already suggesting a next time, and Oliver loved that Eric was keen on the suggestion. As they walked out of the restaurant Eric reached down and grabbed Oliver's hand. Oliver felt the smoothness of the large hand slowly intertwine the ten fingers until they felt like one. Oliver smiled, and his pants got a little tighter as he felt a rush of excitement flood into his groin.

Without saying anything to the other, they both turned and walked away from the restaurant, still hand in hand, toward the park. After a couple of blocks though Nicholas abruptly interrupted the silence to say he needed to end the evening. He was enjoying the silent walk, hand in hand, and he was enjoying being so close to Oliver after all these years, but he knew that he needed to take this slowly — he had to be sure not to ruin what he hoped to achieve with Oliver. After he said his good-byes, Nicholas jumped into a car that had stopped in front of them, almost on cue. His last words to Oliver, after giving him a long, heartfelt kiss on the lips, was that he would call Oliver later. And just like that Oliver was alone again.

CHAPTER TWENTY-TWO

Weeks had gone by since Oliver met Eric in the park, and while they maintained a very flirty conversation via text, they only saw each other once or twice a week. Eric used work as an excuse even though he did not have a job, but Oliver did not know that. Because the relationship was new to Oliver, he did not discuss it with Camilla and Howard the way he might otherwise. He wanted to tell them that he was falling in love, that a man he randomly met on a bench in the park had managed to invoke feelings in him that he had not experienced in a very long time, if ever. He wanted to, but he knew that the moment he told Camilla or Howard any information about Eric they would not stop nagging him. They would want every detail— they would want to meet him; to interview him so they could be sure he was the right guy for Oliver. After all, Eric was the first guy Oliver admitted to dating since coming out to his friends. They would do this out of love, Oliver knew that, but he still felt it would be overkill, and it would certainly scare

Eric away. So, when Camilla or Howard brought up the fact that Oliver was spending more time with his face in his phone, giggling more; appearing to be somewhere other than present with them in any conversation, Oliver would tell them that he was simply chatting with random guys online. He hated to lie to them—and in a way he was not lying since he was chatting, but it happened to be with just one guy—one guy he was falling in love with too quickly—but he could not stop himself. He was having trouble processing how he could have such intense feelings for Eric … they barely knew each other.

When Eric and Oliver did get together it was often at Eric's loft, which was on the outskirts of the city across the street from the park—the same park where the two of them first met. Eric's apartment was in an old warehouse that had been converted to a dozen spacious lofts decades earlier—back when that part of the city was trendier than it is now. In the last financial crisis that part of the city started seeing a lot of one-off restaurants and bakeries shutter, and some of the retail shops—the ones that sold handmade, earth-friendly items, were gone too. The neighborhood had no big block chain stores.

The neighborhood had stood out, back then, as being more bohemian than it intended to be, if it had intended to be anything at all, but had lost most of that swagger over the years. Today there were a lot of empty storefronts—the windows and doors boarded up and layered with various movie and music posters promoting the next big blockbuster, or band tour. The streets were cleaned less often—mostly because the traffic had not warranted that much attention from city services. Depending on what day you were walking through, most likely lost, you would feel like you were on the set of some dystopian movie set—waiting for the Terminator or a pack of zombies to come around the corner and finish you off.

Intermixed with the emptiness were several smaller apartment buildings that were home to four or six apartments per building, and a few loft-style warehouses. Graffiti covered many of the building walls—some vibrant, political and beautiful while others were just an abstract mess of competing graffiti artists fighting for the last remnant of empty space. For as war torn as the neighborhood could feel to a stranger, it was a breeding ground for young hipsters and artists. The storefronts that shown brightly in the night were alive with music, food, and laughter, and from people who lived in the neighborhood. These were not establishments that most people would travel across town to get to—the destinations were great, just not great enough to pull in the distant crowd ... and that is exactly what Nicholas liked about the area. It was hip but isolated at the same time. He could be seen in this area without being "seen," which allowed him to have as "normal" of a life as he could considering his thirst for death.

Nicholas bought the warehouse soon after his father died. He had been watching the area and had been to some of the hole in the wall places with Hunter once or twice, which is how he learned of the area—Hunter was a bigger hipster than most assumed. Nicholas bought the building after his first visit to the area with Hunter, but never told him, nor invited him in. This isolated haven was all part of a larger plan for Nicholas, one that did not include Hunter. He was just a means to an end—part of the puzzle. Only one person would be allowed into his loft—to even know that he had a loft in the area— and that was Oliver. On one of their earlier dates, Nicholas and Oliver walked around the park for hours — talking, and sometimes holding hands. Through it all, Nicholas was always looking around to be sure they did not cross paths with anyone either of them knew. On one of those dates Nicholas took them through the park and to his building. He wanted Oliver to know where he lived. This private space was purchased with the sole purpose of providing a place where he and Oliver could be together without anyone else — to have a safe space where Eric could be as true to his Nicholas roots as possible without revealing that he was Nicholas.

The more time Oliver spent with Eric; the more mysterious Eric became. At times Oliver felt like he would make great progress — learn something new about Eric only to then question something he thought he already knew about the man he was falling in love with — at least he thought it was love. It was a new feeling for Oliver. What Oliver did not know was that Eric was already in love with Oliver and had been for years.

* * * * *

For as quickly as Oliver and Eric bonded and spent endless hours and days together, the honeymoon ended just as quickly as Nicholas pulled away, fearful that he was getting too close, too soon. Oliver spent days sending texts to Eric without any responses. He had been ghosted by the man he was falling in love with—very similar to how things ended with Camila and Nicholas. Angry that Eric was not responding, Oliver threw his phone across the room. It hit the wall with a loud thump before landing in a pile of dirty clothes in the corner. "Oliver!" Camilla yelled from the other room. Up until this point Eric had been very responsive with texting Oliver. It was their constant back and forth texts that kept Oliver excited all the time—the anticipation of what Eric would say or suggest they do next.

It had been several weeks since Oliver spent his first night at Eric's. They did not have sex. Nicholas was not ready to reveal his full self to Oliver while pretending to be Eric. Nicholas was saving that for when he could be himself with Oliver—when Oliver would know Nicholas. With the texting stopped Oliver was trying to relive that sleepover. Did something happen that night that he did not realize? Should they have had sex, he wondered. They had been together since then, but always in the park or out to dinner — never back to Eric's, which was odd given how Eric had pushed them to go there before that night. No more sleepovers, and now no more texting. Oliver found himself stressing out about his relationship and questioning if it was going to last much longer. Part of him realized that he was being overly dramatic, and that he just needed to step back and take a moment to breathe — to see that this was no big deal. Eric could have been away on business or remodeling the loft ... or tired of Oliver.

Sitting on his bed with all these thoughts running through his head, Oliver started to cry. As he sat there sobbing, he realized that he had not cried — not like this — in a very long time. In fact, he was struggling to remember the last time he had a good cry. It was not a loud cry — nothing that was alerting his roommates to the pity party he was hosting for himself in his bedroom. Howard, walking by the room and saw Oliver crying. He went into Oliver's room, got up on the bed with Oliver and gave him a big, strong "I love you and everything is going to be okay" kind of hug. Neither of them said anything. Howard had known Oliver long enough to know when a hug was enough to say all that could not be said. Oliver held Howard tightly, and Howard knew Oliver would be okay soon.

After a few minutes Oliver and Howard loosened their grip on each other. Their bodies were still wrapped up together, with very little space between them—just enough to stare right into each other's eyes. The redness around Oliver's eyes was bright, and his face was still wet from his tears. Howard' shirt was soaked on the shoulder where Oliver had cried into it, but Howard did not mind. He pulled his shirt off and used it to wipe Oliver's face dry. They both smiled at each other but said nothing. Howard did not ask any questions—he knew (or hoped) that Oliver would tell him what sparked the crying. Howard wanted that to happen when Oliver was ready—not to force anything.

The two continued to sit together. Howard would caress Oliver's arm now and again, and Oliver would smile back. No words were needed. But in that moment, something sparked in Oliver that Howard had tried to spark back in college. With the sun shining through the room illuminating the shirtless Howard, Oliver saw him in a new light— literally. Oliver pulled Howard back toward him.

Howard assumed Oliver wanted another hug, but instead Oliver pressed his lips against Howard's lips in more of a "I have always loved you and am just realizing it now" kind of way, which took Howard by surprise. The only thing that surprised him more was how willing he was to give in to the kiss, and kissed Oliver back, intensifying the moment for both in a way that neither expected. The kiss went on for only a few seconds, but it felt like an eternity for both. Their moment was interrupted by Camilla, who was standing in the doorway to the bedroom as she cleared her throat to get their attention. Oliver and Howard both turned to look at Camilla, and the three of them were silent.

The vibration of Oliver's phone in the pile of clothes on the floor broke the silence. It was not a text vibration, but the phone ringing. The three listened to the buzzing for a few rounds before Oliver got off the bed to find the phone in the pile of clothes. By the time he found it the buzzing had stopped. On the screen was the missed call notification — it was from Eric. Oliver's face warmed up quickly as shame, embarrassment, and guilt came over him as he stood there holding the phone — his back to Camilla and Howard now.

* * * * *

While Howard was consoling Oliver with his hug, outside the window—across the street, in a tree, a camera was watching—Nicholas was watching—had been for some time, ignoring the texts from Oliver. Nicholas would go from looking in Oliver's window to looking in Camilla's, and any other window in the house that he could see with the camera. He had been studying the house, and its occupants—had been for a long time. He was ignoring Oliver's texts not to be mean or spiteful, but because he was on a mission to scope out the house to understand if others besides the three roommates and Reed came and went. He had plans for them all and wanted to keep tabs on them. Nicholas knew that Howard, Reed, and Camilla stood in the way of he and Oliver being together forever open and true with each other. He had been working on a plan to change that—to pull those three out of the picture. Nicholas was not expecting to see Oliver and Howard kiss. He should have been the one getting that kiss—not Howard. The only thing he could think to do at that moment was call Oliver—but as he watched the three in the room ignore the phone call for the longest time, Nicholas's anger was fueled more. Had Oliver been mocking him all along, he thought? Did he peg Oliver all wrong? Did all of them have to die now? That was not the original plan, and Nicholas was not sure how to digest all this new information.

* * * * *

"I love you!" Oliver whispered, facing the window but still looking at his phone, and the missed call notification from Eric. As soon as the words were in the air Oliver realized that he did not really know if they were for Eric, or for Howard. When he turned around Camilla was still standing in the doorway looking very confused. Howard, still sitting shirtless on Oliver's bed was tapping away at his own phone.

"I need to tell Reed what just happened," Howard said without looking up. "He is a good man—a great man. I am lucky to have him. I need to be honest with him—we have always been honest with each other. It's not right that—"

"Will the two of you stop it," Camilla interrupted. "You kissed. Big fucking deal. I know better than anyone that the two of you have been fawning over each other for years, even if you could not see it. I am sure Reed knows it or thinks it. He might not want to address it, but it is in the air. Don't think you're fooling anyone, except maybe yourselves."

Camilla was on her soapbox, and the words just kept rolling out of her mouth. Oliver finally sat back on the bed beside Howard as Camilla continued her verbal diarrhea rant. She started citing moments when it was clearly obvious that Oliver and Howard had the hots for each other — little incidents, words, acts that one did to or for the other. Oliver and Howard looked at each other trying to piece it all together. Camilla was the one who convinced them both that Nicholas was a killer, so they were both wary that she was just trying to convince them both that they loved each other.

Oliver stood up, apologized to Camilla and Howard, and left the room. He walked out the front door and down the street toward the park. Eric was still watching the room. He could not understand what they were saying, but when he saw Oliver storm out of the house, and head away from the tree and toward the park he thought Oliver might be heading his way.

Camilla and Howard were momentarily speechless as Oliver left. Once he was gone the two continued talking, but not one lecturing the other anymore. Now they were talking about feelings. Howard even told Camilla about the first night he tried to kiss Oliver back in college — only reaffirming Camilla's diatribe about them belonging together. They moved the conversation to the kitchen because they were both hungry by this point, and as the conversation continued Reed walked in holding a bottle of wine in each hand.

"Who needs a drink?" he asked, holding both bottles in the air. Camilla and Howard both raised their hands as Howard ran over to Reed and gave him the tightest hug and most passionate kiss he could muster up.

CHAPTER TWENTY-THREE

Nicholas was walking through the park when he saw Oliver sitting on a park bench — their park bench. It had been a few days since the missed call, and they had not spoken or texted. Eric sat down beside Oliver but did not say anything. He let his presence sink in. As far as Eric was concerned, he was the one deserving of an apology. It was he who last tried to connect with Oliver. It was Oliver who did not answer the phone.

"Penny for your thoughts," Eric said to Oliver.

Oliver started to cry. It was a quiet cry — mostly a few tears sliding out of his eye and down his face, silently. Eric put his hand over Oliver's just as he had done that first time they met on this bench. His large, soft hand warmed Oliver's, and that only made Oliver cry more. Eric was trying to put Oliver at ease without letting on that he already knew — or assumed why Oliver was upset. He wondered if Oliver would tell him what he had done — that he had kissed Howard.

"I've made a mistake," Oliver managed to spit out. "I think … I have made a mistake, but I am not sure. I don't know anymore. The more I think, the more confused I become."

"It's okay," Eric responded, trying to remain calm and supportive. "Whatever it is, it cannot be that bad. You are not a bad person, Oliver. Everyone makes mistakes. Hell, I have made a shitload of mistakes."

"Have you ever kissed your best friend … and liked it?" Oliver asked bluntly.

Eric pulled his hand away from Oliver's, grabbed Oliver's chin, and turned his head so the two were facing each other. He held Oliver's chin, studying the chiseled face of the young man before him—a man he had fallen in love with long before their first kiss. Nicholas knew what Oliver was thinking, feeling—almost. He wanted to tell Oliver everything in that moment—from the beginning. He wanted Oliver to know—now, more than ever, that he had loved Oliver for a very long time—that had he longed for their first kiss for years. The whole story was running through Eric's head—the voices were speaking loud and proud, but nothing was coming out of his mouth. But he felt quite confident that, even in this moment, if he told Oliver the truth—who he really was—he would lose Oliver for good.

"Everyone makes mistakes. It is what we learn from those mistakes that shape us," Eric continued as if he was the wiser of the two. "If you kissed your best friend, well, that is okay. If you liked it, well, that is okay too. None of that is a mistake. The mistake is if what you do next turns out to be wrong ... then you will have made the mistake."

Oliver, still looking at Eric, but now with fewer tears, told Eric what he did—what led up to the moment. He explained to Eric that he had never felt so 'in love' with anyone as much as he did with him. He was angry and felt shut out by Eric at times, and in the heat of the moment, or the weakness of the moment—he was not sure which—he took advantage of the comfort of his best friend that resulted in a kiss—just one kiss. Eric already knew it was one kiss—he had watched the whole thing, but he still could not tell Oliver that.

"I have loved you for a lot longer than you think," Eric said. "I know that we have not been 'together' for that long, but I feel as though I have loved you for so much longer, and you are the only one I want to spend the rest of my life with. But, if this is not our time—if you need to explore the real meaning behind that kiss with Howard, then you should do that—get that out of your system. I will be here waiting."

"How'd you know I was talking about Howard?" Oliver asked.

Quick to respond, Eric said that he assumed that Howard was his best friend—especially the way he always talked about him. Oliver thought about what Eric said, and thanked him for being so open, and honest. Oliver did not realize then that Eric was setting him up—trying to see who Oliver would choose, if given the chance.

"You do what is right for you, Oliver," Eric continued. "If you need to explore these feelings with Howard, go ahead. Just don't forget about me."

It was killing Nicholas on the inside to say those words to Oliver. He had worked so hard and waited so long to finally get close to Oliver (even if under a false name), and now he was letting him go—to explore life with another man. He knew what he was doing, but that did not stop the pain he felt in his heart. Nicholas was certain that if Oliver did get up from the bench and head back to Howard, then Howard would be next on his list to die. While he had hoped that the killings would stop now that he finally won over Oliver, he realized that the killings would probably never stop—especially when Oliver learns that Eric is Nicholas.

Oliver gave Eric a gentle kiss, one that said, "I love you," then hugged him and thanked him before standing up and walking away. He did not turn around for fear that he would see Eric crying, or Eric would see that Oliver was crying again. Instead, Oliver slowly walked toward home to discover if Howard was really meant to be his one true love, or if he was horny and just wanted to have sex with Howard, finally.

* * * * *

Oliver returned home to find Camilla, Howard and Reed half asleep in the living room. Two empty wine bottles, an empty bottle of champagne, and a plethora of stemware littered the coffee table. It was early in the evening for the that much drinking, even for this crew. Oliver picked up the bottles to see if they saved anything for him—

they had not. Oliver carried the bottles into the kitchen to put in the recycling bin, and to get away from the vision of Howard and Reed — their entangled, drunk bodies on the sofa was not what he expected to come home to see.

Howard heard Oliver in the kitchen, so he stumbled into the kitchen to find out where Oliver had dashed off to after sharing that kiss. While Howard enjoyed a few hours of drinking with his boyfriend, he was having trouble freeing himself of the feeling he experienced with Oliver earlier on his bed. It was just a kiss, he kept telling himself, but he knew it was something more or thought it would be. But he was afraid to share that feeling with Oliver for fear that Oliver would say the whole thing was a mistake — to reject him as he did in college.

"Where'd you go?" Howard asked as he entered the kitchen, rubbing his head trying to ward of a pending headache from all his early evening drinking. "You bolted so fast. Camilla and I were worried."

"Sorry," Oliver said with as little emotion as he could muster at that moment — he was trying to process what Eric said, and how he felt coming home to see Howard and Reed together on the couch. "I needed some air. I am sorry about earlier. I mean ... well ... I mean I am sorry about making you worry. I panicked."

"Sweetie, what are you talking about?" Howard replied. "We kissed—sure. Was it a good kiss? Yes, it was. Did it mean anything? Well, I am not—"

Before Howard could finish his sentence, Oliver had turned around and grabbed Howard and kissed him again. He needed to see if the same euphoric feeling from earlier would return—to see if the earlier kiss was out of anger towards Eric, or love for Howard, or something else entirely. He knew how he felt earlier, and he knew that if he had the same feeling again then he needed to listen to Eric and go for it. Of course, he worried about Reed, or even if Howard felt the same way as he did, but in that moment all of that was moot as Oliver went in for the second kiss. This one was a little longer; deeper than the first. There was more passion, more rage in this kiss. They both gave in to each other at that moment, and as they kissed Oliver knew—he could feel it in his heart, his head, in his pants that he needed to be with Howard. That realization put more passion in the kiss, and Howard reciprocated.

"Are you serious?" Camilla whispered as she walked into the kitchen to find Oliver and Howard kissing. "Reed is in the next room."

Howard let go of Oliver. Not out of guilt, but out of surprise of hearing Camilla in the room. He realized that he was slightly erect from the excitement of kissing Oliver so he did not turn around to face Camilla — partially out of respect and partially out of fear that Reed could be standing beside her. He walked away from Camilla and Oliver, toward the pantry just to buy some time. Oliver had felt the rise in Howard' pants and knew then that Howard felt the same way about Oliver as he felt about Howard. With Oliver and Camilla facing each other, Oliver did not say anything, at first. He did not know what to say — to her. He knew exactly what he wanted to say to Howard but was finding it hard to get the words out with a growing audience. Before he could think of anything to say Reed walked into the room.

"Did you tell him?" Reed asked the room when he realized that everyone was standing around silently as if they just saw or heard something bizarre. Camilla turned around to face Reed, and by now Howard was able to face the crowd, too. He shot a look to Reed as if to say, "No I have not told him—I am still trying to digest the news myself dear," but Reed did not pick up on that at all and proceeded to tell Oliver the news.

"I've been offered a position in Dublin," Reed yelled with the excitement of a child in a candy store. "Isn't that exciting news?"

"Dublin, Ohio?" Oliver replied, more sarcastically or uninterested than he intended. "I am not sure I would find Ohio that exciting." Camilla smacked Oliver's chest.

"You are so daft sometimes, Olly," she snapped. She had not called him Olly in a long time. He knew this was a serious issue and apologized to Reed for being so trite. By now Howard had moved back toward the three of them and the four stood, almost awkwardly, like they were strangers.

"Ireland," Howard said in a bad Irish accent. "Reed is moving to Ireland next week. That's why we were drinking—celebrating, and commiserating. Apparently, some job in Ireland is more important than our relationship."

"Let's not start this again, Howard, please," Reed said. "We have been through this already. I think it is best if we do not even try the long-distance thing."

Oliver could not figure out why Howard could be so upset about Reed leaving, especially considering the two kisses he and Howard shared today. The mixed messaging was about to be too much when Oliver looked up at Howard, who winked back at him before telling Reed that he should go. Oliver was excited about the notion that Reed would be out of the picture — that would make pursuing something with Howard much easier. He had a lot of questions but held off asking for fear that too many questions would get Reed to change his mind, which would make it that much more difficult for Oliver and Howard to get beyond the kissing.

What none of them could know was that Reed was never going to make it to Ireland. The motion of pulling the four of them apart had begun some months ago when Nicholas decided that the only way he was going to be with Oliver was to remove his friends from the scene.

CHAPTER TWENTY-FOUR

It was the night of his flight to Ireland, and Reed wanted to spend it with Howard, but Howard did not have the strength to do that alone. He was torn between these new feelings for Oliver, which they had not discussed again since their kiss a week earlier, and his feelings toward Reed—about their relationship being over. They both said that their friendship would remain strong, but Howard was convinced that those words would mean nothing in a few days when Reed was in another country starting a new life.

Howard and Reed went out to dinner, alone, to bring closure to everything—to try and mend the wounds Reed opened, and to talk about their lives in the future. Reed had been to Ireland many times before—he had family there, so at least he had some comfort in knowing that he was going to a foreign country where he spoke the language. Howard, on the other hand, had never been to Ireland. Just the idea of the rolling pastures, the old castles, and the country living made him uneasy. Howard liked the big city. The louder, the busier, and the more chaotic the better. The city was the white noise that brought peace to his life.

When they finished dinner, Howard and Reed returned to the house to join Camilla and Oliver for one last drink before Reed headed to the airport. When they arrived, the two rolling suitcases that contained Reed's whole life were in the foyer ready to go. In the living room, Camilla and Oliver sat with a bottle of champagne, freshly opened, ready for one final good-bye. While Howard poured some champagne for them, Reed called a cab. As he hung up the phone, Reed realized the finality of everything—that he was really moving to Ireland. There was no turning back now—well, not without being out a lot of money. He convinced himself, one more time, that he was doing the right thing, and joined his friends for their final drink together. Camilla started reliving some of the more hilarious moments of Howard and Reed that she could recall. They all laughed and cried a little. Oliver focused on making sure the night was about Howard saying good-bye to Reed, and not about he and Howard sharing another kiss, even though he was counting the minutes to when that could happen. He was hoping it would be tonight—thought Howard would need a shoulder to cry on, or a hot mouth to make out with. Either way, Oliver was determined to be there for Howard later by being there in this moment for him now.

Their laughter was interrupted by the doorbell. Camilla left the three boys laughing in one room and went to answer the door—assuming it would be the cab driver. It was. She informed the old man that Reed would be right out, and pointed to the two rolling suitcases, asking if the driver would be so kind as to take them now so Reed could focus on his good-byes. The old man, in his late 60s, rolled his eyes as Camilla turned from the door to rejoin her friends. He was tired of "kids these days" who felt privileged and special. He grabbed the two suitcases, which were surprisingly lighter than they looked, and carried them to the curb where he then rolled them toward the trunk of the cab. He opened the trunk and lifted the suitcases in, one at a time. As the driver was about to close the trunk, he felt a sharp pain in his left side. Before he could figure out what it was, he felt another, and another, and then one last one in his neck before he was lifted and thrown into the trunk with the suitcases. Then the lid was closed, leaving the old man trapped in the trunk of his own cab to bleed out and die.

Nicholas, wearing dark clothes, a baseball cap, glasses, and wig and a fake mustache, got into the driver's seat of the cab and waited. He knew it would not be long before Reed would be out. After all, he did have a plane to catch.

Back inside, the four were saying their final good-byes. It was hardest for Howard, and he did the best he could to be strong, but ultimately there were tears—a lot of them. He was mad at Reed for being so focused on himself. He was mad that Reed did not include Howard in the decision process. He was mad at himself for not trying harder to change any of what was happening. Oliver and Camilla left Howard to walk Reed to the door, knowing the two needed one final moment together—to say good-bye, for good.

Oliver stood in the living room, looking out the window at the cab. He could see the driver's silhouette, but not much else. Camilla was sitting on the couch soaking up the reality that she was about to become a third wheel. At the front door, Howard and Reed hugged one more time. They agreed to stay in touch—which they might do for a few months — but they both knew that each would move on, not forgetting the other, but archiving their relationship in their memories. Eventually they would delete photos of each other from their phones — well, Reed might, long before Howard could. Reed let go of Howard and walked out the front door, down the stairs and slid into the cab all without looking back. He knew he had to do it this way — keep the moment from lingering too long. Once the cab door closed with a loud thud, the cab quickly drove off.

Howard closed the door and rejoined Oliver and Camilla in the living room. No one said anything. They sat in silence, continuing to drink the remaining champagne. While Howard was saying his final good-bye to Reed, Oliver had decided to put on some music. Unsure of the best music for the mode, he turned on his classical music playlist and hit the shuffle button. The house was quickly converted into a symphony hall as the collection of instruments played in tune through the wireless speakers. Howard, sitting next to Oliver, had Oliver's arm around his shoulder. It felt warm; comforting even. The three continued to sit silently listening to the calming yet commanding sound of the music.

"I really am going to miss him," Howard finally said as tears rolled down his cheeks.

* * * * *

The livery car was just a simple sedan—nothing too fancy, but not old, or beat up. Reed thought it was quite posh for a cab. Reed took notice of the driver for a moment, but not much more. He had no idea that the real cab driver was in the trunk dripping blood all over Reed's new luggage, and he had no idea that the man sitting in the front seat was Nicholas. Not looking for any small talk, Reed read through some emails and text messages on his phone. Nicholas started the conversation.

"What airline?" he asked, as if he was taking Reed to the airport. Reed responded with "Delta" without looking up from his phone. "If you are thirsty, there's some bottled water for you," Nicholas continued, hoping Reed would cooperate and drug himself by drinking from the bottle. Nicholas knew that it would be a little harder to sedate Reed any other way.

Reed declined the offer of water and continued to focus on his phone. When he was done with emails, he started looking at all the old photos in his phone—specifically those of him and Howard. As he scrolled through the photos, he came across an old video he had taken of the two of them having sex. As soon as he clicked the play button the car filled with loud moans and grunts. Reed forgot he had the volume up so high on his phone. He turned a little red at the idea that his driver heard the sounds, and immediately muted the video, but he continued to watch—Howard slowly undressing, and when completely naked, reach toward the phone to undress Reed. The video was from the perspective of Reed's eyes. Watching this now—it had been months since he shot this and forgot all about it—he was aroused. Watching Howard's naked, muscular body was exciting, almost voyeuristic now in the back of the cab. Howard looking right into the camera—right into Reed's eyes as he started unbuttoning Reed's shirt. Before he could see what happened next Reed clicked the delete icon and the video was gone. He needed to move on, and he did not need to be reminded of what a good man he just let go.

After driving a few miles, and for what Reed thought was longer than necessary to get to the airport, he looked up from his phone. He did not recognize any of his surroundings. He told Nicholas that this was not the way to the airport, and Nicholas responded that there was an accident on the highway, so they were taking surface streets—a short cut, if you will. Reed looked at his watch and started to fear that he might miss his plane.

"Have a drink, sir," Nicholas said, hoping that by now Reed was thirsty. "We will be to our destination in no time at all."

Reed declined the offer again. He was growing impatient with Nicholas being vague about the path they were taking to the airport, so he looked up the airport on his phone and tried to determine where they really were, and how long it was going to take. He realized that his phone battery was now at less than 3 percent, and he was down to one bar of cell service. When his map app loaded and located him, and he still did not recognize the location. He started to type in the airport name when his phone went dead.

"Damn it!" Reed yelled. "Do you have a charging port in his car? My phone just died."

Nicholas told him no and was growing impatient with Reed. Just as Nicholas said there were no charging ports Reed looked down by the bottles of water and saw USB and plug ports. He could not decide if his driver was just being a total prick or not.

"Dude, there are ports right here by the water bottles," Reed snapped. "How can you not know about the simple things in your own car, asshole?"

"Is the name-calling really necessary, sir?" Nicholas fired back, looking at Reed through the rear-view mirror and realizing that his passenger was not going to cooperate.

Reed looked up at the rearview mirror to see Nicholas looking back at him. He could only see his eyes, and they were green. Reed then noticed the Cab ID card hanging from the mirror and the picture was of an old black man. Reed panicked. He tried to roll down the window, but the child locks were on, so he could not. He wiggled the door handle, but the door would not open — the child locks were on the door too.

Nicholas realized that Reed knew that he was not going to the airport — that he might be in danger. He watched Reed squirm a little in the backseat—fiddling with the window and door again, as if they might finally open. After a few minutes of silence, letting Reed soak up the panic of the moment, Nicholas started talking again. He urged Reed to calm down, and to drink some water.

"Who the fuck are you?" Reed shouted. "And stop telling me to drink your water. I do not want any water. It's probably laced with something, isn't it, you fuck?"

Nicholas ignored the questions, and calmly reiterated that drinking some water could be lifesaving. Reed finally picked up one of the two bottles of water and opened it. Then he proceeded to pour the entire bottle out on the floor of the car. When the bottle was empty, he threw it across the car and did the same thing with the other bottle of water. He figured with the two bottles gone, his crazy driver would stop pushing the water, and Reed would have the upper hand. Reed could not have been more wrong.

Nicholas turned the car on to a dirt road. The ride suddenly got very bumpy. The car was not designed for this level of "off roading" but Nicholas did not mind. He was not going to be driving for much longer. After a few minutes on the dirt road

Nicholas stopped the car. The two now sat, alone. Looking out the window, Reed could not see anything but trees around the car and stars in the sky above. They could be anywhere, and nowhere at the same time. If he could get out of the car, Reed realized that he would have no idea what direction to run, or for how long. He was trapped. He could have cried—pled for mercy from his driver, but he sat silently, waiting for the driver to make his move.

Nicholas stopped watching through the rearview mirror and finally turned around to face Reed. He looked at him in silence for only a moment, but to Reed it felt like hours. As Reed looked back, he tried to identify his driver. The cap, the wig and the mustache concealed much of the face. The eyes were green—there was no denying that, and all Reed could think about were the stories Howard and Oliver told him about a green-eyed man. That, and the green-eyed man he saw in the gym. As hard as he studied the man in the front seat, Reed could not conclude that his driver was the same man from the gym. Between the disguise, and the fact that the encounter at the gym had been so long ago, it was hard for Reed to know for sure.

"What do you want from me?" Reed finally asked. He was afraid of what the answer might be, but he needed to ask. "Who are you? I do not have a lot of money on me." Reed started crying, begging his driver to let him go. He was yelling, then whispering, then yelling again, trying to get some response out of his driver. But Nicholas just sat in the front seat, watching Reed fall apart. He worn a grin, Nicholas did, that showed that he was enjoying watching Reed unravel.

"You should have drunk the water like I asked," Nicholas said in a calm, patient voice — like that of a priest in the confessional. No real divider screen between them here in the car, but we did have a sinner and a forgiver. "All I asked you to do was drink some water, Reed. We would not be in this position if you had just done what I asked."

"Okay, I am sorry," Reed said through tears. "Give me a bottle. I will drink it now — please." He begged. The dilemma, as Nicholas pointed out now, was that there were only two bottles of water, and the contents of both were being soaked up by the rug under Reed's feet.

"I had other plans for you, Reed," Nicholas almost sang. "But in true Reed fashion, you were only thinking about yourself—weren't you? You could have opened a bottle, drank it, and we could be someplace else right now. Even better, you could have stayed in town—not decided on your own, to move to another country, leaving your boyfriend behind. Your actions have consequences, and they affect many people. You dumped a man who loved you, and he has now turned his attention to the man I love, making it hard for that man to love me now. Do you see the problem here? Do you see what you have done?"

Nicholas continued to lecture Reed, and the more he did, the more Reed realized that this guy had to be Nicholas, the guy Howard and Oliver had warned him about. What he did not understand was what Nicholas was going to do to him, out in the middle of nowhere. And whatever he did do, how would that solve this triangle of love problem that Nicholas was laying out, he wondered. While Nicholas rambled on Reed was trying to figure out a way to escape. He rattled the door one last time, hoping for a miracle. The only thing that it did was bring Nicholas back into focus. He stopped talking, ending with a question that Reed did not hear. The two looked at each other in silence—Nicholas waiting for an answer and Reed hoping Nicholas would repeat himself. Neither got what they wanted.

Frustrated that his plan was all out of whack, Nicholas grabbed the gun that had been sitting on the passenger seat the whole ride. It was heavier than usual because of the large silencer attached to the end. Nicholas pointed the gun at Reed. "Any last words?"

Reed was crying more now, and as he sat there crying, wiping tears from his face, he felt a warmth in his pants as his bladder drained itself. Like his feet, Reed was now sitting in a puddle. The warmth surprisingly gave him some comfort as he came to terms with the fact that he was about to die. He knew he would die one day — everyone does. He just never envisioned that it would be by gunshot in the back of a car on a dirt road. It was almost too cliché — like he was in some b-rated movie with a dull plot.

Reed heard the almost silent "phist" sound as a bullet pierced his left thigh. He let out the loudest scream. Blood started oozing out, soaking him more. He put pressure on the wound with both hands. He was screaming and crying — and cussing at Nicholas. He still had no idea why this was happening. He heard part of the rant by Nicholas about love and boyfriends, but none of that sounded like a good enough reason to kill someone, especially this way. Nicholas waited for an answer again. Reed, still clueless to the question looked back at Nicholas — his eyes begging Nicholas to stop.

Nicholas got out of the car, closed the driver's door and open the passenger door behind him. Reed was in the other passenger seat, so if he wanted, Nicholas could have gotten in the car and sat beside Reed, but he did not. Instead, he stood there with the door open looking in at Reed, curled up on the opposite side of the car, his body pressed up against the door, hoping that it would open — it never did. Nicholas raised the gun again, pointing it at Reed. Tired of waiting for an answer to a question Reed never clearly heard, Nicholas fired the gun five more times. One bullet pierced Reed's stomach. A second into his other leg. The third and fourth bullets struck his shoulder and his face, respectfully. The final bullet entered Reed's head, just above his left ear. With that fifth bullet, Reed's body went limp. Nicholas could smell the fresh urine mixed with the blood and stench as Reed's dead body shat itself.

He stood there looking at Reed's body, wet from tears, urine, and blood—he could see blood still escaping from the six holes. This is not how he wanted Reed to die, but then he was learning that nothing he did anymore went as planned. Maybe it was time to stop all the planning and killing, and just take life as it comes. The problem was that Nicholas did not like how life was unfolding, so he felt he needed to orchestrate it all to his liking.

Nicholas opened the trunk, pulled the dead driver out and positioned him in the backseat next to Reed. One had been stabbed and the other shot, and it was clear that the two were the victims, neither the assailant. There was no way anyone who found the car the next day, or week—or whenever someone would next come down this road and find them—would believe that these two men killed each other. Nicholas took the knife out of the side of the driver—he forgot he left it in him when he threw him into the trunk. With the knife, Nicholas gashed all four tires and then threw the knife in the trunk. Nicholas took off the driver's gloves he had been wearing and threw them into the trunk, too.

Nicholas slipped out of the dark jumpsuit he had been wearing. It had blood on it—mostly from the driver, but some spatter from Reed. He knew because he felt some blood on his face. Once completely off, he rolled the suit up and stuck part of it in the now open gas tank. He grabbed a bag he had sitting on the front seat and put it over his shoulder, then as he walked away from the car he lit the end of the jump suit, which was almost touching the ground, and he walked in the same direction from which he drove the car. He walked almost 150 feet before he heard and felt the explosion. He turned around to see the car engulfed in flames—looking like a bonfire in the middle of nowhere on a starry night. Nicholas smiled at the success of covering his tracks again, and then let out a single tear. He was tired. All he wanted was to be in the arms of Oliver, but he knew that was going to take some time. He made a promise to be patient and wait for Oliver. And the best way he knew how to be patient was to kill everyone who stood between he and Oliver being together. One down, two to go, he thought to himself as he turned back onto the main road and walked in the opposite direction from where they had driven.

CHAPTER TWENTY-FIVE

"It's been over a week, and we haven't heard from him," Howard was saying to Camilla as Oliver walked in the room. "Something is wrong."

"What's going on?" Oliver asked them both as he grabbed Howard from behind and gave him a kiss on the back of the neck.

Howard pushed him away, almost in disgust—but more in frustration that no one was taking him seriously. He proceeded to tell Oliver that Reed had not checked in since moving to Ireland. Oliver didn't really care about whether Reed made it to Ireland or was having so much fun that he decided to ghost his old boyfriend. He had spent the last week getting very intimate with Howard. He was a little surprised at how quickly it appeared that Howard got over being dumped by Reed—but then this current outburst was proving that Howard really wasn't over Reed. Oliver was having a hard time understanding the emotional roller coaster that Howard was riding. He did not like roller coasters.

Camilla was getting tired of hearing about Reed ghosting them while at the same time constantly walking in on Howard and Oliver, usually naked—their bodies wrapped up in a knot. She needed to get laid—she knew that but was not about to hook up with the first guy to come along. Part of her was still digesting the death of Miles— part of her wanted to be with a man, and part of her just needed a quick hook up. This was not really a conversation she could have with Oliver and Howard. Oliver, sure—and she usually talked with Oliver about these personal issues, but with Howard always in the room lately, it was getting harder to have some alone time with her bestie.

"Maybe he got busy, or maybe he needs time away from you, and just needs some space," Camilla said, although she felt like she was screaming it at this point. "You two are not dating—he does not need to check in with you. And to be honest, if I just broke up with you and moved to another country, you would probably be the last person I would be rushing to call."

"I get that, Camilla. I really do," Howard was saying back, almost through tears. "But he promised me that he would call or text or message me when he made it to Dublin safely. Just a note to say he arrived. That was it. I was not asking him to marry me or check in every ten minutes. One text was all I asked for, and he agreed to — it is not like Reed to go back on his word, even if we did just break up."

Trying to stay out of the battle of words between Howard and Camilla, Oliver was flipping through the newspaper that was on the counter.

"Guys, shut up and look at this," Oliver said, pointing to the newspaper article about a burned-out car with two dead bodies. "It says here that the gas tank exploded, and the bodies were burned beyond recognition."

Howard and Camilla did not look at the article, but they stopped and listened to Oliver read the highlights before asking why he was so interested in the article. Nothing Oliver read aloud stood out as anything out of the ordinary — or were they missing something that Oliver was not reading out loud, they thought. Black sedan, registered livery car, remote dirt road between their house and the airport. When read in snippets there was nothing there, but when read all together it sounded like they might have figured out why Reed had not checked in.

"Don't jump to conclusions, Howard," Camilla said as she watched Howard start pacing the room. "There is nothing in this story that points to Reed. This is not a small town. There are lots of taxis and lots of dirt roads between here, and everywhere, and the airport."

"Yes, but," Oliver interrupted. "It says here that the police say that they believe the explosion happened last Tuesday night—the same night that Reed left for the airport, in a black livery car."

"We have to go to the police station," Howard said. "We just have to." As he was saying all of this, he was putting his shoes on and grabbing his keys. "Let's go, we need to get down there now and find out if this was Reed. I am not going to be able to rest until I know for sure."

* * * * *

Across town Nicholas was reading the same news article, trying to determine whether the police had any idea who, or what, had caused the explosion—and if foul play was at hand. As off-plan as that evening had gone, he felt confident that he left no trace of himself anywhere. From the gloves to the jumpsuit, he was sure he did not leave any DNA at the scene, and given that they were remote, there wouldn't be any CCTV footage. The bullets were embedded in Reed's body. He did remember to pick up the shell casings, but the bullets were the only evidence left behind. Nicholas did not usually use a gun to kill—mostly because he did not like the amount of evidence left from using a gun —bullets, shells, residue—the list was too much for him. Aside from the gun left as part of the coverup, like when he killed his father, he opted for other forms of killing. He knew the bullets lodged into the various parts of Reed could be recovered, and they could give something to the police to investigate, but he was also hopeful that the explosion would have melted the bullets, especially since the bodies were burned beyond recognition.

With the police working yet another case that could eventually lead back to Nicholas, he was already planning his next crime. He was growing tired of waiting for Oliver to come to him—to choose him over anyone else. He partially regretted telling Oliver he would wait, even though it was true. Nicholas had waited almost a decade to be with Oliver. By speeding up the chance to be with Oliver,

Nicholas was risking the chance of never seeing him again — if he were to get caught.

Nicholas was a patient person, and each kill was different enough, and spaced out enough to never draw any attention to any connection the killings might have. The last thing he wanted the police doing was connecting the dots and suddenly knocking on his door to arrest him. He always thought that he would either be arrested on his terms, one day, or die a peaceful death, only to be connected to some cases long after he was dead.

As he thought about his next move, it made more sense to kill Howard, realizing that he might not need to kill Camilla at all. If he could get Oliver to come back to him, he could convince Oliver to move away with him and leave Camilla behind. And if Camilla could be preoccupied with a new man, that might make the whole plan even easier. With this new plan — kill Howard and play matchmaker for Camilla, Nicholas set out to decide how he was going to do both.

* * * * *

At the police station, Howard was asked to do a lot of waiting. He would talk with one officer only to be asked to wait longer to speak with another. Eventually he, along with Oliver and Camilla, were given the audience of the officer in charge of the investigation. It was an ongoing investigation, so to no surprise to Oliver, the officer was not very forthcoming with anything that could be leaked to the press. This officer, Detective Jennifer, made that mistake once before, back when she joined the force. A rookie mistake, sure, but she was new and eager to impress her captain. She just did not realize that telling the hot girl she met at Ginger's happy hour what she did, and what her first case was all about was a bad idea. She swore she would never drink another drop of alcohol after the embarrassment of reading the details she revealed the night before all over the newspaper the following morning. The hot girl took Jennifer home that night, and they were up all night. This was the first time since college that Jennifer went home with a woman. And while she gave up alcohol because of the incident, she did not give up women. She winked at Camilla as she reiterated that she cannot share any details of the case with "Nancy Drew and the Hardy Boys." Camilla was flattered by the wink but insulted at being called Nancy Drew.

Camilla decided to see if flirting back with the officer would make a difference. She was not good at flirting with guys, so Oliver and Howard knew it would only be worse with this officer. Camilla could not wink without making her whole face squish up — it was like watching a two-year-old wink, and not in the cute, funny way. The more she tried, the crazier she looked to Oliver and Howard. But somehow Jennifer found Camilla quite flirtatious, and the winking turned into small talk. It was then that Oliver and Howard realized that both girls were bad at flirting, so Oliver interrupted with a proposition for Jennifer to join them for drinks that night. He mentioned a place called The Rainbow Room not far from the precinct. He had never been, but had seen the name in advertisements, and figured with a name like that how could it be anything other than a gay-friendly bar. To their surprise, Jennifer agreed. She wrote her number down on a piece of paper then grabbed Camilla's wrist. She caressed it a little more than Camilla was comfortable with, and put the paper in Camilla's palm, closed it around the paper and tapped the back of Camilla's hand softly. As much as she wanted to kiss it Jennifer was in uniform, and on duty. She knew she was already breaking several rules just by fraternizing with the three of them.

Oliver, Camilla, and Howard walked out of the police station proud of their accomplishment — well, the boys were proud. Camilla was still trying to figure out what just happened, and if she was going to have to put out tonight just to get the information they wanted. Oliver and Howard were laughing at Camilla — telling her how bad she was at flirting and were mocking and imitating her as they walked to their car. If it were any other set of cute boys, or any boys making fun of her as Oliver and Howard were doing Camilla would have verbally cut them — they would go running to their mamas with their ego between their legs. But not Oliver and Howard. They loved Camilla, and she loved them. She knew they were being silly — and she knew she did not have game. That was part of the reason she was always single. Miles was a fluke. He fell into her lap — literally.

Miles and his friends were at the same club as Camilla and the boys. Camilla and Oliver were sitting at a table at the edge of the dance floor, drinking and commiserating about the dating scene. Howard and a nameless hot boy were dancing a little too provocatively for Camilla's liking. She and Oliver were watching Howard, almost making fun at his expense, when Miles and is group of friends, who were all dancing too wildly, accidentally knocked Miles over. He tripped on the edge of the dance floor and landed on Camilla's lap, almost knocking she and her chair backward. If there had not been the large man standing behind Camilla's chair, Camilla and Miles would have tumbled to the sticky club floor. Camilla was thankful for the large man behind her that night, although he was not happy when the chain reaction caused him to spill his beer on his shirt. That was the night Miles and Camilla met. It would be many nights later before he got the nerve to ask her out, and even more nights before she would finally said yes.

After spending the day searching the internet for any leaks about the car explosion, Howard convinced Oliver and Camilla that they had to get dressed and meet Jennifer. They needed answers—he needed answers. Camilla was resisting. She did not want to end up in a position where she would have to do something with the officer, or touch her — or worse, kiss her. Camilla had nothing against lesbians — she had lesbian friends, and was very comfortable with gay men, but she had enough issues with herself and straight sex that she was not about to try and figure out gay sex. Howard told Camilla that she would not have to do anything she was not comfortable doing, and said that if they all did go out, he would personally snatch block, if necessary. Camilla was repulsed at the term "snatch block," but appreciated Howard trying to be the hero of the night, even though she knew that an hour into the evening she would find Howard drunk and dancing with a stranger — not focused on keeping Camilla safe. She was going to have to rely on Oliver to play hero.

At the club the three got a table and ordered some drinks. When the time to meet Jennifer passed Camilla decided that she had just been playing with them at the station, and she had no real intention to meet a bunch of young strangers at a club. By her third drink Camilla was already asking if they could go home, and just as the three were finishing their last drink — all ready to call it a night, Jennifer walked in and gave Camilla a long, tight hug. Camilla was gasping for air by the time Jennifer released her. She got ready to repeat the act with Howard, since he was closest to Camilla, but he put up his hand to stop her and said he was not a hugger. Jennifer complied and just looked at Oliver. He was too far away for her to hug him without making a bigger scene.

A waiter walked by their table and Jennifer stopped him and ordered a bottle of champagne for the table. Social Jennifer was nothing like the hair pulled back in a ponytail, tight police uniform wearing, serious officer they all encountered earlier in the day. This nighttime Jennifer was relaxed and social—almost a little too much, like she was a caricature of a young party girl. Camilla, Howard, and Oliver were three drinks ahead of Jennifer when she arrived, but by the second bottle of champagne, she was more wasted than the three of them combined. She had sworn off alcohol, but something about the club, and Camilla, had Jennifer chugging the liquid courage. That is when Howard started shifting the conversation to the investigation.

He started asking random, seemingly unrelated questions, trying to ease Jennifer toward more direct questions. Howard really did not care about the explosion as much as he cared about whether Reed was one of the two charred bodies found lying on each other in what was left of the back seat of the car. He was realizing that no matter how drunk she appeared, Jennifer was still quite aware of the conversation, and kept pulling the conversation back away from the case. Camilla could see Howard getting frustrated so she did the only thing she could think of doing, and that was to put her hand on Jennifer's. That simple gesture stopped Jennifer in mid-sentence. She looked at Camilla and smiled, then immediately apologized because she had forgotten what she was just talking about. Howard took that opportunity to turn the conversation back to the burned bodies. It took another bottle of champagne, two shots of Jägermeister, and a kiss from Camilla—on the cheek—before Jennifer started spilling information about the case. And once she did, it was like the end of a gutter in a rainstorm. Fact after fact just came pouring out of her mouth. Much of it was so slurred, and some of it did not even make sense as the three, slightly more sober ones listened, trying to make sense of the gibberish.

From all the nonsense that came out of Jennifer's mouth—in between her having to excuse herself twice to throw up in the ladies' room — the three gleaned one piece of information that helped them confirm the very fear that Howard had been having for days. When she mentioned that one of the bodies was wearing a silver cross necklace — or at least that is what they were concluding it was — the officers could not be 100% positive because the cross had melted from the heat and burned into the chest of the victim, Oliver and Camilla knew exactly what the next question out of Howard's mouth was going to be — was it oversized? Before she could answer with words, her face gave it away. "How'd you know that?" was all she had to ask before Howard broke down crying.

Lots of people have a cross necklace — it is not uncommon. But an oversized cross is less common. Howard bought it for Reed a month after they were dating. Reed had lost the one he had been wearing — the two of them had gone swimming in the Atlantic Ocean and they ended up getting frisky in the water. When they emerged, the jewelry was gone. Howard did not know then that the original necklace had no real sentimental value — it was a cheap replica that Reed bought at a chain clothing store as an accessory to an outfit — bought on a whim. With no back story on its value, Howard found a local jeweler and had an oversized sterling silver cross made, and had a small heart cut out of the center where the two bars crossed. As he described the necklace to Jennifer she started crying. She confirmed that the one she found had melted and had become misshapen, but that it did have a hole in the center — it no longer looked like a heart, thanks to the heat, but it had become very clear to the whole table that one of the bodies in the back of the burned-out car had to be Reed.

It took Howard a few more days to accept the news. The man he loved, had loved for a long time was gone. He was just getting used to the fact that Reed was going to be gone — to another country — some place Howard could visit. The idea that it would be a cemetery where he would have to go to visit Reed was becoming too much to digest. While Howard was coming to terms with the truth, Camilla was trying to recall every little detail of the night Reed left.

Though she did not sleep with Jennifer the night they all realized Reed was dead, Camilla did stay in touch with her — mostly because she was certain that she, Oliver, and Howard could help with the case. The day after the night of drinking too much with Jennifer, Camilla went around the neighborhood to see how many homes had cameras. She did not ask to see any footage but took inventory of the number of homes that might be able to help provide more information about the livery cab driver, or what happened outside the house the night Reed left. She was becoming the Nancy Drew she didn't want to be.

Once Camilla found a few homes with cameras she called Jennifer and shared the information and her theory with her. Jennifer in turn told her supervisor that she got an anonymous tip from a caller about a missing person. Howard made the call and filed a report about Reed missing so there would be a paper trail. That helped Jennifer dispatch officers over to the house to hear about the taxi and the whole story of Reed's farewell. While describing the evening and the encounter with the driver in detail, Camilla mentioned the plethora of video doorbells and other cameras in the area. Armed with this new information, the police went house to house and were able to gather some footage of the night that Reed died.

Back at the station, the police watched the videos and saw the taxi driver bring the luggage from the entry and load it into his trunk, and then they watched a man wearing all black stab the taxi driver and put the driver in the trunk. The man in black never faced any of the cameras, almost as if he knew they were there.

With a starting location and time, the police were able to put together a complete timeline of events right up to the time of death. That helped them set up a radius from the location of the burned-out car to gauge where and how far the man in black might have gone — assuming he was still in the area. To make sure that they left no stone unturned, Jennifer asked Camilla, Howard, and Oliver to come back to the station to review the videos. She and her colleagues were hoping that one of the three of them might recognize the very fuzzy image of the man in black.

Sitting in the windowless room in the police station — one wall home to a large mirror, the three realized that they were, for the first time, in an interrogation room. "Just like in the movies," Camilla said. Jennifer joined them and talked them through what was about to happen. She wanted the three to know that all they needed to do was watch the video and tell her if they recognized the man in black.

"We can pause, rewind, and watch as many times as you need, so don't rush," she said. "We would rather you take your time and give us nothing than rush and send us on a goose chase for someone who might be innocent."

Two officers wheeled a cart into the room with a monitor on it. They plugged it in and gave the remote to Jennifer. Camilla, Howard and Oliver were sitting around the table, all facing the monitor. They had butterflies in their stomachs as if they had done something wrong and were getting ready to receive their punishment. Jennifer remembered the first time she was in their shoes — it is a scary feeling. As much as she could, she let them know it was okay, and that any information they provide would be helpful in solving their friend's murder. Jennifer asked if they were ready and then played the tape without waiting for any response. The first few minutes of the tape were uneventful — the car pulling up, the driver ringing the doorbell. You could make out their silhouettes in the windows — all the lights were on that night. Outside, however, was a different story. The streetlight by their house was out — they thought nothing of it before now but wondered now if it had been out purposely.

Camilla made a little scream and grabbed hold of Oliver when the driver was stabbed. As the man in black moved from the trunk to the driver's side of the car the three of them leaned in to get a better look. Jennifer explained that the footage was fuzzy — it came from a doorbell camera on the house across from them. But as fuzzy as it was, once he was in the car — once his profile was just barely seen in the driver's seat, Camilla and Oliver looked at each other. They did not say anything — they just looked at one another. Oliver knew that of the three of them, Camilla would be the best to identify Nicholas. Oliver had looked at Camilla in hopes that she might see something — but it was when Camilla quickly looked at Oliver that he knew she knew something.

"What?" Oliver asked, almost mouthing it.

"That is him," Camilla said with a quiver in her voice. "I mean, I know that is the killer, but I know who that is — I think. I am sure. Well, positive, maybe." Her flow of second-guessing was not giving the police much confidence. But Jennifer saw something in Camilla's face. She saw fear — real panic. She knew that as much as Camilla was all over the place with her incomplete strings of words, she knew something — maybe even knew the killer.

Howard just sat there staring at the screen waiting for Reed to come out — to see him one more time. He was not paying attention to the others — not very much, so he felt left out when he turned around, after Reed got in the car, to find everyone focused on Camilla. He looked back at the monitor and saw that Jennifer had paused the video. The screen was frozen. Reed was lost in the back seat, out of sight of the camera, which gave Howard no one to look at but the driver.

"Holly shit!" Howard exclaimed. "Is that the green-eyed guy? Guys, look at that image — I'm sure it's him. Holy shit. Come on, Camilla, you dated the guy — you know that's him, right?"

Her bottom lip was vibrating as she bit down trying not to scream. She was trying to understand how it could be Nicholas — if it was the man she knew as Carter. She had spent weeks convinced that Nicholas had been the reason Miles was dead, and then there was the speculation about Hunter. Seeing who she believed to be her old boyfriend sitting in the front seat of that taxi, even as grainy as the image was, she was having the hardest time forming words. She was trying to stay calm, but tears were rushing down her face and a little blood was escaping from the corner of her mouth, from biting her lip.

Oliver was holding it all together. He believed that this guy could really be anyone. They were all still speculating that it was Nicholas, almost wanting it to be Nicholas so they could prove their conspiracy theory. Oliver turned to Jennifer and agreed that they believed that the man in black was someone named Nicholas and started to share their theory. They had no physical proof. Camilla had dated Carter in college for a week, several years ago, and someone who looked sort of like Carter had popped up in their lives periodically over the last year.

"If this is in fact Nicholas, and again, the image is grainy," he said, "then you should know that his father and my mother had an affair 22 years ago. I recently learned that I am the product of that affair. I also recently learned that the man my mother slept with was the father of another boy, who I've only ever seen in pictures as a teenager, so we cannot be 100% sure the person in this video is the guy that we think is both her old fling and my possible sibling—none of us can. But I thought you should know."

Oliver went on to tell Jennifer the name of his biological father—the man who raised Nicholas. He knew that would help Jennifer and her team quickly narrow down photos, at least, of Nicholas so they could try to make a match.

CHAPTER TWENTY-SIX

It was days later, while sitting in their living room and still trying to digest the reality that Reed was dead, when the phone rang. It was the first time the landline had rung in a long time—none of them could remember the last time the landline rang. Camilla looked at Howard who looked at Oliver, who in turned looked at them, giving them a confused look. It rang four times before Howard finally got up from the couch, grabbed the receiver and spoke.

"Hello?" Howard said in a quiet, sullen voice. The last thing he wanted to do was deal with some solicitation from some low-paid worker in a third world country. He was surprised by the clear, well-spoken English-speaking voice that returned her own 'hello' back at him. Howard made several grunts into the phone as he listened to the woman give him the news he was not expecting to get—not this soon anyhow.

"No… um, okay… yes, ma'am… yes, yes, no, yes... we can do that… sure… that is fine. Thank you. We will see you then. Yes… thank you."

When Howard finally hung up the phone he returned to the couch before saying anything. The silence was killing Camilla—she had to know who was on the phone.

"Who was that?" she finally asked as he was getting comfortable once again. "And what did they want?"

Howard told Camilla and Oliver, in as calm a voice as he could, that the police have found who they believe to be the man in the video—Reed's killer, and that they were asking the three of them to come to the station and identify the man in a lineup. They all sat silently for a moment trying to digest the news. They had seen the nightly news repeatedly — they knew that the police managed to catch most criminals quickly, but this seemed sudden. Oliver and Camilla were struggling with how calm Howard was behaving after taking the call.

"How did they do it so fast?" Camilla asked. "We made an assumption about a man in a grainy photo just days ago?"

* * * * *

At the police station, Camilla, Howard, and Oliver sat in the waiting room with countless others. Some were there to receive their loved ones, while others were there to file complaints. Aside from a few men in suits who the three believed were lawyers, the rest of the patrons of the room looked worn out, run down, and out of luck. No one was well dressed—some clearly had not bathed in some time, Camilla could tell, as they got a whiff of the air as they had walked in. Camilla, Howard and Oliver looked like three college preppies, lost in a sea of depressing adulthood.

After sitting in the waiting room for almost 30 minutes a young officer called their names from behind a bulletproof window. By the time they stood up, a door to the right of the window opened. Jennifer stood in the doorway with a big smile on her face. Oliver was trying to determine if the smile was for Camilla or because Jennifer felt good about the man in the lineup. As the four walked toward the room where they would be viewing the men, Jennifer said very little. She did not want to give any indication about her opinions on the individuals who would be on display, specifically which one she and her fellow officers believed was the man Camila believed was Nicholas. She really needed Camilla, Howard, and Oliver to conclude on their own, but collectively. Jennifer was hoping this process would take just a few minutes — she was that confident.

As Camilla, Howard, and Oliver sat in the small, dark room — the only light coming from the room on the other side of the two-way mirror, they watched as seven men were escorted into the lit room — obedient, prisoners of war, being escorted into a firing line. Each man was holding a tablet-sized card with a number on it in a large, thick font. Once they were all in the room they were instructed to turn and face the mirrored wall. As the seven men stood there — all staring at the mirror, almost as if they were struggling to see who was on the other side, the three friends sat in the dark studying the faces of the men before him. None of them said anything.

After a couple of minutes of silence, Jennifer reminded them that they could ask for any one of the men to step forward so they could get a better look at him. They did not really need to do that though — there were a dozen cameras in the lit room capturing every angle of the men. The faces of the men were enlarged, each on one of the seven large monitors in the darkroom. Camilla would look at Oliver, who looked at Howard, then both boys would look at Camilla. Each of their faces asked the question, "Which one looks like Nicholas?" but none of them spoke any words.

"Do any of these men look like the man you call Carter, or Nicholas?" Jennifer asked Camilla. "Please take your time and look at each of them closely. Then tell me if any of these men are your Nicholas."

Camilla did not like the label of 'your Nicholas's as if he was her possession—her responsibility—that she could have prevented the deaths if she had just kept a better handle on 'her man.' Camilla looked at Oliver when Jennifer asked the question, giving him a constipated look as if to say, "What the hell is Jennifer smoking today?"

Oliver decided to be the first one to speak. He felt that had he not, Jennifer would just get tougher with Camilla. "None of them." With those words in the air, Jennifer, an unnamed officer, Camilla, and Howard all turned to face Oliver.

"None of those men in there is Nicholas," Oliver said more clearly. "Number Four, Five and Seven most resemble who we think to be Nicholas — in height and good looks, but number four is too fat. Number five is too buff. Number seven is the closest of them all, but for one thing — his eyes. Nicholas has the most striking green eyes. They almost glow."

Jennifer took in the words trying not to let them crush her spirit, then spoke into her walkie talkie. "Ask any of them if they are wearing contact lenses, please."

Two officers walked into the lit room and stood by the door they closed behind them as a voice over the speaker asked each man to remove any contacts, if they were wearing them. The friends watched as man number one and three both removed contacts from their eyes. The new officers in the room held dishes of eye solution for each man to put the contacts in so they would not get lost. The other five men did not move. The voice came over the speaker one more time, asking the same question. Finally, man number seven put his number card under his left arm and began to play with his eyes, as if he were finally removing his contacts. As he fiddled with his eyes the group sitting in the dark, on the other side of the mirror gasped in unison. When he finally finished playing with his eyes he looked back up and smiled at the mirror. He had not taken any contacts out—in fact he was not wearing any. He was antagonizing his audience, in both rooms at this point. The officers in the room yelled at him, but Oliver and friends could not hear what as being yelled. Oliver looked back over at Jennifer and restated what he had moments earlier—none of the men in the lineup were the man they believe is Nicholas.

Upset, but trying not to show it, Jennifer spoke into her walkie-talkie again to remove the lineup—return them back to their cells or let them go. Camilla, Howard, and Oliver were a little deflated at the idea that Nicholas, if he was the murderer, was still on the loose. Jennifer tried to cheer them up with a pep talk about how the police force was still out looking and would not stop until Nicholas was caught. She had no right making that statement, but knew it was the standard speech she and her fellow officers gave after an unsuccessful lineup. The fact was that Jennifer, and her team were no closer to finding Nicholas, or anyone related to the case. They had zero evidence that would point to anyone. The only clue was that Nicholas was the son of Peter, and while the officers had not yet found that person, they found many others who looked like the man in the video.

* * * * *

Another two weeks passed before the police finally found Nicholas — or rather, Nicholas just showed up. The police had an unmarked car outside Nicholas's fathers house for weeks — ever sense Oliver told them that the person in the video might be Nicholas. With that information, combined with the details Oliver provided, the police were able to identify Nicholas Lawson. As they pieced the puzzle together, the only known address for Nicholas was his father's house. The police were growing weary of their manhunt until the morning when an Uber pulled up in front of the house and Nicholas got out of the back seat with a suitcase. He had seen the unmarked car as his Uber approached but did not acknowledge it. Instead, he headed up the stairs to the front door as if nothing was wrong. Within five minutes of being inside the house the doorbell rang, and when a young Mexican woman, Margarita, answered the door the police were taken aback. They had not seen anyone come or go through the front door. They never thought to check the back of the house — which is where Margarita entered and left through — a back door, every three days to clean the house. Today she was wrapping up her work when Nicholas surprised her. She had not seen Nicholas since before his father died. Right after Nicholas entered, she heard the doorbell. Margarita was a short woman. She was not thin, but not fat either. She was in her late 30s and had worked as a house cleaner for the entire 15 years she had lived in the country. She never received a green card, and always worked under the radar. What little English she did know, she learned from her two American born children. The last people she wanted to see at the door were police officers, but she remained calm, and in her broken English, asked how she could help them.

Nicholas came back to the door when Margarita yelled in Spanish through the house. He was rapid firing Spanish back at her as if it were his native tongue. Neither of the officers spoke Spanish, or any other language aside from English. Nicholas could see that in their faces as he approached them at the doorway, and proceeded to continue speaking in Spanish, just to play with the officers. One of them finally said that they did not speak Spanish and grabbed his walkie-talkie to ask for Spanish back up when Nicholas interrupted him in English.

"Sorry, officers," Nicholas said in English. "How can I help you?"

"Are you Nicholas Lawson?" one officer asked.

"Yes," Nicholas responded.

"Son of Peter Lawson?" asked the other officer.

"Yes," Nicholas repeated. "Can I help you?

"Can you please tell us where you have been for the last month?" the younger of the two officers asked. Nicholas thought this one was the cuter of the two—he was fresher faced, and less bitter from fewer years on the force. Looking at the younger officer, Nicholas was trying to place him—he felt certain he looked familiar, but he was drawing a blank.

"I've just returned from a trip to London. Is something wrong?" Nicholas knew why the officers were there. He also knew they had been in front of the house for weeks. He purposefully stayed away from his father's house just to torment the police. He had enough cameras around the outside of the house that he was able to watch the police stakeout. He even had lunch delivered to the unmarked car one week in and had the delivery boy say that the lunch was from the neighborhood association. He wanted them to know that they were being watched.

The older officer started telling Nicholas nothing he did not already know. They recapped the death of Reed without any details beyond a 'deadly incident' where Nicholas was a person of interest thanks to poor video footage. Nicholas bit his inner lip when her heard about the footage—it turned out that the police were telling him something he did not know. He was recalling that night, and the work that let up to preparing for that night. He was certain that every camera in the area had been addressed. What he had not planned for was new people moving in across the street from Oliver the day before he killed Reed. He remembered canvassing the area one last time the day the moving truck was parked out front. What he did not see was the camera doorbell being installed.

"I am sorry to hear about all of this," Nicholas said, still working his "I was in London" case. He showed the men his passport—and the stamps that put him in London three days before the incident and returning today. The officers reviewed the fake passport they held in their hand and eventually stepped away to call back to the station. The two officers, now standing in the front yard, far enough away that Nicholas could not hear them, were talking with each other, and into their walkie-talkies. The one who had the passport was flipping through the pages but was not finding a lot of activity. In fact, aside from two other entries, one to Canada and a second for London, the passport pages were clean.

The officers finally made their way back to the front door, where Nicholas was still standing impatiently. As the officers moved up the steps, they could see the housekeeper in the window—she was afraid they were there to arrest her for being in the country illegally. Little did she know that they had no interest in her today.

"Thank you for your cooperation, Mr. Lawson," the older officer said as he handed the passport back to Nicholas. "We apologize for the inconvenience and appreciate your time." And just like that they were back in their car and driving away.

Nicholas, back inside the house, had to sit down. He did not like how close he was to being caught. He thought about the night that he killed Reed, and how he ended up on a video. Of course, there was no way to erase the video now — the police had it in their possession. If any new leads came up, or they could make the video less grainy, Nicholas will be back in the hot seat — even with the fake passport giving him an alibi. He saw that Margarita was still standing by the window. He explained to her, in Spanish, that everything was okay — the police were not there for her but were following up on his father's death. She was relieved and returned to cleaning the house.

Nicholas knew it was time to make some big changes or he was going to get caught. Moving away would be the biggest red flag — something in the back of his mind told him that the police did not completely believe the London story even though he had evidence to prove it. It was time to either come clean with Oliver or figure out how to kill off the last two so he could be with Oliver forever — behind his lie. The idea of coming clean seemed harder.

CHAPTER TWENTY-SEVEN

Oliver could not get the grainy image out of his head — was that Nicholas? He was trying to make sense of his thoughts, the video, and most of all, he was trying to understand how he and his friends got so wrapped up in this mess. What did they do, or not do, to put them at the center of these murders? He would ponder that question for many nights, never coming up with a good enough answer. He sent some text messages to Eric even though the two had agreed that they needed some distance while Oliver figured out who he really wanted to be with. The question Oliver struggled with now was about how he felt about Howard as anything more than a friend. The recent kisses were nice and the time they were spending together had been wonderful, but the murder of Reed changed everything.

As he thought more about how his friendship with Howard remained strong, if not stronger now that they had kissed, he questions whether it was just a moment where he needed consoling — needed answers. Howard was the one who was able to give Oliver what he needed at that moment all those weeks ago — mostly because of the relationship that they had built over the years. Maybe that was why they kissed. Maybe it was because they loved each other, or the idea of them being together. Maybe Howard always loved Oliver and used a moment of weakness to his advantage. All these thoughts were running through Oliver's head as he tried to figure out his next move.

Across town Nicholas was busy working on his escape plan. Nicholas was busy pondering the truth vs. more deaths plan. The more he thought about it the more he realized how much he loved Oliver. Maybe they were just not meant to be together. Maybe the solution was to kill them all and move on with his life — put this tormenting behind him so he could find solace in someone else — someplace else. Nicholas was not sure he could muster up the strength to kill Oliver. The others, sure, that would easy. But killing Oliver — killing the one person he had loved his whole life, without really coming to terms with it until recently, sounded like too big of a challenge, even for Nicholas. He had been ignoring Oliver's text messages, not because he wanted to, but because he was grappling with how he was going to respond.

CHAPTER TWENTY-EIGHT

Two months after Reed was buried, life was beginning to get back to normal for Camilla, Howard, and Oliver. The police were continuing to look for a man who looked like someone fitting the description of Nicholas that the three had provided, but with no good leads. Eric resumed texting with Oliver, claiming to be out of town. Through their texting, Oliver did let Eric know the struggle he was having, coping with the death of Reed — he felt that confiding in Eric was okay. It helped with the pain and was easier to do once the police had cleared Nicholas of being a person of interest. Through all the texting, Oliver let Eric know that he and his friends were going to get out of town — they needed a vacation, especially now that the funeral was behind them, and life was starting to get back to some sort of normal. They were headed to Martha's Vineyard. Oliver's mother's family had a home there — a small cottage not far from the beach. It had been in the family for generations but had sat empty for the last few years once the last occupant, Oliver's great aunt Betty, passed away. Oliver had been to the cottage a few times as a child, and his early teen years, but not in the last decade. He had no recollection of Betty other than the photos his mother would pull out now and again for a visual whenever she would reminisce and tell stories about old Aunt Betty.

Eric could tell from the text messages that Oliver was returning to his old self. He was opening more and letting his guard down—and being sweeter—a sign that maybe things between Oliver and Howard had simmered down. Maybe Oliver was ready to move forward with Eric. Oliver did not invite Eric to Martha's Vineyard through their texting, and Eric never insinuated that he wanted to be invited. Eric never gave any indication that he was at all bothered by the fact that Oliver would be out of town, meaning that the two would have to wait even longer to see one another again. Eric was okay with it all—he needed time to think about his next move, and about what he was ultimately going to do with Oliver.

Howard rented a convertible for their road trip. He wanted the three of them to have the best time ever—beach, margaritas, and sun. He wanted to completely leave the world behind them and just relax. While Howard and Camilla packed the car, Oliver made one last visit to his mother's house to say goodbye and to get the keys to the cottage. She had just spent the last few months on the island having the cottage cleaned up for the season. She had grown up spending her summers there, and always shared wonderful memories with Oliver about how much fun it was on the island—how isolated and relaxing it was to be there and leave the real-world troubles behind. It was exactly what Oliver wanted.

* * * * *

Nicholas had been watching the three pack up through one of the many cameras he had pointed at their house. He was still working out how he was going to get rid of Howard and Camilla. He knew that it would be hard to get rid of them both at the same time but that drawing it out and killing them separately was going to take much more planning. He was good at planning—enjoyed it even. The kill was only a small part of the entire ritual that Nicholas went through each time. Stalking his victims and really studying them only to come upon them to interact with them as if he was meeting them for the first time gave him a total thrill. It was enough to get him aroused.

With Oliver's house empty, and the police on to other cases by now, Nicholas was free to enter the neighborhood — being sure not to be seen on his own cameras, let alone any new doorbell cameras that were installed. When he did break into their house — something he had done many times over the years — he would be in there for hours, in the dark. Sometimes he would lie in Oliver's bed taking in the faint odor of Oliver that was woven into the sheets — or he would grab some clothes from Oliver's dirty laundry basket and inhale, basking in the sweaty smell of Oliver. One time — maybe the second time he ever broke into the house, before Camilla had moved in — Nicholas got naked then put on a pair of Oliver's underwear — a dirty pair from the laundry basket. He paraded around the house, in the soiled tighty-whities thinking about all the ways he wanted to have sex with Oliver. That one night, lying on the floor in Oliver's dark room, the odor of Oliver lingering in the air, Nicholas masturbated in those dirty briefs while sniffing a different dirty pair. He wore that sperm-soaked underwear home, and for the next two days just to keep Oliver close to him. He still has that underwear — they had since been cleaned, but every now and again Nicholas put them on and walked around his own house, thinking of a life with Oliver. Nicholas had left his underwear in Oliver's dirty laundry basket — of course they were the same brand and style — and he wondered if Oliver ever noticed that they had been swapped out.

Four days after Oliver and his friends left for Martha's Vineyard, Nicholas broke into Oliver's house again. This time he was more interested in Howard's room. He wanted to see if there was anything that could incriminate him. He had been watching Howard enough to know that he could be holding on to something to share with the police at the right moment. He found nothing. He did learn that Howard was very orderly — the opposite of Oliver. Although the room was dark when Nicholas was in it, the moonlight shone in enough for him to see that Howard was a neat freak. Everything in his room was in order. Even the products on his bathroom sink were perfectly aligned. Nicholas knew then that he had to take extra precautions in

Howard's room unless he wanted to draw attention to the fact that someone had been in there unannounced.

Nicholas took Howard's toothpaste out of the cabinet and took off the lid. Then he pulled a syringe out of his pocket and dipped it into the top of the toothpaste and pushed down on the plunger, releasing an odorless, tasteless poison into the toothpaste tube. He put the cap back on the toothpaste when he was done but was interrupted and left the tube on the sink counter. He heard a noise—almost like someone trying to unlock the front door. Still holding the syringe, Nicholas left Howard's room and crept toward the living room. If someone was coming in, he needed to know who so he could determine what he would do next.

As he stood in a dark corner of the dark room, Nicholas watched as the door slowly opened, lighting the foyer from the porch light. It was Howard, and he was dragging his suitcase behind him as he exhaustedly made his way into the house—home days earlier than Nicholas expected. Nicholas stood silent in the corner. Once Howard pulled his suitcase into the foyer he turned around and headed back out the door, turning the living room light on as he walked out onto the porch and down the stairs to help Camilla with her bag. Nicholas took advantage of the moment to step out of the lighted room and head toward the back of the house from where he entered. He slipped out of the house and into the dark night.

Camilla and Howard had cut their trip short because Camilla had been called back for work. Howard had to go with her because Camilla did not know how to drive a manual transmission. Oliver opted to stay behind at the cottage. He desired a much-needed break from his two best friends, and there was no better place for that than the island.

Camilla and Howard were exhausted from their trip. It was the rest and relaxation they needed but it was too short. Vacations always are. As they unpacked and settled back into their routine Howard noticed his toothpaste on the counter. He knew that was not normal but could not recall if he had forgotten to put it away before they left. He was too tired to think about it and accepted that he probably left it out.

Three days later Howard started feeling sick. Camilla found him on the bathroom floor with his head in the toilet. He was bouncing back and forth—

first his head was in the toilet then he was sitting on the toilet. Whatever it was that was eating him up inside, it was coming out both ends, and he could not figure out why. He and Camilla had ruled out food poisoning. They had both been eating the same thing for the last week. They checked in with Oliver and he was not sick either. Howard almost never got sick, so to find himself living in the bathroom, his throat sore from vomiting and his ass sore from diarrhea, had him very concerned. He had a slight fever, but nothing off the charts. He knew that if Reed were there with him, he would know what do to. Camilla, with no motherly instinct skills, could only mimic what her mother had done to her as a child when she was sick—and it just was not working.

The next day Howard felt worse. He had cramps in his stomach and woke Camilla up with his screaming—the pain was like nothing he had felt before. It would start with the gut-wrenching cramps, then the vomiting—by this time nothing would come up but a little water—mostly dry heaves, and the diarrhea—liquid, but not a lot—then repeat. He could not even keep a Gatorade down, although he needed the hydration. Anything he put in his body can shooting back out. And as the day progressed, the cramps got more painful, and lasted longer. Camilla felt useless—helpless as she watched Howard curled up in a ball on the bathroom floor, filthy from his own vomit and shit. To sit up or move hurt. She finally did the only thing she thought she could do and called 911.

As soon as she hung up, happy to know help was on the way, she called Oliver and told him that he needed to get home ASAP. She said that Howard was getting worse—this was not some flu or bug but something severe enough that she was taking him to the hospital by ambulance. It was late in the day—too late to catch the last ferry off the island, so Oliver was trapped on the island for another day. Before Camilla and Oliver could plan what do to next the ambulance was pulling up to the house—Camilla had to go but would call Oliver once she had more information—and told Oliver to start working on a plan to get home.

Howard and Camilla were rushed to the hospital where a team was waiting in the emergency room to examine Howard. The nurses gave Howard morphine for the pain. Howard was dripping sweat and having a hard time focusing on anyone in the room. He would occasionally yell out for Camilla, who was right there by his side and holding his hand. She had not been this worried since the last time she was in the hospital looking at Miles and all the tubes attached to his body.

Three hours later Howard finally stopped moaning and screaming out in pain. He was still sweating, but his heart rate had finally dropped, and his breathing slowed down. The doctors and nurses felt like they were finally getting Howard's body to stabilize enough for them to really understand what was wrong. Howard still held Camilla's hand, or rather, she was holding his. He was just lying helpless in the hospital bed with tubes slowly dripping liquid into his body to stabilize him.

Camilla felt like she was finally able to take a breath herself. She had been so worried about Howard that she forgot to call Oliver back to give him an update. When she felt that Howard was finally at peace and resting quietly, Camilla stepped out of the room to call Oliver.

CHAPTER TWENTY-NINE

When Oliver hung up with Camilla as the ambulance was arriving to the house, he was so angry with himself for being trapped on an island while his best friend was in trouble. He called his mother for some advice on what do to, and she reminded him that he had come into quite a bit of money—he no longer had to wait for a ferry like anyone else. If he really needed to get to off the island, he should put that money to good use. Oliver realized that he would never be able to spend all the money he inherited, and so he started making a few phone calls, and within 15 minutes he was in an Uber heading over to the small airfield on the island where a helicopter was standing by to bring him to the mainland. The pilot was an EMS helicopter pilot for the very hospital Oliver was trying to get to, so he was able to call ahead and explain the situation to get permission to land on the hospital helipad.

The pilot engaged Oliver in some small talk, trying to get some information about why they were headed to the hospital. Oliver told the pilot what he knew—which was not very much, and the pilot responded with a variety of possibilities—none of which were fatal—all very curable issues, assuming he and Oliver were getting the information correct. Of course, they weren't—neither had firsthand knowledge about what had been happening for a couple of days back home, and that had Oliver gutted.

As the helicopter touched down on the hospital grounds Oliver felt his phone vibrating in his pocket. He pulled it out to see that it was Camilla, but he knew that he would never be able to hear her so he quickly texted her back that his helicopter was landing and would call her right back.

When Camilla looked at her phone and saw the text she laughed. She needed to laugh—the absurdity of Oliver chartering a helicopter—her frugal friend. She was still not privy to the fact that Oliver had come into as much money as he had. He did not want that to change their friendship.

"Which way to the helipad?" she heard herself ask a nurse who was passing her as she read Oliver's text. The nurse pointed and Camilla ran off in that direction.

As Camilla opened the door, she saw Oliver walking toward her. She smiled and laughed again. Neither said a word until they were back in the hospital, sealed off from the loud noise outside. Once inside they hugged for what felt like an eternity. Camilla started crying, then Oliver joined her. The two sobbed onto each other's shoulders, then Camilla took the alpha role and pushed Oliver back so she could face him. She told him the whole story—every detail that she could not when they spoke briefly only a few hours earlier. They were holding hands, walking toward the ICU, trying to block out all the sirens and beeps—the yelling and chaos that made up the ICU until they realized that the immediate chaos around them was for Howard. When Camilla had left him, Howard was in a calm, tranquil state. What she did not know was that Howard's body was shutting down for good. Not long after Camilla left Howard's side, he flatlined, sending nurses and doctors running around trying to resuscitate him. When Camilla and Oliver reached Howard's bed, they were blocked from entering while the hospital team tried reviving him.

Camilla and Oliver collapsed into each other—their bodies holding up the other as tears rushed down their faces, unable to process what just happened. Camilla was mumbling something about it not being possible—about how alive Howard was just days ago. Oliver was listening to her, but not. He was beginning to feel the hurt that Howard felt when he learned about Reed. Oliver was feeling a pain he had never experienced before—not even when his father died. Sure, he loved his father—in the way a son is meant to love his parents, but Howard was different. Howard was his first true love, even if he came to realize it too late.

A nurse finally came out and ushered Camilla and Oliver to some chairs in a private room so the doctor could share what they had learned. When the doctor did join them, he did not bring any news that would help Camilla or Oliver cope with the loss of their friend. He could only tell them that he had symptoms of someone who had been poisoned, but they could not find any poison in his system, and although they did everything they could, Howard's body had already begun shutting down long before he arrived at the hospital.

"Poisoned?" Camilla asked. "Are you seriously saying that our friend was poisoned?"

The doctor replied with a firm no. But only that Howard's body—his condition when he arrived, was like that of someone who had been poisoned. But because they could find no trace of poison in Howard's blood, they ruled poisoning out, and did not have an opportunity to make any other determinations because he was dead before they could do anything more for him. The doctor was being quite firm with Camilla and Oliver that Howard had not been poisoned—he wanted them to be clear about that diagnosis. Of course, only Nicholas knew that Howard really had been poisoned.

* * * * *

Nicholas was able to confirm that he had removed Howard from the picture when he watched Camilla and Oliver return to their house hours later. He had been monitoring the cameras ever since he watched the ambulance pull away. Once he knew the house was empty again, he returned to replace the tube of poisoned toothpaste with a new, slightly used tube. He was not about to run any risk that either someone else die—possibly

Oliver, or that someone would put the pieces together and the police take the toothpaste in as evidence.

Nicholas squirted all the toothpaste out of the tube — letting it ooze out into a dumpster behind a restaurant near his building. He took the mostly empty tube into his house to scrub it clean of prints and put into his own trashcan. He was satisfied that another member of Oliver's inner circle was disposed of and was already planning how to kill Camilla.

CHAPTER THIRTY

Oliver sent a text to Eric a few days after Howard's funeral. It was not so much of an apology text as much as it was a "Hi, how are you?" text—vague, noncommittal. He almost didn't send the text at all. After all, they had agreed to stay apart while Oliver figured things out with Howard. Oliver had so many bad things happen in his life over the past few months that he was beginning to question if bringing Eric back into his life might be a mistake. He was afraid that something might happen to Eric—bad things were certainly happening to everyone around Oliver.

After Howard's funeral, Camilla packed a suitcase and was on the next plane to see her parents. She needed to get away and find her purpose in life. Having lost so many friends in such a short period of time was more than she could process on her own or with Oliver. She needed real adults—people much older and wiser—to help her cope with all this loss. Nicholas watched Camilla through the camera as she got into the cab. He only knew that she was leaving—but to where and for how long remained a mystery. He knew that he needed to talk with Oliver—to get the inside scope on what was up with Camilla. He still felt like he needed to kill her so that he and Oliver could be together.

When Nicholas got the text, he responded almost immediately. He wanted Oliver to feel comfortable coming to him in his time of need. Alone in the house, Oliver thought maybe Eric should come to him since he had the place to himself. Every time he saw Eric it was at Eric's place—or the park near Eric's place. Eric had never been to Oliver's house—so Oliver thought. A few more back and forth text messages and Eric was on his way over.

Nicholas was a little nervous. The man he had loved for so long wanted him, finally. He wondered if it was the best time was to reveal his identity—or if he ever could. Nicholas was surprised that Oliver had not realized that he and Eric were the same person, but then he had done a good job keeping the two identities separate, and Oliver never really knew Nicholas. Any image of Nicholas Oliver would have been very different from the one that Eric portrayed — his white hair and tattoos showing a very different version of Nicholas.

Nicholas could kill off the idea of one of his two personalities and just be the other, forever, but if he did, would Oliver get over Eric enough to want to get to know Nicholas? These were heavy questions to be asking himself as he sat in the back of the taxi. The more he thought about it, the more complicated it all sounded, and he wondered how he let it get to this point in the first place. Thinking back, he should have just killed all of Oliver's friends and then stepped into his life — he realized just how big of a mess he had made his life, and Oliver's too. With that epiphany Nicholas asked the driver to turn around and head to the airport instead. Nicholas needed to get out of town — he needed space between he and Oliver so that he could decide who he really wanted, and what he wanted to do with the rest of his life.

With nothing more than the clothes he was wearing, Nicholas stepped out of the taxi and into the airport. He did not even know where he was going to go just yet, but London was always his go-to place to find peace. As he walked through the airport, he sent a text to Oliver saying that something had come up, and he was not going to make it over today. He never mentioned going out of town, or that he was at the airport as he typed the message.

After one last text message to Oliver of "I love you," Nicholas sent a text message to another number before removing the sim card and snapping his phone into two pieces and throwing it in a trashcan as he walked through the airport. He held the sim card in his hands a little longer, bending it between his fingers before dropping it into a different trash can.

CHAPTER THIRTY-ONE

It had been almost a week since Oliver got the text from Eric with those three words—I love you. He had not responded. He did not know how to respond. Part of him wanted to say the words back, but part of him could not muster up the strength to do so. Oliver picked up his phone multiple times a day over the last few days just to look at the text from Eric. He kept waiting for something more, but there was no other text. He thought maybe Eric had not said anymore because he was waiting to hear the words from Oliver. Finally, Oliver thought it was silly that he was behaving this way over a text. He picked up his phone and sent two words back—Me too. A moment later he got a response that the text was not delivered. Oliver tried again and got the same response, so he dialed the number. Before he could even get the first ring, he heard a recording that the number he was calling was no longer in service.

Confused, hurt, and frustrated, Oliver dialed the number again—maybe there was an error—lines crossed, or something. He got the same response. Unsure of what was going on, Oliver headed out to go see Eric. He figured there would be a perfectly good explanation for the phone issue — there had to be. When the taxi arrived at the destination Oliver looked out the window equally as confused as when he heard the out of service message. He got out of the car to find that he was standing in front of a burned-out building. He looked around and knew he was in the right place — everything else around him looked just as he last remembered it. The only exception being the building before him marked with yellow tape — it had recently burned down. He could still smell the burnt, smoky odor of the water-soaked wood. He could see the piles of bricks — one entire side of the building had collapsed from the heat.

Nothing was making sense. First the text message, then the dead phone number, and now Eric's home reduced to a pile of rubble. Oliver sat on the stoop and cried. He wondered if Eric had been in the fire — which might explain the dead phone. He hoped that Eric had left his phone in the building and was safe somewhere. But he had no way of knowing. As he sat on the steps taking in yet another tragedy in his life a police officer stopped to talk with him. He explained to Oliver that he could not be on the steps—some of the walls could still be unstable. He needed to get away to be safe. Oliver explained to the officer that the building belonged to his friend, and he was unable to find him, and feared that he died in the fire. The police officer put Oliver's mind at rest some by letting him know that no one was in the building when it burned down. They think it was a gas explosion, but investigators were still trying to determine the actual cause.

"Explosion?" Oliver yelled, not meaning to be so loud. The officer confirmed his story before asking him again to leave the steps, for his own safety.

Oliver headed back to his own home. This time he opted to walk through the park. He needed fresh air, and he needed to think about his own life, and what he wanted to do next. Halfway through the park Oliver saw a man sitting on the park bench where he and Eric first met. The man sitting there now looked a lot like Eric. Oliver picked up his pace to reach the bench before the man could have a chance to leave, but when he got up close, he could see that it was not Eric—not the man he vaguely remembered as Eric. He realized at that moment that it had been a long time since he had seen Eric — he was beginning to forget what he looked like.

The man sitting on the bench looked up as Oliver approached then said his name in the form of a question, "Oliver?" Oliver was taken aback as he stopped and stood in front the man, looking down, squinting his eyes from the sun.

"I'm sorry, but do I know you?" Oliver asked. The man stood up, and they were standing eye to eye, but the man's eyes were hiding behind sunglasses. Oliver's initial thought was about how handsome the man looked. He somewhat resembled Eric, but his hair was the wrong color, and his clothing style was all wrong — from what he could remember. And there were no tattoos.

"My name is Nicholas," the young man said as he took off his sunglasses revealing his bright, beautiful, green eyes. "I believe you do."

John Paul's second book
about Nicholas and Oliver,

For the Love of Death

will be published in the autumn of 2023.